For What I Hate I Do

By M.W. Moore

MOORE

M.W. Moore Publications
2005

Production byAxess Printing
www.axessprinting.com

M.W. Moore Publications
P.O. Box 61242
Houston, Texas 77208
www.mwmoore.com

Library of Congress Control Number:
2005910647

ISBN: 0-9776116-0-4

Printed in the United States of America

Book design by Carlfred Giles
Photography by Ferrell Phelps

Although loosely based on some actual episodic events and geographical locations, this work chronicles embellished tales with fictionalized names as part of the author's creativity. There is no intent to disparage likenesses.

M.W. Moore Publications

1 2 3 4 5 6 7 8 9 10

This book is dedicated to the generation of black men and women suffering from rejection, hidden addictions, mental ailments, and terminal scars such as HIV/AIDS. Perhaps they are those we have despised at some point. Even so, they are still our family members, friends, neighbors, lovers.

Although some of these wounded individuals might have contributed a wagonload of pain to the lives of their loved ones, many have taught us the meaning of compassion and forgiveness.

Before redemption, some sufferers might have experienced anger and disenfranchisement. But now is the time that we band together in hopes that we can conquer the illnesses that threaten the people who should mean the world to us, regardless of their compulsive behaviors and damaging decisions.

In Loving Memory

Kermit Bowers, Andre Ramey, Michael Johnson, Florence Griffith-Joyner and my sister, Deborah K. Moore.

Acknowledgements

Thanks to the mercy of God, who is first in my life, I'm still standing. He has sheltered me from Satan's abyss, yet reshaped me for the good of His glory. Thanks to my dear mother, Mrs. Jessie Moore, who has nurtured me since conception – through bitter and sweet times. You are my angel, mom. And gratitude to my siblings: Alvin, Audrey, Debra (who regrettably succumbed to complications from multiple sclerosis during my incarceration) and Ray, for inspiring me, even if unknowingly. The times we spent together, and apart, helped me understand the importance of family.

And much respect to my editor and confidant, L.A. Warren. Your humility and patience are beyond description. You are, indeed, an epitome of God's greatest creations. I believe divine intervention brought us together because of your understanding, tolerance and compassion. I'm further convinced that you, along with others, were directed to help mend my broken spirit so that the Potter could put me back together and reopen my eyes to His bountiful blessings, of which you are among.

My indebtedness to "FWIHID" proofreaders: Albert, Brent, Cheryl, Ferrell, Lewis, Ray, Reginald, Robbie, Valencia.

Also, thanks to friends Alfonso, Lewis, Ray, and Robert for your visits and concern during my darkest hours. And to contributors Lance, Malcolm and Marcus.

*****

Special gratitude to my longtime supportive neighbors: Ernestine Jones, Jessie Sheryl and Willie Pearl Phillips. Appreciation to my college track coach, Bob Kitchens. All of you have been like second parents. Thanks for the discipline, even if I strayed away from some of your teachings.

And a special salute goes to KTSU-FM (90.9). Although the concrete prison walls with steel bars made it difficult at times to pick up the radio station's frequency, I'm thankful to God for allowing the Gospel, both spoken and sung, to miraculously pierce through those supposedly impenetrable walls each Sunday morning. The inspirational sounds from the airwaves were a refuge from despair, a salve from sorrow, a balm from bitterness. I'm also grateful for KMJQ-FM (Magic 102). Its Sunday Morning Live Show kept me abreast of the many challenges and changes arising in this new century of rule and ruin. I applaud KRTS-FM (92.1), as well, for soothing my soul with its repertoire of then-classical music. Another integral source for my endurance was Christian radio station KHCB-FM (105.7), which provided the spiritual substance and teachings for keeping me focused and not feeling forsaken, even when beset by temptations. KHCB's spiritual broadcasting mavens, Tony Evans and Chuck Swindoll, paved the way for my redemption while behind bars.

Thank you all, men and women of God, for revealing my wrongs, redirecting my heart and helping in my restoration.

We are more than conquerors through Christ who strengthens us.

Web sites:
www.forwhatihateido.com
www.mwmoore.com

Character Profiles

The multiple personalities of protagonist **Miguel Morris**, a track star, result from the numerous challenges throughout his life. He uncovers his true identity after haphazardly embracing his weakest links over his pillars of strength. His mother, **Mattie Morris**, relies on faith and tender tolerance to cope with her son's struggles with chemical dependency. A childhood friend, **Caleb Thibodeaux**, helps reveal Miguel's hidden interests. The charismatic **Butch Webber**, Miguel's upperclassman college buddy, proves talent could change a person's life. **Latisha**, a distraught lover, is forced to deal with the reality of her relationship with Miguel. An acquaintance, **Patrick Porter**, becomes Miguel's Achilles' heel. The misogynistic Patrick is perplexed at best and diabolical at worst, often living a wanton life marked by lust and greed. **Lazlo**, a loyal friend, is entangled in a personal quagmire of his own, but his problems magnify after traveling dangerously and figuratively over the rough seas in which he sailed with Miguel. For him, "a quiet storm" was the ultimate oxymoron. *(For other character profiles, see the end of the book.)*

Chapters

Chapter I
Run, Miguel, Run

For America, it was a bicentennial milestone as the nation celebrated its 200th year of freedom. Even though some citizens were still living in economic bondage and segregation in 1976, many had managed to look beyond their circumstances toward a future of prosperity and fulfillment.

It was also an era when I, Miguel Morris, faced a host of new challenges and ventures – an indication that I was definitely coming of age. I would eventually confront forces of evil lurking in the realm of my mind. And those same spirits made unconscionable acts appear normal.

My transformation began in high school with a quest to become more sociable, assertive and competitive. I needed an avenue to display my physical prowess and to start charting my goals. I was a 6-foot, 2-inch tall brother with a dark-chocolate complexion – perhaps to my advantage because of the unforgiving sun that would beat down perpetually onto the Texas landscape. Like a sleek gazelle in the African Serengeti, my structure and athleticism commanded respect. I was a bit vain, but so are many others.

When I had reached age 16, I knew my time for making a decision about college was winding down. With an interest in track-and-field, I mused that sports could be my best ticket to gaining peer status and earning a scholarship to assist me with college expenses.

I was determined to become the second among four siblings to get a formal education, following in my sister Dee's footsteps. She was the older of two girls and attended one of the largest black academic institutions in the South – Texas Southern University, located in my hometown of Houston. I respected my sister, Dee, a young, striking robust woman with a cocoa-butter complexion, a sensual voice and lips like legendary singer Lola Folana, a diva known to dazzle the stage in Las Vegas. Dee might not have been as talented as Lola, but she was just as attractive. And she was a good role model.

Going to college also would be my chance to prove to my brothers that I, like them, could attain success and glory in athletics. Troy, my youngest brother, played football; and David, my eldest sibling, was on the varsity basketball team. They took pride in their athletic successes and often would rub it in my face just to irritate me. But all that was about to change. I wasn't about to be punked by my brothers or anyone else for that matter. So I ventured to squash their bragging.

My time had come.

*****

Despite the fall heat in September, I was excited and full of anticipation about my tryout for the track team. I convinced myself that this decision would have a profound affect on my future.

I grew up in an area called Southpark, which once was occupied by a large Jewish community. Gradually, it became a working-class African-American neighborhood. With white flight, the dynamics of the 'hood changed with an infestation of narcotics. It wasn't a ghetto hood, but oftentimes the media portrayed the predominantly black community as crime-infested. It was also where I attended Ross S. Sterling High School.

The prospect of entering athletics consumed my thoughts, but I still was focused on my other coursework, too. As I left school one late afternoon, I reflected on the turbulent semester involving my drafting class. On one hand, I was happy to have a new teacher, but I bemoaned the circumstances that led to his replacement. The newcomer had arrived to take over for Mr. Weatherbee, a flamboyant instructor who would put the television cast of "Queer Eye for the Straight Guy" to shame.

He practically lived his life as a woman, with an obvious overabundance of estrogen and very little testosterone. He decorated his classroom with floral curtains and wallpaper and accentuated the windows with fresh flowers, trinkets and colorful doodads. He was well-liked by most of the staff and students but hated by some. Even though his eccentric tastes created a fantasyland ambiance in the classroom, he was "way out there." Too feminine. Too gay.

The bold acceptance of his sexuality caused discomfort for some of his detractors, which might explain his heinous execution-style murder. His bullet-riddled body was found facedown, nude in his backyard pool on the southeast side of town. His assailants showed no mercy. A bullet had also penetrated his skull and a cob of corn had been inserted into his rectum in a vile, barbaric hate-crime act that remains unsolved.

While deep in thought, a voice called out my name in the hallway.

"Say, Miguel! You heard the news?" asked Caleb, my best friend. Caleb was a stout, muscular 16-year-old, high-yellow fellow with a medium Afro. He would always meet me in the hall after our last class. Oftentimes pushy, he was still my dawg. Almost too pretty for a boy, he definitely was not soft or a coward. He had an ownership attitude about people, places and things. Matter of fact, he was very deliberate in action and in speech and usually a little too abrasive and reactive to situations not in his control.

"Nah, man. What's up?" I responded.

"It's Willie, man!" he said in a high-pitched voice.

"What about Willie?" I asked puzzled, unable to discern Caleb's expression.

"He finally did it man! I couldn't believe it, but he did it!" Caleb's eyes were teary but still difficult to interpret.

"Did what, man?" I stood in the middle of the hallway irritated at Caleb's vagueness, but his outburst concerned me. He already knew my patience was short and temper explosive.

"He shot him, man! He shot and killed his dad! His neighbor told us in homeroom class this morning how it went down."

By now, I was mortified, simply speechless. I had hoped that my previous thoughts about my slain drafting teacher didn't portend this latest tragedy.

Even so, Caleb seemed to be more concerned for Willie than for the death of Willie's dad.

"He actually shot him?" I said stunned by the news.

Willie was going through some issues with his dad, but I never thought things were that serious, so serious that he would murder his dad – especially after the death last year of his mother, who was killed in a car accident on her way to work by some fool-ass drunken driver.

"You know about the rumor, man. I guess he couldn't take it no more," Caleb said, shaking his head in disgust. "Could you blame him? I couldn't imagine being in that position. Living with a niggah like that."

"But that's all it was, Caleb, just a rumor. We don't know if that shit is true or not," I said, feeling deep in my gut that Willie likely had been sexually molested by his stepfather. Willie previously had hinted about his father's abuse but never went into details.

By now I was feeling heavily burdened.

After we vented for a while over the tragedy, we put our

emotions aside and began to focus on the rest of the day.

"Are we still gonna meet after our last class or what?" a subdued Caleb asked, clearly still affected by the tragic news.

"Maybe I didn't tell you, but I'm gonna try out for the track team today," I said coolly, trying not to sound insensitive after hearing about the ordeal with Willie.

"You told me, man. Why do you think I'm here?

I ignored his acerbic remark and proceeded walking down the hallway toward the back exit.

"Say, man," he said, "Do you want me to hold the bucket at the end of the race for you?" he asked, suggesting that I likely will vomit from heat and exhaustion during the running trials.

"Ha! Ha! Ha!" I said in a patronizing tone. "Why don't you come out there and see me whip some ass!"

Caleb snickered. When we reached the track, he apologetically put his left arm around my shoulders and said, "You know I was just playing with you, right?"

"Yeah, I know, man. I'm just a little nervous. That's all."

As we walked shoulder to shoulder in the muggy weather, I took a vengeful yet friendly swipe at Caleb's right ear before making a getaway. We often played like that to solidify our friendship and as a way to pacify each other in trying times.

Caleb laughed at my juvenile behavior, then slowly walked toward the track to assist me – without a challenge. That was a first.

"So, you really gonna do this, huh?" Caleb asked as I sifted through my bag for practice gear.

"Yeah, man. I told you I was serious about this." I could not have been more serious in my life. I felt it was time that I took control of my life.

The clothes I had worn in the scorching sun made me sweat profusely, so I quickly undressed to put on my nylon running shorts and matching sleeveless T-shirt, both of which soon became saturated, too. Even though I was uncomfortable, I came to realize that this was only the beginning of the pains of competitive track and field.

"Say, Caleb Thibodeaux. If you really want to help, man, take out my running shoes and spikes from my backpack."

Because of my determination to succeed, I had worked over the past summer to save money to purchase the gear. Unlike some other guys from the 'hood, I had to work hard for my earnings. My mom and dad were not as financially secure as the other kids' parents.

As we hastened to prepare for my trials, Caleb and I noticed a middle-age white-haired man plodding toward us. The gravel on the cinder track that was crunched by the stranger's shoes caught my attention as I sat nearby. I glanced up curiously toward him.

"Hi, fellows! I'm Coach Bill Turney. Are you boys here to try out for the track team today?" he asked.

With an impish stare, Caleb took offense to the word "boy" and responded abrasively.

"NO! But he is," Caleb stated bluntly, pointing quickly at me with his right thumb.

He was clearly pissed off at the brazenfaced coach.

"Here, Miguel. These the shoes you wanted?" Caleb asked.

"Yeah, thanks." I attempted to ignore my best friend's anger.

After changing into my running shoes, I stood to formally greet the coach and extended my right hand. As odd as it may seem, I could not recall the last time I had shaken hands with a white man.

"My name is Miguel Morris. I heard you were having try-outs here today for the track team. At least that's what Zac told me."

Zac, tall and dark-skinned with coarse short hair, was a classmate who ran for the Sterling Raiders. He was the top sprinter in the 110- and 220-yard dash. He, too, was a sopho-more hoping to earn an athletic scholarship. I sensed that he

was insincere when he had challenged me to try out for the
team. It was probably just his way to display his machismo.

"Yes, that's true," Coach Turney said, answering my question about tryouts. "I take it you are interested in joining the
track team?"

"Yes, sir."

"What event?" the coach asked.

"The sprints."

"Fine. We'll begin in about 45 minutes. So, why don't you
get warmed up and stretched. We'll meet at the end of the
long-jump pit."

Caleb was still bitter about the coach's greeting. It was odd
though. He and I often called each other the "N" word, but
when someone else of a different racial or ethnic background
used the word or even called us "boy" we'd puff up like an old
toad threatening to piss everywhere.

"Man, can you believe that white mothafucker calling us
'boy?' I bet that old bastard don't know nothing about track
and field. He's only here because this school used to be white,
but now the brothers are taking over. Mothafucker!" Caleb
blared.

"You're probably right, Caleb, but why worry about small
crap like that, man? He's old school and probably don't realize he's being an asshole. Anyway, I gotta start warming up if
I'm gonna make the track team." I had hoped that the red-
faced coach didn't hear Caleb's tirade.

"Yep! You're right, man. But anyway, I'll be here pushing
you to break that world record when you cross that finish
line," Caleb said.

"Yeah, right!" I said as I began my warm-up laps.

While rounding the track, I noticed Coach Turney and
observed him rather closely. He was a middle-age man about
55 years old with a potbelly. His skin was pale and as dry as
the dirt track beneath my feet.

I continued to run pass the coach, drifting into thought.

Caleb was probably right. There's no way this white dude can possibly know anything about sprinting, let alone track and field.

"Run, Miguel, run!" Caleb shouted hysterically at me as I neared the end of my first warm-up lap.

"You're crazy!" I said as I approached him, grinning slightly. Since time was running short, I had to limit my small talk with Caleb in order to focus on the 110-yard sprint that awaited me.

After I completed about seven sprints, I heard a whistle blow. It was time to prove my worth.

I walked swiftly toward the long-jump area, using body language to express my competitiveness. Drenched in sweat, I wondered if I had exhausted myself doing warm-ups in the unrelenting heat.

"OK, Morris, looks like you're gonna be the only tryout today. Is Morris OK, or should I call you Miguel?" the coach asked.

"Miguel is fine, Coach." I then began to experience butterflies in my stomach because I wasn't prepared to run against myself. Hell, I didn't even know how to run competitively. Was this bastard setting me up for failure? Perhaps Caleb was right. Maybe this so-called coach was a fraud. Was he just here for the paycheck and nothing more?

Regardless of what I thought, Coach Turney – with a stopwatch in his right hand – instructed me to prepare for my test.

"OK, Miguel, the start is located a few feet in front of us. Today, all you have to do is run a 440-yard dash, and we will determine your future from there. OK?"

"OK," I answered in a puzzled tone. A 440-yard dash? I thought it would be a 110-yard dash. Anyway, this mothafucker is crazy! He didn't even give me any pointers on how to run this crap, and he expects me to make the team? Maybe he doesn't want me to make the track team, so I won't show up those white runners already on the squad.

The psychological warfare was tearing at me. I had to quickly put aside those thoughts and proceed to the marked area on the red dirt track. As I got into position, I again heard a familiar voice beckoning me.

"Hey, Miguel! You forgot your spikes," Caleb shouted as he ran toward me with his once-neatly groomed Afro thrashing in the hot air under brutal, dry conditions. Hoisting the blue-and-white adidas footgear with his right hand, he wished me good luck.

I thanked him and quickly replaced my shoes with the spikes, then waited for Coach Turney's cue. I stepped into a pair of running blocks, unsure how to run the 440-yard dash. And no thanks to the coach, who didn't bother to offer any pointers. Nevertheless, I had to give it my best.

"OK, Miguel. On your mark. Get set. POW!" (The gun blasted).

The sound ripped throughout the field, causing a piercing ring in my ears as I began my mad dash. I powered my way through the course trying to establish a rhythm while relaxing through every stride with controlled breathing. I continued to zip through the course until I was now halfway in the run. With only about 100 yards to go, fatigue began to plague me, but I muscled on. That's when I noticed Caleb jumping and screaming like an eager cheerleader.

"C'mon, Miguel! You can do it, man!" Caleb assured me.

Feeling as if I were on my last breath, I shot across the finish line, gasping and looking for a place of refuge – a mission impossible because of the ubiquitous and pulverizing sun. The heat only added to my desperation for relief, not to mention the pain I was experiencing in the middle of my ass. It felt as if I had been kicked in the butt by a horse. My throbbing hamstrings were tight and my head light from the dizzying solo run.

"Fifty-point-five-seconds!" Coach Turney shouted incredulously as I crossed the finish.

Unaware of what the time meant, I collapsed onto the infield near the long-jump pit. Despite the grueling task, I experienced a euphoric rush of adrenaline. Was this the runners' high I had heard about? I didn't know for sure. But what I did know was I wanted the glory of the sport.

"Fifty-point-five-seconds? Fifty-point-five-seconds?" Caleb screamed in excitement as he ran toward my weary body to celebrate. He bear-hugged me with Herculean force. I was practically blown away because I didn't know he was so strong. Soon both of us rolled into the infield, frolicking like children. Pure exhilaration! I loved it when he handled me roughly, and I assumed he felt the same.

"OK! OK! OK!" I pleaded while simultaneously being overcome by laughter. "C'mon, Man! Let me catch my breath. Damn!"

Caleb released his potent grip. Shortly thereafter we both stood, staggering to regain our balance – only to collapse to the ground once more. We lie side by side with our backs to the grassy field and our legs spread-eagle.

"Good job! Good job!" said Coach Turney, interrupting our celebration.

"Thanks, Coach," I replied, looking up toward him and the clear blue sky.

After regaining my strength and acknowledging the adulation from my best friend and the coach, I asked a question with perhaps an obvious answer: "Is 50.5 a good time?"

"It was a good time, man. A fucking good time," answered Caleb.

"Well, Miguel, I'll put it this way. You have run the fastest time among my entire squad from last season. An outstanding performance, young man. Oh! And by the way, practice starts Monday at 3:30 p.m."

Coach Turney then turned and walked away.

I knew I was an amateur, but I welcomed the accolades. Of

course, I wondered if this was just a stroke of luck for my would-be ego. Amid the jubilation, I also wondered about my future with the Sterling track team.

"Caleb? How did you know 50.5 was a good time?" I asked curiously. I had no idea what I had just done.

"Damn, Miguel! You never been to a track meet before?"

"Nope."

Caleb appeared surprised. It also seemed he wanted to ask me a personal question, but then he recoiled. Instead, he stood and pulled me from the field. His grip was strong, his eyes sharply focused. He decided to just savor the moment and abandoned his initial thought.

I felt indebted to him for my success during the time trial because he stayed the course and cheered me on from start to finish. This was a bittersweet moment though because we both knew things were about to change between the two of us. I was about to become an official member of Sterling's varsity track team, and my social time would be limited.

But on this day, as victory underscored our long journey home, we relished the time we spent together. And once again we walked shoulder to shoulder.

Chapter 2
What's Up, Tammy?

The weekend was nearly over, and I still hadn't shared the news of making the track team with my parents and siblings. I figured after church on Sunday would be an ideal time. That's when the family would be gathered to devour mother's feast: a mouth-watering dish of candied yams, spicy green bean salad, smothered pork chops, creamed mashed potatoes with brown gravy, homemade buttered sourdough rolls, and a deep chocolate rum cake. The dessert was mom's favorite.

After swallowing my last forkful and gulping the remainder of my iced lemon tea, I shared the news about my accomplishment with mom and my two brothers. Dad, grandmother (known as Big Momma), and my two sisters weren't present.

"Hey, mom," I said, meekly.

"Yes, Miguel," she responded graciously.

"I made the track team on Friday." I was careful to use as few words as possible in the presence of my brothers. They were often brutish and close-minded.

"Well, congratulations! Why are you now just telling us?" she asked curiously, as they all raked through their dinner plates in synchronized cadence.

Not surprisingly, our conversation grabbed the attention of

Troy and David, who sat across from me.

I explained that I originally had wanted to wait until the entire family was together, but I decided not to put it off any longer.

"Well, you know, Dee and Fay are still at church helping Sister Lewis and your grandmother with that Sunday school stuff for next week. And I'm not sure where your daddy is," she said.

Mom, rising from the kitchen table to dispose of her scraps and wash her plate, was an imposing figure. Her red tailored dress, smoky-almond skin and jet-black hair that cascaded over her shoulders accentuated her inner beauty.

As she walked toward the sink, mom unnerved us with an abrupt sneeze, breaking the mealtime silence and catching everyone off guard. After momentarily excusing herself to regain her composure, she returned to the dinner table – her light-almond eyes glistening under the lights. She then glanced toward Troy and David, who were still sitting at the table with me.

"David, Troy. Aren't y'all going to congratulate your brother for making the track team?" she said.

Mom, graceful even when she sneezed, seemed to be wishing that someday her three sons eventually would become closer.

"Oh, yeah. Congratulations, Miguel," they both said, sounding insincere and indifferent – almost envious.

I hesitantly thanked them for their acknowledgement, then left the table, leaving my brothers and their temperament behind.

****

As morning arrived, Big Momma had the responsibility of rustling my siblings and me from bed. Her booming voice would call out to us on school days two hours after our parents had left for work. Big Momma was our maternal grandmother. At 5-foot, 11-inches tall, the 70-year-old matriarch with steely gray hair commanded respect. She suffered from a mild case of glaucoma that she often tried to ignore. Because of her illness and concern for her safety and health, my parents moved Big Momma in with us when they purchased our new home in 1970.

"OK, children! It's six o'clock," yelled Big Momma, knocking at our doors. "It's six o'clock. Get up!" she repeated.

There was no missing school in this household. She made sure we were out of the house by 7:45 a.m.

On this day, I was the first to get up.

"Good morning," I said as I quickly trudged down the hallway toward the bathroom to relieve my bladder.

"Good morning, baby," replied Big Momma, unsure who I was because of my morning hoarseness and her compromised vision.

After removing the "cobwebs" from my eyes and freshening up, my siblings began to follow my lead. Soon thereafter I received my ritual phone call at 7:15 a.m.

"Good morning, Mrs. Bee," the caller said politely to Big Momma. "Can I speak to Miguel?"

"Sure, Caleb," Big Momma said after recognizing his distinctive voice. "Hold on for a moment, baby. Miguel! Caleb's on the phone, baby."

I anxiously picked up the call and told Caleb I would see him in front of my house where we normally met to begin our journey to school. I gathered my books and practice gear and stuffed them in my backpack.

"Goodbye, Big Momma," I yelled as I left the house.

While waiting outside before Caleb arrived I had a few minutes to reflect on the track team and my accomplishment. The entire experience left me dazed but spirited. Then Caleb startled me when he suddenly crept from behind during my meditation. There was something different about Caleb today. Oddly, he was much taller. I then looked down at his feet and discovered he was sporting platform shoes.

He was now almost two inches taller than me. His lime-green shirt and heavily starched bell-bottom designer blue jeans made him more alluring and debonair. We shared similar styles, particularly when we would hit weekend garage parties decked out in our finest under strobe lights.

We sometimes coordinated our attire to project an image of distinction and uphold our best-dressed reputations. Today, though, I wore a lavender and white nylon shirt, along with bell-bottom blue jeans and high-top white Chuck Taylor Converse tennis shoes.

I complimented Caleb on his platforms before veering the conversation to track and field. I reminded him not to meet me after school because of practice.

"Speaking of practice," Caleb said, "Did Troy and David tease you about making the track team?"

"Nah, Man! They just gave me a funny look. You don't remember me telling you that yesterday after church?" I said hastily – not really wanting to talk about my brothers.

"Man, you were saying so much yesterday I guess I forgot."

Before heading into our homeroom classes, we noticed Caleb's cousin, Tammy, puffing hurriedly on a cigarette. Her high-yellow complexion was similar to Caleb's. She was wearing a pleated skirt that revealed her long seductive legs. Her black shoulder-length hair was perfectly groomed and hung flawlessly even as she leaned over to extinguish her cigarette. For a smoker, her white teeth showed no signs of stain and accented her beautiful smile. At that moment, I developed an infatuation so badly that I imagined myself salivating and yelping like a dog in heat. My virginity was on the verge of being lost.

"What's up, Tammy?" asked Caleb, nudging me in my left side with his right elbow.

Was that my cue?

"Oh! I'm just trying to get ready for these boring ass teachers today," she said flirtatiously while walking toward her class and looking back into my lustful eyes. Her stare caught me off guard, but I maintained my composure.

I reciprocally teased her by winking and then assured her that we would see each other again soon. As the first warning bell rang, we all marched toward our classes.

*****

The advent of the track-and-field season began under a crisp February sky. The first meet was scheduled for the weekend – three short days away. With football season over, my time had arrived to steal the family spotlight. My brother Troy, a ninth-grader, had previously hogged the attention from my parents. My eldest brother, David, wasn't a factor anymore because he had graduated from high school the previous semester and was now working for the City of Houston water works department.

Near the end of practice, I finally noticed Caleb, who was trying to conceal himself. Strangely, the wooden bleachers where he stood provided a nearly perfect camouflage as he peered from the west end of the structure. Not to be outsmarted, I pretended that I didn't see my "cloaked" friend and continued my workout. As I moved closer, Caleb sought deeper cover. When I veered toward him to bust his childish prank, it was clear that he was embarrassed.

I mocked him.

"So, you spying on me now, Caleb?"

"Nah, man!"

He lied.

"I just didn't want to disturb you. That's all," he said.

"You're my boy, Caleb; you're never a disturbance, man," I said, resting my hand on his right shoulder.

"I'm really your boy, huh?" asked a grinning Caleb, showcasing his gleaming teeth. "I really wasn't hiding. I wanted to see if you're serious about running, Miguel. That's all."

"Now, you know, huh?" I said, playfully patting him on his ass like ballplayers do. Shortly thereafter we strolled through the chilled wind, trying to ignore the weather as we gathered my gear and headed to the locker room for a hot shower.

*****

On the day before my track debut, I was hyped after the morning announcements urging students to support the track team by attending Saturday's 10 a.m. meet. When my first class ended, I thought about my coronation into sports. I suddenly realized that my rivals were not my brothers, but rather my teammates and opponents from other schools. It also dawned on me that I would be on exhibit for all spectators: my family, classmates, neighbors and friends, including Caleb and Tammy.

After I gathered my belongings for my drafting class, I meandered down the long corridor, running into a cheerful Tammy. Her cousin Caleb was close behind adjusting his full-length black leather coat over his broad shoulders, admiring himself on the cool. Vain bastard.

"Hi, Miguel. I heard your name over the intercom," Tammy said seductively, as if she really wanted to experience my chocolate pipe.

"Yeah! Tomorrow's my big day," I said confidently, pretending not to be sweating over the upcoming event.

"What's uuuup?" asked Caleb, offering a high-five and his trademark pearly-white smile.

"Hey, Caleb," Tammy said unenthusiastically after Caleb busted onto the scene.

There appeared to be some tension between those two.

"What's up, Caleb? I was just telling Tammy about my big day tomorrow."

"Yeah, tomorrow's your big day, huh?" he asked rhetorically as he got eye to eye with me and ignored his cousin after her dry-ass greeting.

"Yeah. Miguel's gonna run circles around those guys," Tammy said boastfully as she searched furiously through her purse.

"Yep. I'm gonna do my best, y'all," I said modestly. As I adjusted the buttons on my waist-length leather coat, I noticed an arm reaching over the top of my head and a silver-coined necklace being placed around my neck.

"This is for good luck, Miguel," Tammy said with a sparkle in her eyes.

I admired the token, thanked her and told her she didn't have to do that.

With a hint of envy Caleb said, "It must be nice to have all the ladies running after you, huh, Miguel?"

"Oh, boy! Stop tripping," Tammy demanded.

"BOY!" belted Caleb, taking offense to the word that got him riled up when Coach Turney used it on the first day of tryouts.

"Well, 'MAN,' then!" replied Tammy, patronizing him.

I wondered if Caleb was suddenly tripping.

I'd learned from him long ago that you have to manipulate women before they get the upper hand. He said most of them were nothing but groupies and bitch-ass gold diggers and a good lay when convenient. Although he felt that way about females, I did not subscribe to that belief.

"Say, are we gonna walk together or stay here all day?" I interjected to defuse the senseless squabble between the cousins.

"I'm ready when you are, man," Caleb said.

"I'm going to catch a smoke," said Tammy, adjusting her white Fox coat. She told me she would see me tomorrow. She then galloped between us, slightly rolling her eyes at Caleb.

My eyes stayed fixed on Tammy as she walked away firing up a cigarette. I wondered why a girl so pretty would smoke. Were there other problems in her life? Maybe it was just a way to calm her nerves for whatever reason.

"Miguel! Miguel!" Caleb shouted to snap me out of my daze.

"Yeah, man. I'm ready. Let's go."

Later as we prepared to walk home, a rare occasion given my practice schedule, I wondered if Caleb were upset about the gift Tammy gave me.

"Say, man! Do you think your cousin likes me?"

"I don't know, man! Why don't you ask her?" he snapped.

His sour response baffled me, so I assumed that dating his cousin was off-limits.

"Well, I guess her chain says it all, huh?" I uttered as I examined the gift, holding it in my hand as we walked home. At first glance, Caleb appeared to be either indifferent about my interest in Tammy or insanely jealous.

After a long silence and a quicker than usual walk home, Caleb finally answered: "I guess she does really like you."

"I'll call you later tonight, so we can make plans to leave together in the morning," I said.

The growing tension between us was so obvious that even our routine departure was different. We didn't bother to give each other our traditional hand and finger-popping dap.

*****

When my parents arrived home from work later that evening, I reminded them of tomorrow's track meet.

"Well, Miguel, your father and I are to meet downtown with the attorney to do some paperwork for the land in Corrigan. Maybe your brothers can make it there. But I'm not sure about David, since he works on weekends, baby. We'll make it up to you," mom promised.

In actuality I wasn't expecting dad to make the meet anyway.

Dad was a stout man at 5-feet, 10-inches tall. He had sandy red hair and honey-brown eyes. He grabbed me firmly on my left shoulder to show his support of me in the track competition. My father didn't embrace me often, but when he did it was welcomed. I just wished that he didn't smoke so damn much.

Dee said she could not make the event because she had to

meet with a study group for college algebra. David, watching
television in a different room from everyone else, chose not
to attend either but didn't offer a reason. It was safe for him
to stick with mom's excuse: work.

Troy said he wouldn't be there because he needed to
focus on his classes now that football season was over.

Yeah, right!

Fay, my youngest sister, was a seventh-grader. She was the
only one who appeared to take interest in my sport.

"I'll go! I'll go!" she shouted with excitement.

"Girl, you can't go to no track meet. You will stay here
with Dee and watch your grandmother!" mom ordered before
starting the evening dinner.

After being let down by my family, I stormed out, passing
Big Momma's open door.

A moment later, I heard a faint knock at my door. It was my
God-fearing Big Momma coming to soothe my fragile ego. She
reminded me that even when man wasn't there for me that
Jesus wouldn't forsake me. She told me to read Isaiah 41:9-13.

I reached for my Bible next to my bunk bed to read the
inspirational passage aloud:

*"I brought you from the ends of the earth. I called you
from its farthest corners and said you must serve me. I did
not reject you, but chose you. Do not be afraid - I am with
you! I am your God. I will strengthen you; I will help you; I
will uphold you with my victorious right hand. See, all your
angry enemies lie confused and shattered. Anyone opposing you will die. You will look for them in vain - they will
all be gone. I am holding you by your right hand - I, the
Lord your God - and I say to you, don't be afraid; I am here
to help you."*

When I had finished, I was filled with assurance. I believed
nothing could shake me, or my faith. My grandmother then
instructed me to keep God's words with me always. As she

continued to show signs of deteriorating vision from glaucoma, she exited my room by touching the walls to locate the door.

I then telephoned Caleb and made arrangements to meet him in the morning. After that short conversation, I called Tammy and thanked her for the gift and to verify her presence for my track debut. But, to my surprise, she wasn't home.

A male voice indicated she was out for the rest of the evening.

****

"Runners. On your mark. Get set. POW!" The blast of the starter-gun reverberated throughout the field, commencing the 440-yard race. I ran in Lane 4 and had a good start out the blocks.

The loud cheering interfered with my concentration at first, but I managed to establish a smooth rhythm that drove me into second place as I approached the curve. My teammate, Zac, was leading, but I began to gain momentum to even the race. With only seventy-five yards to the finish, I nudged ahead, pulling away gradually. A few seconds later I would glide to victory, breaking the finish-line tape in championship form. Zac finished second, with other cross-town rivals following.

A burst of cheers greeted my victory.

"Forty-eight seconds," the timer yelled when I had crossed the finish line.

"You won! You won! You won!" an exuberant Tammy said.

Although tired from the race, my confidence was punctuated by the crowd's support. I basked in the celebration. I fell in love with the taste of victory. How sweet it is.

When I glanced at Tammy, I noticed her joy. I also noticed she was carrying a small child on her hip.

I waved toward her direction before heading to get my official time and clothing from the arena.

Caleb entered the field to assist me.

"Man, I told you that you were gonna beat them punks," he bragged.

"Yeah, man! I thought Zac had me for a minute there."

"Yeah! I almost had you, Miguel," uttered Zac, who walked up behind us. He gave me a congratulatory pat on the ass.

But before he walked away, Zac warned that he would seek revenge.

I then turned my attention to Caleb. "Say, man. Is that Tammy's little sister or something."

"Yeah. That's her something – her little girl," Caleb answered.

"Oh!" I said, speechless and stunned.

Then Coach Turney walked up.

"Good job, Miguel! Good job!" he said, walking with a clipboard and stopwatch. "Well, we clocked you at 48.7, which may be the fastest time this year. We won't know until the middle of the week."

Still looking at his stopwatch in his right hand, Coach said, "But I'm sure that you're leading in the district so far. Congratulations, Miguel! Oh, by the way, keep yourself warm from this cool air because you, Zac, Bob and Roland are running the mile-relay for the finale."

"Well, you heard him, Speedster. Put your clothes on and keep warm," Caleb ordered.

I then followed the coach's, and Caleb's, orders even as my mind kept wandering back to Tammy and the baby. I panned the crowd to find her. When I spotted her she was still standing near the finish line as if waiting on me to cross it again for a final lap.

"Say, Caleb. I'm gonna holla at your cousin for a minute, OK?"

"All right, go ahead, man. I'll be here waiting for ya. Hurry back, niggah."

I then approached Tammy with a sparkle in my eyes and a plan to get into her panties sooner or later.

"Hi, Miguel. Boy, you looked real good out there today."

"Thank you. And who's this pretty little thang on your hip, Tammy?" I asked, pretending not to know.

"This is my daughter, Olivia."

"And I'm 4!" Olivia said.

"You're 4, huh? You sure are small to be 4 years old, Little Pretty," I said touching her small hands.

"Say thank you, Olivia!"

"Thank you," said a smiling and coy Olivia, tilting her head downward and nibbling on the tip of her thumb.

"You're welcome."

"So you wanna come over after the meet? I have the place all to myself until eight o'clock tonight," suggested Tammy.

"Yeah! You know I do! I'll be there about 3 o'clock, OK?

After our brief conversation, I dashed back onto the field to rejoin Caleb and prepare for the next competition. I was anxious for the track meet to be over, knowing that I was, perhaps, hours away from getting some ass.

After my victorious 440-yard race, I was really pumped for the finale. The Sterling Raiders men's track team was unstoppable. We not only won the finale (the mile relay), but the team won the overall meet.

Tammy and I eventually met up, but I decided to make a good impression on our first date. I avoided risqué behavior; instead I decided to shower her with praise and prove to her I was a perfect gentleman.

For the rest of the season, I ran times I never imagined. I won the regional meet in my events and finally excelled to the state competition, where I fared respectably in the 440-yard dash as the season neared its peak.

My junior year as a competitor produced similar stellar results as I began to further lay the groundwork for my future. I received encouragement from my coach, fellow teammates and classmates, who all saw my potential to make a name for myself as a professional athlete. But I had to focus first on getting through high school and eventually college.

****

With school out for my junior year I began training even harder because I knew my senior year had to be my best ever if I expected to obtain a college scholarship. So I began keeping myself in shape by lifting weights and doing extra work on the weekends. I also was seeing Tammy in my spare time and promised myself not to lose focus of my goals. I also sensed that Tammy was seeing someone else – maybe the baby's daddy.

One particular Friday in June, Tammy and I were alone at her parent's home. I was highly excited because the last time we met she held out on me, playing hard to get. Eventually, our hormones raced out of control. First, the kissing then the removal of our clothes. As we left the sofa for her bedroom, I gently picked her up by her 24-inch waist, while softly stroking her bare breasts with my moist tongue. She reciprocated by wrapping her long, seductive legs around my waist, resting her calves around my muscular round ass while plowing her lips, tongue and teeth into the crevices of my moist neck.

Not missing a beat, I carried her toward the bed, which was neatly draped with pink-and-white linens. Her legs were still locked around my body. I then lowered her seductively onto the firm mattress, lying between her smoothly shaved legs, which were spread slightly apart into the air for easy entry. It was time to get my ol' jimmy wet – to pop that ass like I had envisioned for weeks.

"Oh, Miguel, Oh, Miguel," moaned Tammy, melting into a state of ecstasy. "I want it, baby! Ohhh! I want it."

Perspiring profusely, I began working my moves in rapid succession that we both began panting and howling like two Chihuahuas fucking in a pepper patch.

I gradually slowed down but continued to stroke her desire as she continued to moan.

Then all of a sudden, it happened.

"Miguel! What's happening?" Tammy groused.

As I was attempting to get my freak on, I suddenly lost my erection. It was one of the most humiliating moments. How could this happen to me? I wanted her so badly, but I could not perform. So I just lay there between her warm sex, crumbling like a fragile cookie.

"Don't feel bad, Miguel," a disappointed yet supportive Tammy said. She wanted the jimmy just as bad as I wanted the ass. "It happened to Kelvin, too," she said, speaking about my best friend's brother, her cousin.

Surprised, and with my mouth slightly ajar, I slowly peered into Tammy's hazel eyes. I wondered if I had heard her correctly.

"Kelvin? But ain't Kelvin your first cousin?" I thought. I wanted to ask, but I kept quiet. I was dumbfounded. She had actually slept with her first cousin. Maybe that explains the baby. And come to think of it, Olivia does look like Kelvin. Could this be the reason Tammy smokes so damn much. Perhaps she's bothered by the fact that her first cousin is her baby's daddy.

I snapped out of my daze.

"Oh, really. It happened to Kelvin, too?" I asked coolly, trying to subdue my shock.

"Yeah! You sure you don't want to try again?" she asked.

"No. I think I'm gonna make it home and take a rain check. It's getting late."

We gathered our clothes from the front room floor and called it a night. We hugged and kissed goodbye. After Tammy heard Olivia's voice, she bid me farewell.

I left perplexed, wondering which was more haunting – not getting an erection or finding out that the father of Tammy's child was her first cousin. This struck me as abnormal and unacceptable.

Chapter 3
Booty Call

I was anxious for Saturday morning to arrive. It marked the big Day After – the day after my embarrassing escapade with Tammy.

I was still livid over my failure to copulate with her. I thought long and hard about calling her, but I was disgraced. So I decided to call Caleb instead. He always seemed to comfort me in times of need.

For a moment, I entertained the thought of telling Caleb about my fling with Tammy. But I remembered how he acted the last time I had mentioned Tammy's name to him – jealousy in his voice and eyes.

"I can't tell Caleb shit about this," I mumbled while waiting on someone to answer my telephone call. "He'll laugh at me until there's no tomorrow. I just know it."

"Hello!" a voice answered.

"Can I speak to Caleb?" I asked, still weighing my decision whether to spill the beans.

"Yeah. Hold on."

I eventually realized the voice on the other end was Kelvin. I squirmed at the thought of him sleeping with Tammy.

"Hello," Caleb answered.

"What's up, man?" I asked.

"Nuttin, man! What's going on with you?"

"Well, I was thinking maybe you, me and Zac could hang out at AstroWorld today, man. You down for that?" I asked. My desire to be in Caleb's presence was stronger than ever now. Perhaps I was looking for an escape after the embarrassment with Tammy.

"Zac! When you and Zac start hangin' out, niggah?" Caleb asked curiously.

"Man, calm down! He's my teammate. Zac's cool. Do you wanna go or what?" I asked. I was a little miffed yet a little flattered by Caleb's retort. He was becoming territorial about our friendship. It was somewhat sexy, albeit unnatural. I was vibing his attitude, but feeling odd thinking that another dude could arouse my interest on such a level. I slapped myself, figuratively speaking, and dismissed the notion.

"Yeah, OK. What time?" Caleb finally conceded.

"About 2 o'clock. I think Zac can get the Volkswagen then. I'll call and make sure," I said.

"All right. Call me back. Oh and, Miguel, you wanna spend the night over here at my house? We can go to church tomorrow," Caleb asked.

"Yeah. That's cool, man." My excitement increased at the thought of Caleb and me hanging out together all day and night.

After ending the call with Caleb, I called Zac to confirm our outing and transportation.

I informed my mom, and she approved of my arrangements – but not without a mild tongue-lashing. She reminded me to always consult first with her or my father before accepting an overnight invitation. She then admonished me for not inviting my younger brother, Troy, to AstroWorld.

"Why didn't you ask Troy if he wanted to go?" she asked with her hands resting on her robust hips.

"Because Troy always starts trouble with me. That's why!"

"Well, you and your brothers had better start getting along

because one day y'all gonna need each other, Miguel." She then stormed toward her bedroom.

"Well, he can go if he wants," I said softly, as she disappeared into the back hallway.

I then began to reflect on the time Troy used to tease me during childhood when I suffered from incontinence. We shared the same bed even though I had recurring bouts of involuntary urination. The bed-wetting was just another humiliating point in my early life – second only to my recent experience with Tammy in a failed attempt to consummate our relationship. But was it all about sex? Maybe not.

As the afternoon minutes ticked away, my telephone rang about 2 p.m. It must be Caleb or Zac calling, I thought. To my surprise, it was Tammy, asking about my plans for the day.

"So, you already made plans for today, huh?

"Yeah! Me, Zac, Caleb and Troy are going to AstroWorld in a lil' bit," I answered.

"I guess I'll talk to ya later. Bye!" Tammy said abruptly – slamming the receiver down before I could respond.

To hell with her. It was just the way it was, whether she liked it or not.

Later, I heard the doorbell, and mom yelled for one of us to answer. Zac had arrived with the car.

Troy! Let's go!" I was still fuming over the short conversation with Tammy and thinking how rude she was. Selfish bitch!

"Y'all be careful," mom cautioned. She got out of her bed to confirm that Zac was driving.

Zac greeted her from his Volkswagen Beetle.

For several hours the guys and me spent the day bonding, enjoying the amusement park rides and watching girls. It turned out to be a beautiful day – even my brother Troy enjoyed himself.

When we returned from a day of frolicking, Caleb and I gathered my personal items and headed to his house two blocks away. I wrestled with my inner demons and the uncharted feelings for Caleb. Even so, I would not let those things unnerve me. This was going to be a day to remember.

Approaching Caleb's house, we noticed Kelvin sitting on the trunk of his dad's Buick LeSabre with both feet resting on the chrome-plated bumper as if he were a James Dean action figure.

Kelvin, a slim fellow with a large Afro and light-brown eyes, had a sinister countenance, despite the neatly groomed moustache that highlighted his vibrant, red lips. Many people called him Red because of his high-yellow complexion.

When Caleb and I approached Kelvin I became more bitter at the thought of him sleeping with Tammy. I chose to focus on the sleepover instead.

"What's up, Kelvin?" Caleb and I asked in unison.

"Nuttin', fellas. How was AstroWorld?"

"It was all right," Caleb answered, as he and I walked through the garage door carrying my belongings.

When we entered the house, Caleb's mother was sitting in the family room chatting with a friend. They both waved and smiled as we passed.

After entering Caleb's room, I absorbed the ambience of his room. As we began storing my clothes, his mother knocked on the door to formally welcome me.

Scouting the incense-filled room with the aroma of honeysuckle, I began to admire Caleb's walls. They were filled with album covers of various artists, including Donna Summer; Parliament Funkadelics; Prince; Earth, Wind & Fire; and Rufus featuring Chaka Khan.

Pulling music from his audio rack system, Caleb blasted the sounds of *"Brickhouse."* As I reclined on the full-size bed, I became enraptured by the lyrics of Lionel Richie and the Commodores. Caleb's room felt like home away from home.

After dinner and more music, we showered and dressed for bed. It was clear by now that Caleb and I would be sharing the same bed. All I had to do was stay on my side of the bed and everything would be all right. There was no way I was about to reveal my hidden feelings and risk ruining my friendship with Caleb. Besides, I wasn't a fag.

As I kneeled to pray, I thanked God for the day, my family and friends. Afterward, Caleb loaded more music and I could still smell the honeysuckle. *"Reasons"* by Earth, Wind & Fire, featuring Phillip Bailey, piped through the room.

With Caleb quietly singing in the background and the tranquility of the black light and incense, I drifted into a deep sleep. I began to fantasize about caressing and kissing a small, breasted woman as our bodies infused each other – her hands stroking my back and ass ever so gently.

Caleb's face suddenly replaced that of the female in my dream, with our lustful thoughts advancing to full erections and grinding. I fought hard to control my emotions. But the visual images intensified, causing me to jerk involuntarily in my dream and ultimately awakening me. My shit was as hard as steel. I sensed Caleb had noticed my erratic behavior and was secretly watching me.

Suddenly, I was stricken with a jolt of reality. I began to physically experience the gentle strokes I had only dreamed about earlier. Only this time it wasn't from the female of my dream, but from the actual hand of my bedmate, Caleb. I felt his warm, masculine hands gently rubbing up and down my buttocks in the darkness.

I simultaneously experienced anxiety and pleasure, even wondering if I had lapsed back into a dream. But then when my eyes narrowly opened, I was in disbelief. Caleb was unaware that I caught a glimpse of him fondling me.

The room began to fill with a high-intensity tempo as Earth, Wind & Fire's *"Kalimba,"* with drums and bamboo woodwinds like those at an African dance ritual, blared in the background. The pounding of our hearts next to each other was fast and furious.

Lying stunned, I began to feel the fingers of Caleb's right hand entering the narrow passageway of my ass as I lie on my left side. As uncomfortable as it felt, I still pretended to be asleep and not bothered by the intrusion. Then I gently turned on my back to retreat from the anal assault from Caleb's fingers. But when I again opened my eyes slightly, the assault continued. But, this time, my stiff "jimmy" was the target.

Caleb's hands, lips and tongue zeroed in on my hard jimmy. It was my first experience with a male, but I welcomed the forbidden sex, as I knew it. The sensual oral experience and euphoria made me squirm. My toes began to curl, my ass locked and a gusher of viscid liquid erupted from my hard sex.

I couldn't believe what had just happened in Caleb's bedroom. I was supposed to be the one despising and avoiding this "fag" shit, but it turned out that my best friend was the one who set this whole thing up. What a slick motherfucker! This was a booty call, and I answered.

Shame on me.

After it was over, guilt and fear overwhelmed me. I lie in silence scared to move or speak. If mom or dad ever found out that I had performed such a despicable act they would "skin me alive," torture and tar me or perhaps even worse disown me.

Caleb then got up and headed for the bathroom to clean himself.

When he got back, I shamefully turned opposite of him and wrapped myself with the bed covers, eventually falling asleep and not knowing what the next hour or morning would bring. But I was certain that that would be the last time Caleb and I would ever do that again.

****

"Caleb! It's nine 'o clock. You and Miguel get up for breakfast," his mother ordered as she knocked on the door.

"OK!" Caleb replied. He leaped out of bed as if everything were normal.

The smell of bacon and coffee filled the house, and I could still hear the sound of metal utensils hitting the skillets from the kitchen.

"Miguel, you up?" Caleb asked quietly.

"Yeah," I answered softly.

After I got out of bed, I wasn't sure what to say. The quietness was ominous as I was too ashamed to make eye contact with Caleb. I quickly dashed to the bathroom across the hall to brush my teeth. As I looked in the mirror, my face registered guilt. "FAGGOT!" I shouted within.

To my surprise, Caleb entered the bathroom and stood next to me to brush his teeth, too. As we stood there, we glimpsed at each other's reflection in the mirror. Suddenly, Caleb broke the gloom by using the faucet to squirt cold water in my face. I grinned and engaged in water combat, relieved the tension was over.

"Man, stop tripping!" I demanded, while laughing like a hyena with water dripping from my forehead and cheeks.

"You ready for breakfast, man?" a smiling Caleb asked.

"Yeah. Whenever you are, man."

Caleb made it seem so easy to move on. Had he been in this position before, I wondered. And, if so, with whom?

After finishing our Southern-style breakfast, Caleb and I prepared for church, not once mentioning our sexual encounter. It was a mutual understanding that a code of silence was best for something so taboo. The fact still remained: I hated what I had done even though I welcomed the act that would surely haunt me. Was I becoming a full-blown faggot, or was this just a phase?

Chapter 4
A Starry Night

My senior year was finally here, so I began consulting with my school counselors about college. Unfortunately, my academic performances in math and science were poor. I had taken only an intermediate algebra course and introductory physics, which weren't sufficient for my planned major in architecture.

I needed to take two more upper-level math and science courses to try to improve my chances on college entrance exams. Over time, I took advantage of several study groups to obtain an acceptable GPA. During this stressful period, I avoided friends and relationships. Caleb and I would still meet as usual, but my relationship with Tammy had ended with that telephone conversation we had the day the fellas and I went to AstroWorld.

This was also a pivotal year for Troy, who was now a freshman running back for the Ross Sterling High football team. It seemed that we were still competing with each other for attention.

As November rolled around, the school prepared for homecoming, and Troy was ready to shine as he had done all season. He had already gained record-breaking yardage for the school, in addition to scoring an impressive nine touchdowns.

At 6 feet, 180 pounds, Troy was about two inches shorter than me. He had brown eyes and sandy red hair that matched our father's, making him a striking young replica of dad.

During Thursday morning's homeroom classes, an announcement from the intercom indicated that star players Troy Morris, Reggie May and Henry Kuntz were to be recognized Friday for their outstanding athletic contributions. In addition, the homecoming king and queen were to be selected at Memorial Field. Finalists were Caleb Thibodeaux and Roland Cox; and Anita Ross and Amelonee Shelby.

When Caleb entered the school cafeteria, followed by Zac and me, many heads turned, followed by congratulatory greetings – especially for the king nominee.

As I panned the cafeteria, I was struck by an image in a far corner that made me uneasy. I saw Kelvin and Tammy observing us with insidious stares. I quickly looked away and redirected my attention to the activity swirling around my table.

"Hey, Miguel! Ain't that your brother, Troy?" asked Caleb, pointing and waving at Troy to join us.

Zac, sipping on his lukewarm orange soda, asked Troy if he were ready for tomorrow night's game.

"Yeah, Troy, 'cause I know ya gonna kick some ass, huh?" Caleb chimed in.

Troy, a quiet and shy freshman, regaled in the attention.

"Yeah. I guess I'm ready, y'all."

I looked on without saying a word. A bit envious, I suppose.

"That's my boy! 'Cause we gonna need to win that game against Wheatley to complete our celebration when I march down that field as homecoming king tomorrow night," Caleb said boastfully.

Troy, showing little emotion other than a slight grin, nodded and said, "OK! I'll see y'all later." Then he walked away.

****

This festive homecoming night was filled with hopes of

achievements and 5,000 maniacal fans. Powerfully striking hues adorned Memorial Field. As the supercharged bands were jamming, the athletes revved up for action and cheer-leaders pulled out all the stops with extraordinary acrobatic feats. The teams' mascots gyrated around the field as howling fans from both sides rocked the stadium to an unimaginable crescendo. The thirst for bragging rights was apparent. Only one team would experience the crowning glory, and to the victors would go the spoils.

It was time to play ball.

Destined to battle to the end, Ross S. Sterling football play-ers strutted out in their blue and white team colors.

While awaiting the start of the game and the eventual half-time, the homecoming nominees scouted the sidelines. A snazzy Caleb wore a beige-and-white double-breasted tuxedo with a lavender shirt and black shoes. Roland, my teammate, was Caleb's competition. He stood far field in a light-blue tuxedo, white ruffled shirt and white patent-leather shoes. He wasn't as confident as Caleb, but he was just as handsome and charismatic. Indeed, a worthy adversary for the homecoming king crown. I also wondered why all the light-skinned dudes got all the attention.

While walking through the crowd, Caleb spotted Zac and me as we gorged on hotdogs and popcorn and gulped down sodas.

"Say, fellows! Y'all make room for me," Caleb said.

"Damn, Caleb! You lookin' good, niggah, in those threads."

I realized I had used the forbidden N-word that mom had warned me about. I made an exception this time since she wasn't around to scold me.

"Yeah, man, it ain't no way Roland gonna beat ya tonight," Zac bragged.

"Thanks, fellas. Man, ain't y'all cold drinking those sodas?" said Caleb, trying to warm his large hands by rubbing them together on this cool, crisp night.

Adjusting and zipping our jackets just to mock him, we both looked at him and laughed.

"Nah, man. We ain't the ones half-dressed trying to be pretty and freeze our asses off," I joked, just as the referee began the coin toss, which was won by the Wheatley Wildcats. The crosstown rivals chose to receive the football.

As the game commenced, the Wildcats displayed their adroitness. On their first possession they successfully moved the ball all the way down onto our 20-yard line and ultimately earned the first points on the scoreboard. The sounds of cowbells and a sea of purple-and-white pompons were out in force as the opposing band got jiggy with the beat of *"Blam! Ain't We Funky Now"* by the Brothers Johnson.

It was now getting close to halftime and homecoming activities, and the Sterling Raiders were down 7-0, but our punt-return specialists with extraordinary coverage and a gallant gallop toward midfield put us within striking range.

I watched intensely and noticed my brother Troy, wearing No. 23, approaching the field from the sideline. After the ball was snapped and strategically thrown into his hands, the crowd went wild. Using his speed and massive thighs to cut a swath through the field of muscled mass, Troy broke several tackles on his way to the end-zone for a magnificent touchdown. The celebration shifted as frenzied Sterling Raiders' fans roared.

Even I had to acknowledge my brother's swift-footed movements and joined in on the hoopla.

"Touchdown! Touchdown! Touchdown!" I shouted to Caleb and Zac, watching them leap to their feet and pumping their fists in the air like warriors.

"Yeah! Yeah! I told you your brother was gonna come through, niggah," Caleb shouted as he prepared to march toward the field before the sound of the canon signaling halftime.

Standing proudly, I thought of my family's conspicuous

absence during our sporting events. Mom and dad should have been here to witness Troy's spectacular night. Unfortunately, dad was out of town as usual on Fridays, and mom couldn't drive.

By now, Caleb had already exited the stands, and made his way toward midfield, where the other homecoming nominees had assembled. As the nominees for king and queen were being announced, Caleb appeared to be fidgeting, as if questioning his chances at winning.

I wondered where all his confidence had gone. He seemed less nervous and more self-assured in the bedroom during our little escapade than on the field.

Then the master of ceremony announced the winners: "Ladies and gentlemen, the 1977-78 homecoming king is ... Caleb Thibodeaux; and his queen is ... Anita Ross!"

Applause ringed the field, and the two winners embraced each other and walked toward the platform for their crowning moment.

Caleb admired Anita's lavender arm-length gloves and matching satin gown. Their 15 minutes of fame was utopia as they stood midfield waving and smiling at the cheering crowd before being chauffeured around inside the stadium in a new 1977 convertible Cadillac El Dorado.

Once the halftime activities ended, the Sterling Raiders went back to business.

Throughout the game, Troy would be a major factor as he had been in the past. Before the evening was over, he would score three touchdowns and rush for a 120 yards, amassing a school record. Troy and the Sterling Raiders routed their rivals 24-7, leaving the battered Wheatley Wildcats languishing in humiliation. The Raiders' fight song sent fans to their feet: "Wildcats, Wildcats why can't you attack? Can't stop these Raiders from breaking your back!"

Chapter 5
Breakup to Make Up

Caleb was still on a high on this sunny Sunday morning after the previous night's homecoming victory. He replayed the celebration in his mind over and over. As he washed his school shirts in the bathroom sink, his thoughts were interrupted suddenly. His brother, Kelvin, began to interrogate him about the bitterness between me and Tammy. Since Caleb was unaware of the acrimony, he gave his brother a blank stare.

Kelvin then told Caleb that Tammy and I had had sex.

"Who told you Miguel and Tammy fucked?" Caleb asked curiously, somewhat annoyed.

"Tammy did, Caleb!" Kelvin answered harshly. "She also said the punk couldn't even get his shit hard, man!"

"So! What are you telling me for?" Caleb asked.

"Tell that niggah he better stay outta her face!" ordered Kelvin, angrily walking away toward the family room.

"I ain't telling him shit! You tell him, niggah!" shouted Caleb, his head slightly outside the bathroom door.

While trying to regain his composure, thoughts of Miguel flashed in his head. He wondered if Tammy and Miguel actually had sex. But even if they did, he didn't see a problem and wondered why Kelvin exploded. Anyway, Tammy is not his girlfriend, just a cousin he impregnated, Caleb mumbled.

Once he finished washing his shirts and putting them in the dryer, Caleb called me on the telephone to arrange a private afternoon meeting at Crestmont Park to shoot basketball and chat.

The small park was only four blocks from my house.

After hanging up with Caleb, I wondered why he would arrange a basketball game since he had never done so before.

The only thing that came to my mind was the forbidden act that he and I experienced during the June sleepover. I became uneasy.

My thoughts were interrupted by another phone call. When I dashed toward my room to answer I ran into Troy, who was heading to the bathroom. Before answering the telephone I once again offered my congratulations to him for an indisputable homecoming win.

"Hello!" I answered hurriedly.

"What's up, Miguel?"

I instantly recognized the voice. It was Zac.

"Nothing. What's up with you?" I said.

"Well, I was just wondering if you wanted to go to Hermann Park today to scout out the girls?"

Forgetting my promise to Caleb, I accepted the offer. Then I had to retract my statement. "Oh, no I forgot. Caleb and I are going to Crestmont at three o'clock. Damn!" I said disappointedly.

"Well, tell Caleb I'll pick y'all up and all of us can go," said Zac, inviting himself.

"All right. I'll call ya back," I said, forgetting that the meeting between Caleb and me was supposed to be private.

I instantly called Caleb and told him of the change in plans.

Caleb, bitter about the change, said, "Man, I thought we were gonna get together alone and play ball. If you don't wanna hang out with me just say so, man!"

"Man, stop tripping! What's wrong with Zac going?"

"Well, fuck it then, niggah!" Caleb said, hanging up after he verbally lashed out at me.

"What a bastard!" I thought.

Standing in my room with the receiver still in my hand, I was jolted by Caleb's attitude. I then attempted to call him back, wondering what his problem was. After a few rings, Caleb answered angrily. He ripped into me again like a bull targeting a matador. I asked him what was wrong.

Clearly lying, he said sharply, "Nothing's wrong!"

He claimed he just needed to ask me something, and he wanted to ask it in person with nobody else there.

"All right, man! I'll let Zac know what's up, and I'll see you at three o'clock."

*****

As I pressed toward my rendezvous, the sound of a basketball reverberated throughout the park that was nearly empty. I watched from afar as Caleb attempted a free-throw. I then joined him in a game of 21.

Figuring I could use my eye and feet coordination to outmaneuver his slower movements, I passed the ball around my pelvis to my left and successfully faked him. The game quickly neared an end as I got the better of him.

SWOOSH! "Two more points for Miguel," I bragged. "Wanna play another one?" I asked after winning 21-15.

"Nah, man. Let's rap," Caleb said.

Several yards away from the south end of the basketball court, I noticed Caleb's brother, Kelvin, charging toward us. I immediately sensed trouble.

"What's ya brother doing here, Caleb?" I asked nervously.

"I don't know."

His answer was short and evasive.

As his brother approached, Caleb turned in the direction of the basketball goal to shoot a free throw, intentionally leaving me face to face with Kelvin.

"What's up, Kelvin?" I asked.

"Niggah! You know what's up!" Kelvin fumed.

Caleb then walked over. He stood next to his brother in what appeared to be the start of an uneven duel.

"Kelvin, what are you talking 'bout, man?" I asked again, still clueless.

Caleb joined the attack.

"Yeah, Miguel, Tammy said you and her was screwing, niggah."

"What?" I asked, trying to deny the truth. What was more unbelievable was that Caleb was turning his back on me – even after our own sexual tryst.

Kelvin suddenly pushed me in the chest and issued a staunch warning.

"Punk! You betta leave her alone and stop calling her! You hear me, niggah!" demanded Kelvin, pointing his finger in my face.

"Bitch-ass punk!" I said in silence, fearing retribution if he heard me.

"Man, leave that niggah alone, and let's go," ordered Caleb, who turned away from me, although with a hint of regret. But his words defied any remorse.

"Tammy is family, niggah! And you don't mess with family!" blurted Caleb as he walked back toward his house. To some degree, he appeared more frightened than me.

I was in total disbelief as I stood near the goal where Caleb and I had played basketball only moments earlier. I then slowly walked to the north end of the court to meditate over the incident that left me stunned. The more I thought about it the angrier I became.

"If Caleb feels that way about me, then fuck him!" I thought. "I don't need him anyway to accomplish my goals. All I need to do in the coming months is to obtain a college scholarship and shoot for the 1980 Olympic trials."

*****

Nearly five months had passed since Caleb and I had spoken to each other. It was probably best that we didn't communicate anyway – particularly with the nightmares I've been having about us having sex.

Although we didn't talk, we saw each other almost daily in passing. We were too stubborn to try to resolve our differences. I sensed that we were still emotionally, and perhaps physically, vulnerable to each other.

In the meantime, I had been hanging out with Zac, who avoided asking questions about my fractured friendship with Caleb.

Anyway, with track season in full swing, it was our hope that we would be inundated with promising recruitment offers from universities throughout the nation. As it was, Zac and I had dominated most of our events during competitions throughout Texas.

The state meet was only two weeks away. Zac and I were running times that qualified us for the long-awaited Texas Relays in Austin.

I was in the best condition of my track-and-field career and on a winning streak with nine victories in the 440-yard dash.

Unlike Zac's more glamorous 110- and 220-yard dashes – which he dominated – my 440-yard dash was less prestigious but still required a committed effort. Zac had won six consecutive titles. He and I basked in the attention from our peers at school and from universities pressuring us to commit. As far as we were concerned, the state meet was to become our theater to display our talents and lure the ultimate recruiting offers.

Since we weren't going to be competing before the Austin trials, we sought permission from Coach Turney to practice on a high school track similar to the University of Texas surface known as Mondo Rubber. To do that, we would have to travel 12 miles to a wooded enclave known as Memorial – an exclusive white area of town that had everything our neighborhood school lacked.

Pine and palm trees lined the median of each upscale boulevard, decorated with exotic plants and flowers. As we drove into the community, luxury cars populated the streets. The landscape's manicured evergreen and modern architecture, with large arched columns, made Memorial High look like a small university.

After parking near the track, I was shocked to see four black students walking across the campus. I nudged Zac, who was resting on my new 1978 Oldsmobile Cutlass Supreme Brougham coupe that I bought from money saved while working throughout the summer and holidays. The vehicle was metallic brown with crushed velvet over-sized bucket seats and equipped with an AM-FM stereo and eight-track tape deck. It drew a lot of attention.

"Say, Zac! Check that out." I nodded my head in the direction of the black students.

"Man, I didn't know black people went to this school!" an awestruck Zac said.

By now, the two of us had grabbed the attention of students nearby who probably assumed we were part of the student body. They didn't seem to care much about our presence or race but were rather impressed with my car. It was parked next to a student's red-and-white convertible Mustang.

"What's going on, fellas?" a blond student asked.

"Nothing, man. Just trying to get this practice over with," I answered. I then reached in the back seat of my car to retrieve my backpack stuffed with my track gear.

Zac went ahead of me, singing *"Jungle Boogie"* by Kool & the Gang, as he headed toward the track to begin training.

Because I embraced all races, it was refreshing to be with Zac, who unlike Caleb, was more tolerant of whites.

*****

The school bell echoed throughout the halls of Ross Sterling High School as the fourth period ended.

After I left my trigonometry class, someone tapped me on my shoulder in the hallway. The intruder was Zac.

"What's up, Miguel? Check these out, man!" said Zac, showing me opened recruitment letters from several universities.

"Where in the hell is West Texas State?" I asked curiously as I glanced through the letters.

"Somewhere outside Amarillo, in the Panhandle," Zac answered.

Sifting through his mail, I discovered a letter from a location I was familiar with because I had received one, too. It was from Oklahoma State.

Zac and I then walked toward the back exit leading to the track to begin our short practice.

Afterward, we would meet with Coach Turney, with whom we shared the news of our recruitment letters. With graduation just a month away, Coach was unaware of the many universities trying to woo us. He was pleasantly surprised.

He had assembled his squad to offer thanks and farewell to his outstanding senior athletes, followed by trophy presentations in the locker room, which reeked of athletic balm and sweaty bodies.

With the humidity and muggy conditions, track team members – some half-naked in a quest to cool off – struggled to focus on the coach's final speech.

"This has been a year of triumphs for our track squad. Therefore I would like to present these trophies to our outstanding track and field seniors – Roland Cox, Zachary Finn and Miguel Morris for their achievements and for landing attractive scholarship offers from various universities throughout the country," Coach Turney proudly proclaimed.

Cheers rang throughout the locker room as teammates were recognized. The emotional celebration helped us to ignore the muggy atmosphere. But the buildup of moisture on the concrete floor created a slippery hazard, causing Roland and Zac to lose their balance after being stampeded by ecstatic peers.

After all the hoopla, Zac and I lingered in the humid locker room to ponder and discuss our college options. As time passed, we decided to take a break from the discussion so we could shower before heading home.

The thought of the refreshing water prompted us to make a beeline for the wet area.

As I began to lather my body, I lapsed into a deep trance about my past as a youth and my future as a college student. I thought about my family, sibling rivalries, track and my absentee best friend, Caleb. I couldn't forget our little sexual tryst.

After telling myself I was not gay for the millionth time. I was unaware I had developed an erection. I snapped out of my daze only when my bar of soap slipped and torpedoed toward my foot. My outburst over my clumsiness caught Zac's attention. When I quickly turned to retrieve the soap I inadvertently exposed my erection. Damn! I was busted.

Zac must have figured I had been fantasizing about someone.

I did a quick about-face to hide my erection from Zac, who was showering nearby. I took a few deep breaths to try to relax and deflate. Zac pretended to be oblivious to my shit. When I sneaked a peek toward him, I saw that he, too, had developed a hard-on. We pierced into each other's eyes.

"Oh shit! What's going on?" I asked myself. These thoughts weren't supposed to ever happen again. Not with anyone. I had promised myself that I would never get excited over another man. Caleb was my last time! "REPENT! REPENT! REPENT! You fool!" I tried to psyche myself out.

Suddenly, the locker room doors burst open, startling us. It was Coach Turney screaming from the front to remind us that the van would leave at noon on Thursday for the state meet in Austin. After Coach left and our hearts resumed normal rhythm, we quickly exited the showers. We said nothing to

each other about our arousal.
  Temptation was averted.

Chapter 6
College Bound

The month of May was full of promise for Zac and me. The state track meet was behind us and so was the locker room scene. We could now concentrate on our academic finals and decide on a university.

Our performance in Austin was highly impressive. Matter of fact, three universities invited us to visit their campuses in June.

One of them was Oklahoma State, which agreed to pay for our airfare and room and board. Texas Tech University and West Texas State were the other Top 2 schools bidding for us. We vowed to sign with the same college.

This was also an exciting time for my oldest sister, Dee, who was completing her freshman year at Texas Southern University.

She gave me pointers on how to handle classes and professors:

"Remember, Miguel, once you get settled in your dorm, keep a copy of dorm rules and regulations so that you will be informed at all times of your rights. Registration is going to be a trip, too, so get a map of the campus from the student center and learn the campus and your routes. Professors hate it when students are late and interrupt their classes," she continued. "And, Miguel, make sure you introduce yourself to the

dean of your department because one day you may need him
or her. And you better go to class!"

Troy and David, sitting in the family room watching baseball, eavesdropped on the conversation as they drank soda
and munched on buttered popcorn.

David, in almost predictable fashion, chimed in with a bit
of sarcastic advice.

"Yeah, Miguel, make sure you don't wear your running
shorts too high 'cause people might think you're a punk!"

Troy roared in laughter like an impish child, giggling at just
about anything to entertain himself.

"Oh, boy! Stop acting silly!" Big Momma demanded.

"So y'all think that's funny, huh? Sounds like you're jealous
to me," I said as I lashed out at their stupidity. It seemed that
any time I attempted to accomplish something they tried to
rain on my parade.

"They jus' kiddin' you, baby," Big Momma said, feeling her
way to a seat at the kitchen table as she tried to ignore her
failing vision. "Them boys just silly."

"Here, Big Momma. Sit here," I said.

She again told me to remember to keep God with me at all
times and that He would supply all my needs.

Coughing to clear her throat, she struggled to talk.

" 'Cuse me, y'all! You know Big Momma's been suffering
from this long cold," she said, trying to convince herself that
she suffered a minor health problem. Fact is, she didn't know
what was wrong with her but also didn't believe in going to
the doctor. She relied on home remedies but, foremost, she
believed her faith in God would deliver her from all evil and
ailments – including her "minor" cold.

Her conversation was interrupted by her rambunctious
grandsons.

"Yeaaah! Run, niggah! Home run! Home run!" David shouted as he and Troy celebrated a score by the Houston Astros.

"Hey! What did I tell you and Troy 'bout using that word?"

mom asked angrily.

The N-word was forbidden in our house. And she meant business, too. After her admonishment, she zeroed in on Dee's potato chips and bologna sandwich as she joined the conversation between Dee and me.

"Miguel! Have you and Zac decided which college you're going to visit yet?" mom asked.

I explained that we might go to all three, but that we must score adequately on the SAT first to qualify.

*****

The last weekend in May was a joyous time at my house. Out of 582 seniors, I graduated No. 214.

With Coach Turney's influence, Zac and I decided to attend West Texas State in Canyon, Texas. The track team is led by Joseph Durham, his friend and colleague.

When I arrived home from school, my mom handed me my mail. Moments later, the phone rang for me.

"Hey, Miguel. You get any mail today, man?" Zac asked excitedly during the call.

"Yeah. Why?" I asked.

"Well open it, niggah, and look inside," he ordered.

Not knowing why Zac was hyped, I opened it. To my surprise, there were two sets of round-trip tickets to Amarillo on Ozark Airlines.

I shouted jubilantly, startling mom as she sat on the sofa sifting through her bills.

"Look, mom!" I said. I showed her my plane tickets as Zac listened through the phone.

Mom eyeballed the tickets and then became teary-eyed. The bittersweet joy of her son entering college was overwhelming.

"Oh, Miguel, I'm so proud of you!" she said.

"Thanks, mom. I love you!" I then returned to the call with Zac and told him that I would come over to his place to celebrate – but not before first giving thanks to the Father above.

While dashing down the street with tickets in hand, I noticed Caleb, who was walking toward me. It had been awhile since we talked. Our eyes locked onto each other like heat-sensing missiles; we stopped suddenly, finally facing each other again. And thanks to singing robins soaring above, a whistling calm settled over us. God knew we both had been stubborn.

"What's up?" we said in unison, both cracking a smile. A feeling of relief permeated throughout my body. We clasped hands as we had so often done in the past. His grip was still strong.

"Man, I'm sorry. I just let Kelvin trick me," Caleb said apologetically and quickly as if he'd been waiting for this moment. His sincerity was unmistakable.

"Yeah, man. It's OK." I responded. "I knew Kelvin had to have lied to you about something to cause you to completely shut me out the way you did." I was very cautious not to say anything offensive or appear vindictive over an issue that was never clearly explained in the first place.

We talked and walked. And as I now stood near Zac's driveway, I caught a whiff of the honeysuckle from the nearby tailored lawns and evergreens dotting the neighboring homes. The sweet smell of the flowers capped our special reunion after a bitter feud that lasted much too long between old friends.

I began to have flashbacks to that time in June of last year when Caleb had invited me to his house for a sleepover. The honeysuckle incense in his room helped climax an evening that would change my life forever. And since then it seemed that sex was attempting to control me, and I was powerless to fight the urges. I questioned whether it was normal to have such feelings.

Caleb rattled me from my daze, asking me what I was carrying in my hand.

A letter with plane tickets to Amarillo, I answered. "Zac

and I decided to go to West Texas State in August to run for their track program."

Noticing an oncoming car fast approaching, I quickly, but gently grabbed Caleb's left arm to pull him to safety into Zac's driveway. He thanked me and nodded with approval as I was about to exit his life for an extended period of time.

But with a sad expression, he asked, "So ya really gonna leave us, huh?" He really wanted to ask if I were going to leave *him*, but he shunned away from that question.

"Yeah, man. It looks that way. I just wished we could have been together more this year so you could have seen me run," I said.

"Well, if ya really wanna know the truth, I saw you run at Butler Stadium in March and at school for the regional meet last month," a smiling Caleb said.

"What!" I asked gleefully. I was so happy to hear that Caleb supported me even during our separation. I instantly began to feel closer to my old friend once again. Talking to Caleb made me realize the huge void in my life – something much deeper than my big plans for college life and beyond.

"So, man, you were really there supporting me during my competitions?" I was grateful.

"Yeah, Miguel. I was. Because I … I love ya, man," Caleb said nervously, uncertain how I would respond to his verbal affection. He caught me off guard.

"Damn, man. I love you, too." I spontaneously grabbed his right shoulder and embraced him. Hugging another man publicly may have been taboo before, but not this time. It felt right, and I felt empowered – even outdoors in the middle of the day.

Several minutes had passed as Caleb and I stood in the hot driveway reminiscing. I then remembered Zac was waiting for me.

I invited Caleb to join us since we were already in front of Zac's house. That way we could all celebrate the scholarships together. Yet, for some reason, I sensed that this meeting with Caleb was the beginning of an end for us.

"Can I come to visit you one weekend?" Caleb asked.

"You know you can," I said, gazing into his widened eyes as I winked surreptitiously. But even with all the titillation I figured a visit was just a remote possibility, although I could not rule it out based on the look in Caleb's eyes. We were like fragile glass as we prepared to confront our varying emotions in the coming months and perhaps the coming years.

*****

The sounds of jet engines echoed on this warm August day as Zac and I approached Houston Hobby Airport in the back seat of my dad's Buick Electra 225. I wanted to take my car to the university, but freshmen weren't allowed to have cars on campus. I was really starting to miss my Cutlass Supreme Brougham, which I voluntarily allowed to be repossessed.

Looking quietly into the clear blue sky and at the monstrous metal aircraft preparing to land, Zac and I scoped the familiar sights around us, realizing we would have to get used to another city soon as we prepared for our destiny.

Shortly before arriving at the airport terminal, mom reached beneath the car's plush seats and grabbed two packages, handing one each to me and Zac.

"Those are gifts from Big Momma," said mom. "So, don't open them until you get on the plane, OK?" She then reminded dad, who was holding a cigarette, that he could smoke only when the kids were out of the car.

Zac and I promised to abide by her request but were anxious to know the contents of the packages.

"There's Ozark Airlines!" mom said to dad.

"Honey, I see it!" he snapped. He was a little testy because he craved a cigarette.

Dad, a quiet but no-nonsense man, viewed women as subservient. He didn't particularly like being told what to do or how to do it. He guarded his ego.

"Now, Miguel and Zac, when y'all get to Amarillo ..."

"It's Canyon, honey," said mom, correcting my dad.

"Well, Canyon! Call us when y'all settle in your dorms," dad instructed – his stern eyes directed at my mom. His annoyance toward my mom for correcting him was obvious.

"Yes, sir," we answered simultaneously.

When dad parked near the curbside, mom exited the car swiftly before dad could open the door for her. She zipped toward the back door where I was sitting and stared into space as dad unloaded the baggage from the trunk. Mom then tapped on the back window alerting her young charges to exit.

This was our first flight.

"Are y'all scared?" she asked.

"Yes, ma'am!" Zac answered quickly.

She smiled and said, "Y'all will be OK."

Minutes later, we were met by cool air gushing through the wide corridors as we proceeded to our terminal.

We were awestruck by the many Ozark aircraft, some of which were propelled and others jet-driven. Since Zac and I didn't know the difference between the two, dad enlightened us. He pointed out that jet-driven craft are much faster and smoother than propellers. He then gave us a short history lesson:

"BMW started off as a company that made small engines for airplanes in the '30s and '40s. Did y'all know that? Pilots flying with those powerful BMW engines noticed that the rotating propellers formed a colorful illusion, which eventually led to the blue-and-white BMW logo. So you see, with a reputable company like BMW, flying is as safe as driving a car," he said.

Now armed with that information, I hoped for a smooth ride to Amarillo's Airport with a jet engine that was as smooth as a BMW engine.

But the moment of truth soon arrived.

"Flight 191 now boarding to the Golden Triangle area. Amarillo, Midland/Odessa and Lubbuck now boarding," a woman airline agent announced on the PA system.

It was also my parents' cue to bid their farewells. Zac and I then headed toward the Jetway. And much to our chagrin, we were led to a propeller plane.

Once inside, two blondes with pronounced Texas accents greeted us. One led us to our adjoining seats as the other greeted boarding passengers.

After getting settled, we noticed large propellers slowly turning. There were no blue-and-white colors to indicate that this was an aircraft engineered by BMW.

So, to take our minds off the fear of flying, Zac and I retrieved Big Momma's gift packages from beneath our seats and discovered Bibles with $100 bills in each. The money was strategically placed atop a marked scripture.

As the plane began its ascent, I closed my eyes temporarily to affirm my courage. I then began to read the passages: Isaiah 41:9-13. It was the same scripture that Big Momma shared with me when my family didn't make it to my first track meet. As turbulence rocked the aircraft, I read it softly to Zac:

"I brought you from the ends of the earth. I called you from its farthest corners and said to you, "You are my servant!" I did not reject you, but chose you. Do not be afraid – I am with you! ...

Chapter 7
Butch Webber:
American Sports Idol

As Zac and I traveled down the long stretch of highway that led to campus, a huge billboard greeted us: "Welcome to Canyon, Texas – Home of the West Texas State University Buffaloes."

While in the back of Coach Durham's canary yellow Cadillac Coupe DeVille, he pointed out landmarks along the 15-mile course such as Paladora Canyon, an expanse of land with long-horned cattle grazing on the vegetation. It was an eyeful. For those who actually think Houston is too country, West Texas takes the cake.

Coach Durham was about 34 years old, 5-feet, 5-inches tall – a short man by most standards – with a reddish tan, neatly combed brown hair and hazel eyes. He had a fatherly image and a seriousness about himself that put you in the mind of actor Robert Redford.

As we continued the journey down the highway, our noses were put to the test.

The smell of cow dung and ammonia from a buildup of cattle urine and molasses – used to enrich production of milk – assaulted our nostrils like the force of a proverbial West Texas twister. This was an instant reminder that we were far from the big city. Coach Durham appeared to be amused by our reaction as he noticed our contorted faces. He assured us our noses would adjust to the smells before long.

When we arrived on campus, I noticed a maroon-and-white water tower, depicting the colors of the West Texas State Buffaloes. The aura of the campus, encompassed by large dorms and huge administrative structures, was a paradox to the small town outside the university.

After reaching the athletic dorm, we noticed athletes unloading luggage and packages of various sizes. Zac and I followed suit, hauling our electronic equipment and other gear and goods from the trunk of our chauffeured Cadillac.

"Well, guys, this is it," Coach Durham said.

"Yeah! This place is pretty big," I said.

"Sure is," agreed Zac, surveying our new home.

I observed the campus with doubts about fitting in. Time would definitely tell.

As we approached the front doors of the five-story burnt-orange brick dorm, Coach Durham struggled with a piece of luggage while leading us toward our room. It had become obvious that Zac and I would be roommates. Could he and I handle the apparent attraction we had for each other?

"Whose heavy baggage is this?" asked Coach, leaning awkwardly.

"It's Miguel's," Zac answered with a chuckle.

"OK. Here we are. Room 24B." Coach was relieved as he sat the heavy luggage down to retrieve the door keys from his pocket.

The white-walled room was large and spacious with double beds made of soft pine. The smell of incense reminded me of Caleb's home back in Houston. Matter of fact, a few things began to remind me of Caleb: the scents, window shades, and even Zac's presence. Although Zac and Caleb did not look alike in the face they shared some other physical characteristics. They were both masculine with an athletic build.

"Welcome to West Texas State once again guys. I'm going

to leave my home number with you two, and as soon as you settle in give me a call before 5 o'clock and we will go out to dinner. OK?" Before leaving, Coach placed the door keys on one of the pine desks. He walked out, rattling coins in his pockets – perhaps happy that he had no more bags to carry.

"So this is what it feels like to be in college, huh?" Zac asked.

"Yeah … lost," I answered, still unsure if I really wanted Zac as a roommate.

"Yeah. Me, too, Miguel," responded Zac, not having a clue about what was going on in my head.

We postponed our unpacking and selected our beds, then immediately crashed from the long travel. We stared at the white ceiling of Buffalo Towers, listening to music pumping throughout the corridor from rapper Kurtis Blow and the Sugarhill Gang.

Soon thereafter, a hard knock at the door interrupted our rest. I quickly glanced toward the door as it opened slowly. A large, muscular, shirtless dude stood in the doorway juggling a football. The visitor, no doubt an upperclassman, exuded confidence.

"What's up, fellas?" he asked in a deep, raspy voice and a wide bright smile.

"What's going on, man?" I asked, admiring the stranger and his leather pigskin.

"Freshmen, huh?" he queried.

"Yeah, we're from Houston," Zac said proudly as if it were a big deal.

"Yeah! Me, too," said the interloper.

"I'm Butch Webber. I'm across the hall in 25B."

He made his way over to offer a friendly handshake.

As we sat up in bed, we took in Butch's towering presence. From our supine position, he came across as a hulk of a man, like that of "Andre the Giant" – the French international wrestling star from back in the day.

Yes, Butch was huge. At 6-feet, 4-inches tall with bulging biceps and triceps, he flaunted his King Kong hairless chest. His skin was chocolate brown. Large veins protruded from his massive arms that had a few nicks, apparently from aggressive football action. His chiseled face resembled a young O.J. Simpson, and his colossal hands swallowed Zac's and mine when he reached out for a formal greeting. This guy's body was serious, a human machine that appeared invincible. Hell, his smile alone was lethal.

"So, what part of Houston you from?" Zac asked.

"Southpark," Butch answered quickly.

"Southpark! We're from Southpark, too." All of a sudden, I was now proud to be from that part of the 'hood.

"Yeah. Where?" Butch asked curiously as he tossed the football in the air.

Crestmont area, we answered, as we observed the football player's movements, his deep eyes and his cockiness.

"Man, this is a small world for sure. I'm from there, too!" said Butch, acknowledging his homeboys.

"So, what grade are you in?" I asked.

Judging from Butch's look, I realized I had made a stupid blunder.

But Zac didn't make it any better when he chimed in.

"Yeah, Butch, what grade?"

"Grade? There's no grade here. You are classified as freshman, sophomore, junior or senior, which is what I am," a proud Butch explained. He repeated it for effect. "I'm a senior. You're a freshman."

Embarrassed, I said, "Oh, we didn't know." And before I could get another word out, our new cocky friend interrupted.

"Now you do," said Butch, twirling the football on his right index finger. The boy had skills and a sharp tongue.

As the conversation carried on a few minutes longer, Butch began to dance to the funky sounds of George Clinton and the Parliament Funkadelics. He then made his way to exit the door while chanting to the tune of "*Flashlight*."

"*Flashlight, Red Light, Neon Light, Stop Light*," he continued.

"Oh. By the way, fellas, welcome to Big Boys Territory!" said Butch, gesturing goodbye and leaving Zac and I a tad envious.

*****

When the alarm clock sounded early Monday we struggled to get out of bed to prepare for registration that was a couple hours away. We also got a telephone call from Coach Durham, checking in on his investments and making sure we didn't oversleep. Before ending the call, Zac assured the coach we would register on time.

As I surfed the television for the latest sports and weather updates, I saw a familiar face on the screen. It was Butch Webber being interviewed by a local sports reporter about the upcoming scrimmage game with Texas Tech in three weeks. Zac and I marveled at how well the "local celebrity" skillfully and articulately handled the questions. His professional demeanor captivated us. Because of Butch, I began to imagine myself in the spotlight one day just like my Southpark homeboy.

After the alarm sounded again, we shifted gears and prepared to bolt out of the door.

*****

Registration was a maze of booths, signs and endless lines. Anxious students could only hope that class space was still available.

I was surprised when Butch and I stood together in one of the lines. I wondered why a senior would be enrolling in freshman literature. Nevertheless, we both registered for the same course and time for 9:30 a.m. Tuesdays and Thursdays. This seemed to be an ideal situation for me because I would have a study mate – and who better than my neighbor, Butch Webber?

After finishing with his registration, Zac located me. I was still attempting to sign up for my final class – an 8 a.m. algebra course.

As I acknowledged Zac, the young lady assisting me inquired about our geographic background.

"So, where are you guys from?" she said.

"Houston." This was a question that we quickly learned we were proud to answer.

"Big City guys, huh?" she replied.

"It's an OK city," I answered modestly.

"My name is Patsy. Patsy Pollard." She reached out to shake our hands.

Patsy was a 22-year-old white senior pharmacy major with straight brown shoulder-length hair, hazel eyes and a silky tanned complexion. She seemed a bit flirtatious, judging from the way she kept flipping her hair while talking. She was not drop-dead gorgeous but still rather attractive. And it was obvious that she was digging us black men. Digging me.

I introduced myself, and then Zac as my roommate.

She told us that the algebra class I needed was closed for the time I wanted but that another class time was available.

Disappointment brushed my face, but I chose a later class instead.

"By the way, I tutor freshman algebra at Buffalo Towers on Wednesday and Friday evenings from 7 p.m. to 8 p.m. if you need help, Miguel. Many of the athletes know me, so just ask around and I wouldn't mind tutoring you."

I thanked her, and she acknowledged me again with a handshake, this time holding it firmly as if it were hers to keep. She was being overly hospitable.

"Thanks. I'll remember that," I said and walked away, this time exuding some of the same cockiness as my gridiron classmate Butch. I was puffed up like a loaf of fresh oven-baked bread.

"I think she likes you, Miguel," Zac said, nudging me in the side, much like Caleb would do.

"You really think she likes me?" I asked.

"What do you think? You know what they say! Once you go black, you never go back!" Zac said rhythmically.

"I know that's right!" I was glowing as I left the auditorium for chow time.

Butch caught up with me and asked if I were ready for class next Monday. I said of course, because I was now in "Big Boy Territory" – to borrow his phrase. All I had to do was market my skills, and I was on my way to a successful season. Could it be that simple? I was hopeful.

Days after registration, Butch challenged me to a flex test as we stood facing the vertical mirror that hung from my closet door. Despite being two inches shorter, I accepted his flex challenge. On this hot day, it was a good excuse to showcase my goods, too. I knew I was no match, but I was proud of my slender muscular body and chest.

His dominating presence intimidated me to some degree. Whenever we walked in the hallway, I admired his Herculean calves that supported his razor-cut thighs, which fit snuggly inside his Levi khakis shorts. As usual, this shirtless Trojan carried his prized treasure – his football, much like the Charlie Brown character Linus with an affinity for his blanket.

Butch was obviously proud of his killer abs. Forget the six-pack, this man had an eight-pack.

After throwing his football to me, he offered some fitness and nutritional advice.

"Say, fella. If you want to grow, you gotta start lifting weights and eating right," Butch advised. "You know, I used to be about your size when I was a freshman. Football gave me the size and strength I needed, not to mention an appetite as well."

"But I don't play football, so how can I grow like that?" I asked envying his biceps, triceps and abs.

"Well, there's a weight coach, and he's there for every

sport. So you just get hooked up with him. It won't take much for those little birds of yours to grow like these eagles. To work with me you gotta stay focused," he said pointing to his bulging biceps. "You're halfway there already," Butch said squeezing my biceps - unaware he was sending chills throughout my body.

Damn, he was confusing me. I didn't know how to separate his advice from my lust. Even though I had done it before, it still oftentimes felt strange being touched by another man, other than my dad. And even that was rare. Matter of fact, the men in my immediate family didn't express much affection at all, verbally or physically. We were definitely deficient in that area.

"Where's Zac?" Butch asked.

"He's visiting some girl at Jones Hall," I said, elated that Butch and I were alone.

Butch then walked toward my side of the room to rest. He sat down to sift through the many albums in my record collection. He gently placed one onto the turntable and gracefully lowered the diamond cut needle onto the third selection of the album.

The crisp sounds of The Isley Brothers' "*Fight the Power*" bellowed.

I then picked up Butch's football and tossed it to him. He lowered his back to my bed and tossed the football above his body as the music filled the room. I then rested alongside him in my bed as if everything were normal. I decided to heed the sweet sounds of the lyrics that told me to fight the power - more like fight the lustful temptation building inside me.

Lying next to "my" American idol was a majestic moment.

After several songs, Butch raised from my bed. Even with my eyes closed I sensed a force hovering over me as I continued to absorb the music. I opened my eyes and saw Butch staring at me.

"Say, fella. You wanna throw some ball?" asked Butch, reaching for my right hand to eject me from bed.

"Yeah! Why not?" I answered in delight. "Say, Butch." I hesitated at first. "How come you're not with your girl today?"

"Man, I don't have no girl! I'm about to go pro, and the last thing I need is to be tied down right now with some hoochie tied to my back." He then led us out of the room as we trotted toward the warm, sunny field, where fellow student athletes were playing volleyball.

"Heads up, Miguel!' Butch shouted throwing the football in my direction.

I caught the ball with a single hand, impressing Butch.

"Looks like you got some good hands, fella."

"Yeah. That's from playing that backyard football," I said proudly.

"Well, let's see how good you are. Go for this in-and-out pass to the left." He threw the spiraling football on target into my hands.

"Yeah! You thought I couldn't catch it, huh?" I bragged holding the pigskin high above my head.

Our bodies were being nourished by the shimmering sun as the intensity of our game increased just like our conversation. We sweated through each throw and challenge while discussing our career goals and future.

Butch talked about his role as a strong safety and backup quarterback with the Buffaloes. He had big dreams.

As the sun began to set and the sounds of mating locusts became deafening, I decided to pack it in.

"You're quitting?" Butch asked with a hint of disappointment.

"Yeah. Those damn locusts are getting on my nerves, man. Anyway, I'm somewhat exhausted."

"Well, let's hit the showers," said Butch, drenched in sweat.

"What's for dinner tonight?" I asked, trying to avoid the topic of showering. I wasn't sure if I could handle being alone naked with him.

"I think sirloin and baked potatoes. I'm not really sure." Butch answered. As we walked toward our wing of the building, he recognized a familiar, yet distinct scent.

"I smell gunja, man. Gunja," said Butch, smiling and sniffling as if he'd been craving the joint.

"Yeah, man. I ain't smelled Mary Jane in a long time," I said, reaching for my key that was clipped to my belt loop. "That shit sure is strong," I said. It intensified as we got closer to my dorm room.

When I opened the door we noticed Zac lying in his bed. He smiled at Butch and me as we entered the smoky room that gave us an instant buzz. I quickly closed the door after realizing Zac was the culprit.

"What's up, fellas?" asked Zac, blowing smoke toward the ceiling. "Yeah I saw y'all getting y'all play on out there. I decided to wait for you to see if you wanted to catch the munchies with me," a smiling Zac said.

"You the man!" said Butch, reaching for a chance to inhale the stimulating herb.

I stuffed a white bath towel at the bottom of the door to try to conceal the smell. I then joined Zac and Butch as the three of us indulged in the high that we knew could get us in trouble in the long run. We were like reclusive bats in a cave.

*****

On Sunday morning, the eve before my first college class, mom called. I, of course, had a hangover. It was 9:37 a.m., and mom wanted to know if Zac and I were going to church. She then put Big Momma on the phone, and she asked the same question. So to satisfy their curiosity, I said "Yes, I'm going." I lied, even as I explained to her that there was a chapel on campus for us to attend and that service started at noon. I then told mom I went to bed late last night, and I was exhausted. I gave her a rundown on my class schedules and asked her to pray that I make it through the semester.

"Baby, you can do it," said mom, sipping on coffee.

Knowing her it was probably a hot cup of café mocha. Folgers style.

Big Momma offered her encouragement, too.

"Just remember what I always told ya. Pray and things will happen. That algebra and graphics stuff can't beat ya, baby. Just study and pray, OK," she advised. She then asked about Zac.

I knew I couldn't tell her we had been smoking dope. How could I be so easily influenced by cannabis?

Before ending our small talk, she told me Caleb had asked about me.

As I prepared for a soothing shower and an upcoming lunch, I noticed the extinguished marijuana joint and incense and began to have pleasant flashbacks of my best friend in Houston. How I wished he were here now with me. It was just wishful thinking. Unfortunately, Caleb decided not to make college a part of his future. Instead, he opted to work as a shift leader at his uncle's restaurant in Houston.

Caleb liked cars, though, so I never thought he would start a career in the restaurant business.

After reminiscing about Caleb, I undressed. Zac uncovered his head and noticed my slightly disrobed body. The lust in his eyes made me nervous, but I regained my focus. I was determined to make sure that Zac and I would never go down the same road Caleb and I had traveled. I did not want to reawaken the beast inside me that had caused so much self-hatred, angst and disgust. I dressed quickly.

"Say, man" where you goin'?" asked Zac.

"To wash up, man." My eyes didn't meet his. "What are you going to do today – church?" I asked, mocking him on the sly.

"Yeah."

He lied as he crawled out of his bed with a morning hard-on.

"And you?"

"Church." I lied, too, trying not to notice the bulge in my

roommate's boxers. I then left the room for the shower. I imagined Zac discovering the partially smoked joint, lifting the dorm window, firing up the joint while blowing smoke out of the window as he contemplated whether to attend church services.

After entering the wet area, my heart fluttered at the sight of Butch Webber standing butt-naked in the center of the shower flashing all his goods. I was paralyzed, my heart pounded rapidly. I couldn't stop myself from staring at strategic places on his body. This was not good for me. I pulled myself together and remembered the words Butch shared with me: "To work with me, you gotta stay focused."

With that, I spoke to him and showered.

*****

A light haze settled over the open field as Coach Durham journeyed to Buffalo Towers. It was 7:05 a.m., and he hoped that he could catch Zac and me for breakfast. When he entered the towers, the sizzling hickory sausage, potatoes and homemade bread stimulated his nose. He scanned the cafeteria in search of his athletes and, with his hands planted firmly in his pockets, spotted and joined us.

We were told that this was his daily ritual before heading to his office.

After breakfast, my first day of college classes began.

"OK! Everyone, please! May I have your attention?" an authoritative voice demanded through the rumble of voices in the massive auditorium.

I lifted my head out of my algebra text and gazed at the salt-and-peppered hair instructor standing at a lectern. He appeared to have a hangover.

"Good morning, my name is Professor Hagley, head of the mathematics department at West Texas State University. Today will be very simple. I will call roll and once I've completed, you are dismissed. On Wednesday, I expect everyone to have his books before class begins."

The auditorium was silent, but the mood was far from somber because everyone was happy the day would end in a short New York minute. Previously, I considered dropping the class after learning the instructor headed the department, but I knew Coach Durham would not accept my lame excuse.

After my morning classes, I decided to visit Coach Durham at the athletic office. On my way, I noticed a teammate named Kevin Knight approaching me. He was the second fastest quarter-miler in Texas and had attended high school in South Dallas. He was slim, about 175 pounds, and had a long torso. His medium-brown Afro highlighted his chestnut brown skin. I saw him studying me with his piercing dark eyes.

"What's up, man?" asked Kevin, who was unsure of my name.

"I'm just going to see Coach Durham for a bit."

"Yeah. I just left his office. You know where it is, huh?" Kevin asked slowly.

After chatting with him, I stepped inside the glass doors of a large circular complex. I went to the second floor to the coach's office. With the door ajar, I noticed that Coach Durham was on the telephone. Judging from the conversation on the intercom, the party on the other end was the coach from the Missouri Valley Conference.

Coach Durham, leaning in his black leather chair, eventually noticed me and motioned for me to come inside. I entered the trophy-filled office and sat my backpack on one of the two cushioned chairs in front of the maple wooden desk. I was in awe as I scanned the walls and bookshelves covering each side of the mammoth desk. Achievements, accolades and records covered the office walls.

"Well, Coach, it seems like the second weekend in January next year would be ideal for our guys to run there in Des Moines," Coach Durham said to the Iowa State track coach.

"Well, let's make it official then," said the Iowa coach, ending the call.

"Morris! What's up?"

"Oh, nothing Coach. I just thought I should pay you a visit. That's all," I said, lying.

"Well, how was the first day?"

"It was OK."

"Well, by the sound of it, I think you're lying," said the coach, at his desk with his elbows and clasped fingers supporting his chin.

Smiling with embarrassment, I took a seat next to my backpack and explained the reason for my jitters.

"Coach, don't you know I'm one of only two black people in my graphics class, and some of those white guys look at me as if I don't belong there," I explained. "And I know you have to know Professor Hagley in the math department, huh?"

"Yeah. He's a character, Miguel, so take him very seriously. He's failed many athletes."

"Well, I thought about …" I paused, and Coach interrupted.

"I know you are not thinking about dropping the class, Miguel. Right?" asked Coach Durham, rising from his chair to close his office door. "Well, let me tell you, Miguel. If you're going to quit, you might as well start packing because I will not train a quitter. Is that clear?"

"I didn't say I wanted to stop running track, Coach."

"Then keep in mind, Miguel, that education is our No. 1 priority here at West Texas State University. Academics, not athletics."

"Yes, sir."

"Is there anything else you're concerned about Morris?"

"I didn't know Mercury Morris ran track here." I had glanced at the list of records on the back wall of Coach's desk.

Mercury Morris was a superstar football player in the '70s, playing for the Miami Dolphins. He was the crème de la crème of running backs – an unstoppable force.

"Yeah. Mercury played football primarily but ran track as well, setting school records here. Now if he could excel during those times when integration was just taking shape, imagine what you can do, Miguel."

"You're right, Coach. I'm not a quitter. So, I'll see you at 3 o'clock for practice."

I felt a little foolish, but maybe it was for the good.

"OK. I'll see you then Morris."

Chapter 8
Tutor Me, Please

The sun's rays were beating down on us during the first day of practice in August. After running about four miles on rough terrain around campus, the squad headed for the track in a futile attempt to find refuge from the heat. The black tar surface added to the searing 100-plus temperature. The only protection from the sun was a green screen-covered fence on the west side of the track.

"OK, we have only about 300 yards to go, guys," Kevin shouted to the other 16 guys. Before we could catch our breaths, Coach approached the team, instructing us to listen to the workout mapped out for the day. Damn, I had hoped that this guy wasn't going to be a slave driver and torture us in this heat.

He told us to do a set of ten, 100-meter sprints up and down the track with Kevin in charge.

The first day of practice was grueling.

After it was over, Zac and I went back to the dorm and collapsed onto our beds like falling timber in a forest. The fatigue made dinner an afterthought.

After about twenty minutes of rest, the silence was broken by a knock on the door.

"Come in!" Zac shouted.

It was Kevin. "You guys going to dinner?"

Raising my head, I glanced at the time on the clock. Six o'clock was closing in.

"Yeah, man. We're going. We'll meet you there."

"I know you guys not tired, huh?" said Kevin, taunting us.

I sensed that this dude was going to rub me the wrong way before long. He bounced out the door on his toes, probably laughing at us on the inside. Pompous Bastard!

*****

After five weeks of grueling workouts and classes, I prepared for my first big algebra test Friday.

I combed through my copious notes that Wednesday, and relied on my tutorial sessions with Patsy Pollard in the basement of Buffalo Towers. Unlike the affluent school districts back at home, my school then didn't have tutors, advanced algebra or computers. So I had to make do with my limited resources.

"Miguel! What's up, fella?" Butch shouted through the crack of the small opening from my dorm room door before entering. He was eating a banana and holding a spiral notebook and a business law textbook under his arm.

"What's up, Butch?" I was actually happy to see him, preferring his company over the algebra text in my hand.

"Just getting ready to go to this study session on tort laws," he explained.

"Oh, yeah. What's your major?" I didn't remember him ever saying before.

"Business administration. I didn't tell you?" He appeared surprised.

"You probably did. I just don't remember."

"What's yours?" Butch asked.

"Pre-architecture."

"I didn't know you like to draw, Miguel."

"That's my first love," I said, glancing at my clock. My tutoring session was minutes away.

"Yeah. Maybe one day you could draw a picture of me."

"Just let me know when you're ready. It'll be a new experience for me. Having a live model. You'll be my first."

"So, where you headed?" he asked.

"I'm going to the tutoring class for algebra in the basement."

"That's where I'm headed, too. You know the honey that tutors algebra is good. I mean real good," Butch said with extra emphasis.

"You know Patsy?" I began to wonder what he meant by saying she was "real good."

"Yeah, fella. I sat in her sessions when we were sophomores. She started tutoring for extra dollars to pay toward her pharmacy degree. I used her services on several occasions. And I tell you I wasn't disappointed. Get what you can get out of her and scram."

"So she's smart, huh?" I asked, ignoring his comment. What was Butch really trying to tell me?

"That's only half of what she can do. So be on point. You dig?" We then left my room and headed for the study sessions.

*****

The smell of buttered popcorn filled the basement foyer, exciting my taste buds as we arrived for the tutoring sessions. As I entered the small study session marked algebra, I noticed Kevin sitting in the front row with a handful of popcorn.

I stuffed the buttery snack inside a red-and-white hand-sized bag, then sat next to Kevin.

After the hour session, I headed toward the exit. Before I could leave Patsy appeared to intentionally drop her books. And in a display of chivalry, I turned and scooped them from the floor. I noticed her glimpsing at my buttocks as I bent over.

"Thanks, Miguel." Her eyes left no doubt what she was thinking.

"No problem."

"So, did the tutoring session help you?"

"Yeah, it did," I told her in a rather reserved tone. Actually I began to even like math – not so much because of Patsy's presence but more so because I now understood it.

"Great. I'm glad you did."

"Here you are – all nicely stacked," I said, handing Patsy her books and papers.

"Thanks, again. Has anyone ever told you that you have nice eyes, Miguel?" she asked, touching my hand as I gave her the last of her belongings.

"No, not really."

"Well, they are," she said flirtatiously.

Kevin then interrupted our conversation.

"Say, Miguel. You coming?"

Is this niggah cock-blocking? I wondered.

"I'm sorry, man. Was I interrupting something?" he asked rhetorically.

Patsy said goodbye, but not before handing me a piece of paper with her phone number.

I told her I would be seeing her for the next session. A bitter Kevin became envious.

"What's up, Kevin? You trying to cock-block, man?"

"Niggah, please!"

"Well, something's up, man."

"Say, man, I was just checking to see if you wanted to play some Backgammon before it got too late. That's all. But if you gonna make a big deal about this tutoring shit, fuck it!"

"Oh, really," I said, still suspicious of his ass. But I decided to ease up on him a bit.

"Really," Kevin said, patronizing me.

"Well in that case, I'm down, man. You need to be schooled anyway."

He was a snake, and he probably sensed I knew.

*****

I basked in the celebration of my 19th birthday after

receiving a special card from my family. Earlier that Saturday morning, my father, mother and grandmother had called to congratulate me for the high scores on my first semester exams. They also told me that my sister Dee was doing well as a sophomore at Texas Southern University. But the news about Troy was not as pleasant.

With all the talent he possessed, Troy decided to drop out of high school in his junior year. When he was younger I remember him struggling with reading and math. But I never believed that he would give up on school completely. The news shocked me. Troy and I had our differences, but I did not want to see him give up on a promising athletic future.

Later that day, the sound of bass drums and horns filled the air from a neighboring field. The band was preparing for the start of the MVC (Missouri Valley Conference) football season. West Texas State was hosting New Mexico State today.

Listening to the music through the opened window, I felt somewhat lonely, so I decided to call Patsy.

"Hello," a voice answered.

"May I speak to Patsy, please?" I asked, attempting not to sound too anxious.

"Patsy speaking."

"This is Miguel."

"Oh. Hi, Miguel. This is a surprise. What have I done to deserve this call?"

"You're not busy are you? If so, I can call you back."

"No, I'm just sitting on my apartment balcony listening to the band. What about you?"

"Doing the same from my dorm window, trying to decide if I'm going to the game."

"What do you mean trying to decide? Do you want to go?" Patsy asked, playing right into my trap.

"Well, since you asked, yeah!" I said, smiling to myself.

"Good. It's almost noon now. How about if I pick you up at 1:30 p.m. from your room?"

"Yeah, that's cool," I said.

She confirmed my room number, and I asked her how she got it.

"You wrote it on the check-in list at my tutoring class, remember?"

"Oh, yeah." I felt stupid.

"Well, I'm glad you called because I thought you had brushed me off, Miguel."

"No. I'm just kinda quiet. But I'll be ready at 1:30, OK?" I said, trying to quickly end the conversation so I could prepare myself.

*****

"Let's go, Buffaloes. Let's go!" the cheerleaders screamed. One in particular caught my attention. He was a light shade of ebony and very muscular, yet a bit on the effeminate side. His husky voice and athletic build didn't match his mannerism.

The roars from the crowd and cheerleaders echoed throughout the packed Buffalo Stadium that afternoon as New Mexico State threatened to score. When the ball was snapped, the two left side receivers mixed their signals, allowing the defensive strong safety to intercept.

Then the great pursuit began for the home team.

Number 25, identified as Butch Webber, sent the crowd screaming when he plowed through the field for a touchdown. Patsy and I joined the excitement, embracing each other and crushing our box of popcorn. Eventually our eyes zeroed in on each other. We slowly released our seductive grips and continued to celebrate. I could only imagine what was next.

Butch's skillful efforts helped launch an assault against New Mexico State. At halftime, the score was 35-10. Patsy and I agreed to leave the game and headed back toward campus to become more acquainted.

I would later discover that Butch went on to score two

additional touchdowns and switched to quarterback for the entire fourth quarter. He threw for 212 yards and two touchdowns to further seal the victory.

Once Patsy and I reached her apartment, sexual sparks began to fly immediately. I felt the breeze from the evening air on my legs. I noticed Patsy's soft lips and leaned in to kiss them. She was the first white woman I had kissed, and it seemed weird at first because her lips were not full like I was accustomed to. But I adjusted.

We began to get passionately involved as I eased my hands around her thin waist. My heart rate picked up momentum. I actually felt a sexual chemistry with Patsy, unlike my first experience with Tammy. I wasn't quite sure what made this encounter different, so sensual. Was it the color of her skin, hazel eyes, shoulder-length hair? I couldn't say for sure, but I was ready to get my rocks off.

Patsy's warm body next to mine intensified my hard-on. I grabbed her hand and placed it on my throbbing jimmy. I put my hot tongue on her neck and trailed it toward her rounded breasts as she unbuttoned my shirt.

Patsy then eased her soft and warm hands underneath my shorts, grabbing my hard sex like a pair of vice grips. I nearly ejaculated prematurely. Moaning loudly, Patsy abruptly stood in front of me and lowered her khaki Bermuda shorts to the floor. I wasted no time ripping off my clothes, exposing my hard black sex. I was ready to mate and nothing was going to stop me this time. Old jimmy was hard and throbbing, and I was ready to get down to business and dive in for the kill.

Suddenly, a jet-black cat brushed against my leg, and I leaped forward. Patsy then assured me that Felix was harmless. She then lowered me by my shoulders to the heavily carpeted living room floor for some of her sexual healing.

"I just want you to lie back and let me do the work," Patsy suggested, as she squatted to my abdomen.

I still felt the soothing breeze from the open French doors

as Patsy lowered herself onto my hardened sex. She was so hot inside, so soft, so wet. So this was what sex felt like with a woman? Damn!

"Yeah, baby. Let me do the work," Patsy offered. "Let me do the work for you. Let momma work it." Her eyes began rolling back. "That feels good, Miguel?"

"Oh, yes!" I answered. That feels real good." I was almost cumming. I realized I had to learn to control my movements and timing if I ever wanted to be good at this.

Patsy was a freak, just as I had assumed. She rode my jimmy and caused me to push even harder as the sound of her passion filled the room. She was like a wild animal. Even Felix got in on the act with a loud "meow." That made Patsy ride even more forcefully. I could tell that she was a freak. I was more surprised that she didn't pull out whips, chains and handcuffs and shit like that. But I wasn't down for that crap. If anyone were going to do any whipping, I had already decided that I was going to be the "numero uno" ass-spanker.

Even after a long evening of passion Patsy wasn't done yet. She leaned over and grabbed my broad shoulders, bucking and twisting like a Texas rodeo steer as she continued to ride me. She asked for it, and I obliged. I firmly grabbed her with both my hands around her thin waist and drilled deeper into her soft sex.

"Oh, Miguel. I'm cumming! I'm cumming!" Patsy screamed, not caring that the French doors were wide open and her voice echoed throughout the apartment.

"Yeah! Yeah! Oh, shit, baby. Me, too!" I shouted. I gritted my teeth and curled my toes, as a gush of fluids flowed from my hard jimmy. "Damn, Patsy. Damn!" I shouted, wondering where she had learned to make love like that. A stellar performance, indeed.

Considering this was the first time I had intercourse with a female, let alone a white one, I felt I did good. I was impressed with my endurance. I promised myself that pussy was definitely in my future.

Preparing to shower before venturing outdoors to catch fireflies, Patsy wished me a happy birthday. She then kissed me on my forehead and touched my nose softly with her right index finger. I wasn't sure what that action meant, but I accepted it and then asked how she knew it was my birthday. She told me there wasn't much she didn't know about any athlete on campus.

A date with Patsy was a definite climax to my birthday celebration – literally.

Chapter 9
The N-Word

The track team was bound for its first outdoor meet of the season, the Drake Relays.

"I didn't know Des Moines had skyscrapers," Zac said looking into the horizon from a window seat of an Ozark aircraft.

"Yeah. Des Moines has skyscrapers, man." I knew because I had studied city structures from my architectural books.

"Yeah, we forgot. You're Mister Know-it-All," Kevin blurted out.

"Sounds like you jealous to me, niggah!" I said angrily. Actually I was just still upset about a racist note left on my dorm room door calling me a niggah and telling me to "leave our white women alone!" This was because I was kicking it with Patsy.

I was used to being the only black athlete in my electronic classes and oftentimes the only black face in some area restaurants but wasn't used to being called a niggah by white racists. Yet, there I was using the same racial epithet to malign a fellow athlete.

"Morris!" screamed the coach, "what did you say? There will be no use of that word anymore – not in front of me or anywhere. Do I make myself clear?" he demanded.

"Yes, sir," I said apologetically but still looking menacingly at Kevin.

No one was more surprised than me for using the word and then being admonished by the coach. Heck, the word was forbidden in my household. Mom argued that the term was degrading and especially devalued blacks when used in the presence of other races and ethnicities.

After we had arrived at the hotel, coach still seemed upset with me.

"Listen up, guys," Coach Durham said as the 17 squad members stood in the hotel lobby waiting for their assigned rooms. "I'm going to give keys to groups of four, and after y'all settle down we will meet in my room for a team meeting, OK? Miguel, Kevin, Tony and Charles, y'all are responsible for having everyone out of their rooms for the meeting at 3 p.m."

Tony and Charles were sprinters. Tony was a sophomore and ran in the mile and sprint relays. Charles, a senior, competed in the 110-meter and 300-meter hurdle events, which he had dominated the past two years in the MVC. Charles did not talk much. He was from Clovis, New Mexico, and led the state with the fastest 110-yard times in high school. He was a 5-foot, 8-inch sandy-red blond with curly hair.

In contrast, Tony was 5-feet, 5-inches tall with a medium Afro. The hyperactive 20-year-old was from Muleshoe, Texas, and had a penchant for obese women.

*****

Seated at the wooden desk in his hotel room, Coach Durham talked with his wife over the phone.

"Honey, these kids are at each other's throats already. It may be because they're just nervous; I don't know. But I'm going to set the record straight here and now," he explained.

"And Zac, I'm not sure he's going to make it through the year because he flunked three classes last semester, and the dean is jumping down my throat about him. He's already on academic probation. And that Morris kid. I know he knows better than to use the N-word."

A knock on the door interrupted his conversation, so he

abruptly ended his call with his wife to start the team meeting.

"Come in, guys. It's open."

The atmosphere was intense as the squad gathered in the small quarters. Coach Durham assigned us our specialized events for Friday and Saturday.

Before the meeting ended, he gave his final words.

"As we all know, we are here as a team. And in order to be a successful unit, we must all stick together as one, right? So let me again make myself clear. There is to be no fighting or name-calling like the one used on the plane earlier. That word will not be tolerated. PERIOD! Dinner's at five. I'll meet everyone in the lobby."

Never before had I felt so bad about using the N-word.

*****

Tony, Zac, Charles, Kevin and I qualified for Saturday's showdown. A large, crowd gathered in the warm, outdoor multi-purpose complex.

The West Texas State squad sat on the west side of the starting line. The final jump on the pole vault was in progress. After teammate Adam failed to clear the distance, Coach gave lane assignments to those who qualified for the finals in their events. The 400-meter race with Kevin, me and other rival athletes was scheduled to start in 60 minutes.

Kevin was entering the finals with the fastest time, and I burned with envy despite my third-fastest run ever. I realized that I shouldn't be complaining since we were separated by only a 400th of a second, and I could still take first place overall.

As time wound down, we got into our starting positions.

The announcer instructed all 400-meter runners to report to the clerk of the course and approach the starting line.

Anxiety swept over me as I received the rules and instructions about the race. I noticed Kevin trying to keep warm by doing a series of jumps. I stared coldly at our rivals in an attempt to shake their confidence and wear them down psychologically.

After three warm-up sprints, the quarter-mile showdown was about to commence. The speed-hungry crowd was anxious and ecstatic. The TAAF (Texas Amateur Athletic Federation) apparatus used to calculate the official times was put in place.

"OK, runners, on your mark." There was a pause. "Get set … POW! POW! The gun sounded twice to indicate a false start by an Oklahoma State runner in lane six.

"OK, guys, let's get a clean start this time," the announcer said.

I quickly glanced over at Kevin in Lane 3 and Brian in Lane 4.

"Runners, on you mark, get set … POW!"

A clean start.

The six runners sprinted into the tight curve. It seemed as if the Oklahoma State runner in Lane 6 was leading the race. But the staggered lanes into the eastside straightaway were misleading. As we approached the 100-meter mark, Kevin and Brian had taken the lead by a few yards. I trailed close behind in Lane 2.

"Ladies and gentlemen, in Lane 4 we have Brian Newberry of Kansas State leading the race, followed by Kevin Knight in "3" and Miguel Morris in "2", both from West Texas State. This is going to be a race people!" the announcer said.

The crowd was pumped.

"Twenty-three two! Twenty-three three! Twenty-three four!" Coach Durham screamed from the sidelines as Kevin and I crossed the 200-meter mark.

I then began to move faster as we neared the 300-meter point, where I would normally make a stronger kick.

Coming into the last curve, Brian, Kevin and I were dead even going into the final straightaway. With Brian as MVC's indoor and outdoor champion last season, I knew this was going to be a fight to the finish.

Only 100 meters remained.

"Here we go, ladies and gentlemen! It's Newberry of Kansas State! Newberry! Now it's Morris of West Texas State in Lane 2. They're close; they're close. Oh! Here it is. I think it's … it's Morris of West Texas State!" the announcer screamed to the boisterous fans in the arena.

"It's Morris of West Texas State," the announcer confirmed again.

"Way to go, Miguel!" shouted Coach Durham, rattling the coins in his pocket, as he approached me.

I was still bending over to catch my breath.

"I think you may have broken the record here today, Morris. I clocked you at 46.4 seconds," Coach Durham explained.

"Really!" I said slowly. I then stood upright to fully grasp what Coach was telling me.

"Good run, Miguel," said Brian, the competitor from Kansas State.

"Ladies and gentlemen. The race you just saw was a new record. It also qualified Miguel Morris and Brian Newberry of Kansas State for the NCAA Outdoor Championships in June. So let's give them both a round of applause," the announcer said.

It was indeed a crowning moment.

Chapter 10
Picture Perfect But Seductive

"OK, Butch. You gotta stay still man if you want this figure drawing to come out right."

On this pleasant spring Saturday in April on the West Texas State campus I had finally arranged a session to sketch the muscular body of this pro-bound safety. The scent from the magnolia trees swept into the room as Butch, sitting atop his pine desk, inhaled the outdoor air as he posed in a pair of red nylon running shorts, imitating the famous pose of "The Thinker" by sculptor Auguste Rodin.

"So, Miguel. You're ready for the outdoor championships this summer?" asked Butch, glancing at my shirtless body.

"Yep. Sure am. I'll finally get a chance to meet some big-name people this time," I said focusing on his face, brow and strong ethnic features.

"You didn't meet any last time?" Butch asked curiously.

"Nope."

"Why?"

"Because I was too busy trying to qualify for the finals."

"Oh, well, how is everything going with you and Patsy?"

"Fine, man," I answered as I focused on the finer points of Butch's detailed frame and abs. "We're supposed to go to a club in Amarillo – the Gray Gaspy. Have you been there?" I asked while stealing a quick glance at Butch's thick crotch and massive thighs. Surely, he must have noticed my wandering eyes.

"I've been there many times, fella," said Butch, repositioning himself as his tight shorts made a slow crawl up his large thighs.

"Keep still, man!" I ordered. It felt great being able to assert my authority over this massive hunk. I had to get something out of the deal because I had to endure fighting my temptation not to touch him. In reality, I knew I couldn't because I promised myself that I would not turn into a "faggot" like my high school drafting teacher who was murdered in his backyard pool. But whom was I fooling? No matter how long I suppressed my feelings for another man, I knew they would always be there! "Repent! Repent!" I kept telling myself.

"I'm trying to adjust something. Do you mind?" asked Butch, explaining his reason for so much movement.

"Like what?" I boldly asked.

"Something I don't think you wanna adjust," said Butch, putting his right hand between his legs as he repositioned his crotch while, at the same time, staring into my soul.

I ignored his comment. When he was done I asked if he were now comfortable. He was really testing me as my heart raced like African drums at a hunting ritual.

"I'm not as comfortable as I could get. There's nothing better than the nude, fella," Butch said without hesitation.

Would he actually let me draw or do a nude painting of him? Perhaps he would, but I couldn't handle that.

"You're tripping, man." By now I was really turned on by this Herculean figure posing in front of me. It was definitely time for me to change the conversation. "Say, you wanna go with Patsy and me to the club tonight?"

"I'll be there," Butch said revealing his partially hardened sex that crept down the side of his right inner thigh. "You need to learn how to use your assets, man."

"What!"

"You got skills and don't even know it. Look in the mirror, Morris. You're a magnet and people are drawn to you."

It seems my effort to veer from sensual subjects didn't help at all. We were right back on the topic. This time I did not comment and changed the focus again.

From head to toe, I carefully analyzed the nearly completed drawing. I almost wanted to sketch that snake creeping down his thigh. My final touches included his piercing eyes and dazzling gleam.

"There. I'm finished," I said.

Butch then lowered his feet to the floor and stood to adjust his semi-hard sex. He was eager to see the final results. I still couldn't figure out how he managed to maintain an erection for so long?

"Can I see it?" he asked.

"Yeah."

"Damn, Miguel! You did good!" said Butch, grabbing my hand and shoulder simultaneously.

"Thanks," I said modestly, hoping for something more than just a handshake and simple thanks.

I then heard the phone ringing in my room across the hall.

"That's my phone," I said, breaking away from Butch and unlocking the door. "I'll be back."

"Ain't Zac there?" Butch asked. It seemed he didn't want me to leave.

"I thought he was," I said, shouting from across the hallway. While heading to answer the phone, I noticed Kevin walking toward my direction.

Here comes trouble.

"Hi, Miguel. What's going on?" Patsy said when I answered the call.

"Nothing much, just drawing a picture," I explained.

Then Kevin approached. He glanced across the hallway and noticed Butch wearing only a pair of tight red running shorts. Kevin, clutching the latest Track and Field magazine in his right hand, gave me a puzzled look after noticing me leaving Butch's room just seconds before. He did a double take.

"We're still on for tonight, huh?" Patsy asked.

"Yeah. Nine o'clock, right?" I asked while observing Kevin's reaction to Butch's half-naked body.

I ended the call with Patsy quickly, telling her I needed to finish drawing Butch's picture. I purposely lied to cover my actions as Kevin, loitering in the doorway, pretended to thumb through the magazine.

Suddenly, Butch slammed his door, startling Kevin.

I finally acknowledged my intruder.

"What's up, Kevin?" I asked. Inside, I was boiling. This Negro is notorious for cock-blocking – even though I really wasn't sure that I was ready to experience sex with a man again.

"I just wanted to show you the mile-relay rankings this month. We're No. 12 in the nation with 3:07.25." He handed me the magazine.

"Damn! Look at Tennessee. They got two of the top five times in the nation, too," said Kevin.

"Who's leading the 400?"

"Willie Smith!" Kevin answered.

"Damn! 45.26. That boy is bad," I said.

"Yeah! Look what Renaldo's running," Kevin said.

Renaldo "Skeet" Nehemiah ran 13.21 seconds in the 110 hurdles last season, aiming for the world record.

"Skeet's gonna break the world's record. Just watch."

I then glanced at the women's statistics.

Evelyn Ashford – the top female sprinter in the nation in the 100 event – was burning up the track, too, along with Edwin Moses and high jumper Dwight Stones.

"Well, we'll be there with all of them in June at the NCAAs, right?"

"Yep. We sure will," Kevin agreed. "Well, I just wanted to show you that. That's all. I hope I didn't disturb you and

Butch." His sly comment left a bad taste in my mouth.

I then closed my door, which Zac had carelessly left unlocked.

When I returned to Butch's room, I asked if he were OK.

"Yeah, I'm fine," said Butch, buttoning his IZOD aqua blue sports shirt. "I don't like that cock-blocking ass Kevin Knight," Butch said.

I agreed with him on that issue.

"Kevin always has something up his sleeves," I said as I examined the finished product.

"So, who was that on the phone?" asked Butch, changing the subject.

"It was Patsy. She was making sure I was still hooking up with her tonight at nine. So, where are you going now?" I asked, watching Butch dress.

"To dinner. It's five o'clock. You're going?" he asked, looking in the mirror as he brushed his naturally wavy hair.

"Yeah. I'll head down there with you, buddy."

"Buddy! I like that," said Butch – his smile reflected in the mirror as he continued to groom.

"So, what you gonna do with your picture?"

"Frame it and put in my house when I go pro, 'buddy,' " he said as we left the room.

"Butch. Question."

"Shoot." he said.

"You like having a room all to yourself?" I wondered how he managed to get such privacy. Two words came to my mind: "Alumni. Perks." Of course, he is the biggest college football star in the Southwest.

"It feels like heaven, buddy. I wouldn't have it any other way. It's total privacy for me. You feel me?"

Hmmm. If he only knew I wanted to do just that!

*****

A shimmering glow filled the rooms of Patsy's apartment as I lie next to her with a hard-on Sunday morning – our naked bodies clinging to one another. As usual, Felix, Patsy's cat, was nearby begging for attention at the foot of the bed. He even leaped onto the bed. He was as graceful as Butch was spinning records last night at the club.

"Oh, Felix, not now," Patsy said softly as she covered her head with her perfumed pillow.

"What's up, buddy?" I said to the cat as I rubbed its thick, black coat.

Trying not to disturb Patsy, I gently got out of the bed, taking Felix and a terrycloth robe with me. And since I wasn't going to make it to church, I headed into the living room to find a gospel radio station.

After a few minutes of surfing, I found an Amarillo broadcast that featured black gospel music from 6 a.m. to 3 p.m. on Sundays.

I opened the French doors leading to the balcony. I sat down in one of the four metal patio chairs that surrounded a glass table, listening to the joyous sounds of "*Oh Happy Day*" by The Edwin Hawkins Singers.

When hunger pangs struck, I went to the kitchen – with Felix in tow – to prepare breakfast.

I fed the cat first, filling his kitty bowl near the dishwasher with an array of treats.

"This is DJ Webber, giving you sounds from across town. And to the WTSU listening audience, good Sunday morning. It is now 10:15 a.m.," the radio announcer said.

Hey, wait a minute. I couldn't believe what I was hearing. With a carton of brown eggs in my grip and the aroma of hickory sausage filling the air, I froze in my steps. Were my ears playing tricks on me?

"That sounds like Butch," I whispered to myself. Then it hit me. On the previous evening at the dance club, I was surprised to learn that Butch was the featured DJ. And now, I'm discovering that he's also a radio DJ for a popular Amarillo station.

This explains the incident months ago why he was able to handle my stereo equipment so flawlessly when he gingerly placed the turntable needle on the third track of one of my albums. I won't ever forget that moment when he rested next to me in my bed while listening to The Isley Brothers' "*Fight the Power.*"

Strangely enough, I've been battling my "Butch Webber urges" ever since. And at my weakest moment, he possibly could have had his way with me and put a positive spin on the term "molestation."

Minutes later Patsy, stretching her muscles and inhaling the aroma of the mouth-watering meal, entered the kitchen. She kissed and thanked me for feeding Felix and preparing our breakfast.

"Patsy. I didn't know Butch was a DJ for an Amarillo station.

"Yeah. That's his station you're listening to right now, huh?"

"Yeah, it is. He shocked me last night when I found out he was the DJ at the Gray Gaspy. Now this."

"You'll come to learn that he's full of surprises, Miguel."

*****

After I exited Patsy's car, I thanked her for a great time and headed to my dorm room. But a strange feeling came over me when I returned to the nearly empty campus.

As I reached my floor of the dorm, I heard faint laughter. I then realized the sound was coming from my room; music was playing in the background.

I gently knocked on the door to alert my roommate Zac that I had arrived. It was obvious that he had company.

"Who is it?" Zac asked.

"It's me. Miguel," I whispered. As I stood in the hallway waiting for clearance to enter, I crept toward Butch's door and heard slight snoring from his room.

Zac finally opened the door.

"Man, come in. Why you knocking?" asked Zac, standing in the open doorway looking dazed and his breath reeking of alcohol.

"I didn't want to walk in on you, man," I explained. He indeed had company.

"Hi, Miguel," Judy said as she sipped rum and coke from a foam cup.

"What's up, Judy?" I said in a gruff tone, clearly annoyed with this private party.

Judy was from east Amarillo. She was Zac's girlfriend, 5-feet, 5-inches tall with light-brown complexion and dark, brown eyes hidden by a pair of wire-framed glasses. She was not a student at WTSU but often visited the campus like many other females chasing athletes.

Her excuse for being in the room with her "baby" was to help him study so he wouldn't flunk out of school. Notes from his kinesiology and physiology classes lay on the bed, but apparently the only studying going on was sex education. And that wasn't even part of Zac's curriculum. They both shared blame for screwing up his future.

I told them I just came by to get a change of clothes and my textbooks for classes tomorrow. Then I asked if my mom had made her usual call.

"No. Not since we've been here," said Zac, rolling several marijuana cigarettes.

I figured I would try to go to Butch's room. Instead of pounding on his door, I telephoned him. I remembered him saying how he enjoyed his privacy. After three rings, I was about to hang up before he finally answered.

"Hello," he muttered, sounding lethargic.

"Hi, Butch. This is Miguel. I'm sorry for waking you, buddy."

"Oh, that's OK, Miguel. What's up?"

"Well, I was wondering if I could spend the night in your room because Zac and Judy are studying. She wants to stay the night with him," I said, as Zac handed me one of his herbal cigarettes.

"Sure, man. Come on over. I was about to get up anyway for dinner."

"OK, I'm out the door. … Oh, Butch."

"Yeah."

"I need to use your phone to call home. It's a collect call."

"Yeah, buddy. No problem. And maybe after dinner we can walk over to the complex and lift weights, all right?" We ended the call, and I went across the hallway for my sleep-over.

As I entered, Butch smiled broadly. His room smelled like Downy April fresh fabric softener.

"You can put your stuff in the closet," he offered.

"I hope I'm not intruding."

"Man, stop tripping! You know you're OK with me," said Butch, walking toward the closet in a pair of white briefs that hugged his buttocks ever so firmly. "If you wanna use the phone, it's under the bed."

"Thanks." I still was having trouble getting comfortable with his half-nude body. Lust was eating up at me.

I studied the clothing in Butch's closet. He had a wide selection of adidas jogging suits that were lined meticulously at one end; athletic shoes, IZOD shirts and a variety of pants lined the other shelves.

"I sure hope someone's home," I said phoning my people back in Houston.

Finally, an answer.

"Daddy?" I said.

"Yeah. Is this Miguel?" asked my father, who was probably smoking because I heard a slight cough.

"Yeah, daddy, it's me. I didn't recognize your voice. Is everything OK?"

He paused.

"Well, not really. This morning your mother found Big Momma in her room, son."

"What do you mean found her in her room?" I said. I knew what he was insinuating, but the news stunned me.

"Well, I think it was cancer!"

"Cancer! Big Momma had cancer?" I asked.

"Yeah. That's what your mother said. The doctors told her a few months ago. I guess she didn't want to worry you while you were in school.

"Where's mom? Is she OK?"

"She's in the bedroom gathering Big Momma's belongings. I believe she's fine because she kinda prepared herself."

"Hold on. I'll get her."

I was in shock. The walls in Butch's room seemed to close in on me during my phone conversation as Butch listened while leaning over the sink to wash his face.

Mom confirmed that cancer took grandmother's life. I asked why they hadn't called me sooner.

"You have to complete your classes. I just didn't want you worrying. Are you OK?" mom asked.

"Yeah, but …"

"And I know you probably can't make the funeral next week, either, so concentrate on school, OK."

"Yes, ma'am."

"We know that you loved your grandmother. So don't feel bad about not coming for the homegoing, baby. Your brothers and sisters said hello."

"Tell them I'll be home sometime in June after the NCAAs."

"OK, honey. We love you, and don't worry. I'll be fine. Don't forget to write and go to church next week if you can for Easter. Big Momma would like that," mom said cheerfully – even through the pain of losing her mother.

After ending the call I lapsed into a trance, hoping dad would kick his own habit to reduce the risk of suffering another family loss.

Butch approached to offer condolences.

"I'm sorry about your grandmother, Miguel."

"Thanks."

"Are you gonna be OK, buddy?

"Yeah. I'll be fine."

"I just can't believe Big Momma is gone. That's all."

"You gotta stay strong for your family, Miguel. You're a man now," he said. "Pull yourself together, then figure out who you are and how you will handle the pressure when it is really on, man."

"Even if that means death?" I asked teary-eyed.

"Yeah, Miguel, even death. You know I lost my grandmother when I was 16, and I thought the world had ended. But my father told me that no one could change God's divine plans. And we cannot question it."

"So, you're saying this is a test of my maturity or something."

"Well, Miguel, you'll be 20 this year, won't you?"

"Yep, in September." It seemed as if it were just yesterday when I celebrated my birthday with Patsy during football season.

"So, figure it out, buddy, because now you're on your own. And much as I'd like to be around you, I can't stay. There's money to be made and goals to be accomplished. I'm not sounding too harsh, huh?" asked Butch, resting his right hand on my shoulder, encouraging me.

"Nah, man. You're right. I'll tell you what. You go on to dinner. I'm gonna stay here and order a pizza. I need some time alone to think."

"You're sure?"

"Yeah. I'll be all right, man."

"Don't you mean, 'Buddy'?" asked Butch, smiling as he rose from the bed for chow time.

Of all my battles, this seemed to be the greatest one. I never had a chance to say goodbye to my grandmother, and I was full of guilt. Instead of ordering the pizza as planned, I settled for quiet time. I dropped to my knees in prayer after

Butch left. Tears began to flow as I talked in-depth to God and my Big Momma about my sexual sins and the trials I was facing:

"Lord, I have struggled with bad feelings about myself all my life, and I really don't know why. It just seems that everyone has more to offer than I do. I envy the guys who are better looking than I am – even the ones who are more athletic or smarter. Sometimes I feel that I'm so different, even at times feeling gay, and I don't know why. I know I don't want to be that way. I can't control my feelings at times and lust tries to take over me. What's wrong with me? I just don't measure up to my own standards. And I know I could never please you living a life of sin. I guess most people can't. So please Lord, hear me and answer my request. Show me a way out. Show me the way to feeling normal again – like a man should feel for a woman, a responsible feeling, Father. Amen!"

Tears flowed with great intensity until comfort miraculously descended upon me. I felt like the biblical figure Paul who faced extraordinary challenges. I didn't know how to control my behavior, let alone the affliction that was causing so much pain. So I lie on my back to meditate and absorb the serenity. I felt assured again, even if I still had a few doubts.

After Butch returned, I assured him that I would be all right.

"So, buddy, I guess lifting weights is out of the question, huh?"

"Yeah. I've lost the desire, man."

"Well, that's OK. There's a good movie coming on at 8 o'clock, *'Guess Who's Coming to Dinner,'* with Sidney Poitier.

"Have you seen it before?"

"Yeah. I have. It was a long time ago. But I don't mind watching it again."

"Do you want some shorts to put on?" asked Butch, peering into his closet.

"Yeah. That's cool because I don't think I put any in my backpack."

"Here. These should fit," he said, checking the size. "By the way, I thought you were gonna order a pizza, Miguel?"

"I was, but I lost my appetite. I still can order one if you eat it with me."

"Sure. Why not. I can use the extra calories. Besides it would go good with the movie."

Inconspicuously watching Butch undress, I noticed he was not wearing underwear. His naked body was now adorned with only a gold chain around his thick neck. I wondered who was the biggest freak: Patsy or Butch. I felt my heart rate increase.

I then took off my blue jeans, keeping my briefs glued to my lower body, but revealing my muscular thighs. I quickly leaped into the borrowed yellow running shorts.

As I walked over to the side of the bed to get the number for Domino's pizza, Butch laughed.

"Say, man! When was the last time you put lotion on those legs?" he asked teasingly.

"This morning after I showered at Patsy's." I was slightly embarrassed as I watched Butch search for lotion.

"Here, man. Give that skin some relief."

He gave me some Nivea body cream lotion just before the pizza arrived.

After we consumed our large pepperoni pizza with sausage and green peppers, I offered a different kind of dessert.

"You got dessert? What kind of dessert?" Butch asked, lying on his back.

Reaching into the pockets of my jeans folded in a chair, I revealed my secret – gunja!"

"Yeah! That'll work." Butch's eyes seemed to glow from the sight of the neatly rolled cannabis.

A glow from the stereo's yellow light added to the building sexual tension as a jingle from a Coca-Cola commercial echoed throughout the room: *"I'd like to teach the world to sing in perfect harmony. ... "*

Butch covered the bottom of the door with a towel to trap in the smoke as I opened the window and watched him fire up the herb. It relaxed us and took our minds off the death of my grandmother, among other things.

After a few more drags from the joint, Butch and I peered at each other; the drug left us spellbound. We were drawing closer and closer together.

"Say, Miguel, have you ever had a massage?"

"No. Why?"

"Well, I tell you what. Now is your chance to experience one from the best," said Butch, sitting up in the bed extinguishing the half-smoked herb. "Lie on your stomach and turn toward the movie and relax. I'll have you in nirvana before you know it."

If he only knew, that is what I was afraid of. I wasn't sure if I wanted to go there. But I was curious and welcomed a massage by Butch, who gently applied the lotion to my severely dry legs. His strong masculine hands were as skilled with lotion as they were with a football as he pressed his fingers deeply into my calf and thigh muscles, causing me to tense up a bit.

"Damn, buddy! Loosen up a little," Butch ordered as he saddled my back, pinning me down on the mattress.

"I'm trying, man." I was a nervous wreck. It's funny how I was never once uptight when Patsy and I hooked up. Even though it was the first time I had intercourse with a female, I was calm. Perhaps, I felt it was a more natural act with a woman.

Anyway, I justified this moment because of my grieving.

"How does that feel?" Butch asked in a breathy, sensual voice.

"Good," I said, swooning. But I was still scared. I wondered if we were moving too fast. A short while later, my anxiety lessened. "Come on with it buddy," I said.

And he did. He began to inch his way to the small of my back, slowly descending to my buttocks.

"OK, Miguel. Just relax. I'm gonna slide your shorts down a little, just to massage your lower back. It's tight man. So tight."

"Where did you put that joint?" I asked.

"Here it is. Fire it up."

I obliged. Then Butch passed it and then calmly removed my running shorts and stared at my chocolate ass as I faced the television.

"What are you afraid of Morris? Relax man."

"I ain't afraid of nothing man." I was lying because I didn't want anyone to find out about my attraction to Butch and expose our immoral behavior.

"Then prove it and relax, man."

My heart continued to pound as Butch applied the cool lotion onto my buttocks. It sent a delicate tingle down the middle of my spine, arms and gapped legs. This was an invitation for him to dive right in.

I then felt the warmth of his massive inner-thighs resting on my outer thighs as he massaged my lower back with precision. He then slipped my shorts over my feet, tossing them to the floor.

It was too late to release myself from seduction now. I really wanted to please him, and I wanted him to like me.

"What are you gonna do, Miguel? Smoke the whole thing?" Butch asked. Without warning, he had completely disrobed, exposing his hard sex. I could feel him resting it in the curvature of my back, cradled in warmth.

"No, I'm passing it. Just don't rush it, man."

He continued the massage after he had finished the herb. The titillating therapy led me to spread my legs even wider. I knew then that I was under an enchanting spell or, perhaps, some deep dark voodoo shit.

He lowered his body onto my warm soft frame and began licking my ears, neck, back and extremities before finally burrowing his tongue into the cavity of my moist buttocks. I had never experienced anything like this before. Was he turning me out? Was he taking advantage of me? Hell no! How can one rape the willing?

"Damn! That ass is fat. Let me in," Butch whimpered. I submitted by putting out the welcome mat, and he became my guest – even though I was a visitor on his turf.

My body pulsated as he anchored himself inside me.

He gently rocked my world.

The night was made whole as we explored the greater depths of our bodies.

His force was delicate enough to cause simultaneous volcanic-like eruptions that spewed "lava" along the edges of our bodies.

After it was all over, we had finally gotten the answers we wanted about each other – and then some.

Lust, passion and forbidden firsts with a man replaced the gloom that had threatened to define my day. Just that fast, I had forgotten that I had asked God to deliver me from sinful acts such as what I had just engaged in with Butch Webber.

Even for all the things I hate, I still do them.

Lord, help me.

Chapter 11

The Freshmen Years

Rain pounded and thunder roared on this early Monday afternoon in May. After class and finals, Zac and I relaxed in our dorm room to view the local news. A weather advisory indicated a funnel cloud had been spotted in our viewing area.

Later in the newscast, there were reports of devastation elsewhere as camera shots of the Wichita Falls, Texas, area showed horrific images of flattened and twisted structures wrought by one of the most powerful tornadoes ever. The city looked like the 1969 scene from Hurricane Camille, which devastated the Gulf Coast with its 190 mph winds.

In Wichita Falls, there was destruction as far as the eye could see: leafless trees lined with metal, toppled vehicles and downed power lines. Scores of emergency personnel and rescue squads were dispatched.

We were glued to the television coverage when Coach Durham called.

"Miguel, you guys watching the news about Wichita Falls? That's horrible, huh?"

"Yes, sir. That's terrible. I hope I never see one of those things," I said, still gripped by the devastation.

"Well, how did your finals go?" Coach asked.

"Fine, Coach."

"Good, good. So, where is Zac? Is he there?"

"Yes, sir. He's here. You wanna speak to him?"

"Yes."

Seems another storm was about to brew, and it had nothing to do with the weather. I passed the telephone to Zac, who was failing classes miserably and had missed a substantial amount of days. Also, his performance on the track team had suffered because of excessive use of marijuana and alcohol.

"What's going on Mr. Finn?" asked Coach Durham, using a rare formal greeting.

"Just sitting here with Morris watching the news, coach."

"Yeah, isn't that something?" Coach asked as he prepared to shift the conversation to academics.

"Sure is, coach."

"But anyway, Zac, I want you down at my office around 3 o'clock today before practice. We need to talk."

"Yes, sir," Zac said worriedly.

"Well, I'll see you then, and tell Miguel we will practice inside today due to the bad weather, OK?"

During the hours before his meeting with Coach Durham, Zac tried to prepare himself for the worst.

He sat. He paced. He sat more. He paced more.

Zac knew he was in hot water.

"Zac. Come on in and take a seat. Do you want something to drink?"

"Yes, sir."

Coach then asked his secretary to bring him two cokes.

Zac needed a minimum 2.5 GPA for the school to honor another semester of scholarships, but Fs and Ds had plagued him all semester. He failed kinesiology, physiology and advanced mathematics, and he was already on academic probation. Coach Durham said there was nothing he could do to reinstate the scholarship and that Zac's poor performance athletically, too, had effectively severed his relationship with

West Texas State.

He was embarrassed because he knew he would have to tell his girlfriend, Judy, and eventually his family. After his meeting with Coach Durham, Zac returned to empty the dorm room of his belongings. He called Judy and wrote me a short letter about his abrupt departure. He couldn't bear the thought of facing us

He reserved a seat on the Greyhound bus to high-tail it out of West Texas for Houston. He didn't even tell Coach Durham about his departure.

Zac skipped out of town as fast as the tornado that cut a wide swath of destruction through Wichita Falls earlier in the day.

*****

"Hi, mom. I'm doing fine. I just wanted to let you know I'm in Chicago, and I'm here for the NCAA championship."

That was the message on the postcard that I wrote to my family during my layover at O'Hare International before traveling to Champaign and the campus of the University of Illinois. On Friday, the track teams were preparing for the evening's events. The dry air flowed down the rubber track as we gathered for the mile-relay and other events. Unexpectedly, the mile-relay competitors were informed that there would be no semi-final race. Instead, the finals for the mile-relay event would be held tomorrow due to numerous withdrawals.

My teammates and I were surprised to learn that such an elite event would yield so many withdrawals, especially for an NCAA competition. This meant that we automatically qualified for the finals.

Hooray!

On Saturday, the day of our automatic qualification, the team came up short. We were creamed by our more experienced opponents. Despite that, the crowd cheered wildly for us, the underdogs. I had struggled through the last 50 meters of the race.

Although blitzed by some of the best in the track and field world, I was surprised by the crowd's sportsmanship and cheerful support. The encouragement led me to complete the grueling race.

The official time for us as the last finishing team was 3:07.45.

"Way to go, Miguel. Way to go!" Coach Durham shouted as Kevin, Tony and Kenny looked on.

"Thanks, Coach," I said, gasping for air as if it were my last.

"Good run, guys, and congratulations," said Willie Smith, the country's top quarter-miler at that time, running in at 45.10 seconds.

"Thanks," the squad said in unison.

At that instant we realized we had gained respect and experience from true champions. It was also a historic moment for our West Texas State squad, which discovered that it was the first team of three freshmen and a sophomore to compete in an NCAA final mile relay.

*****

As the pulsating water from the shower relaxed me, I began to daydream about my friend Zac, who was now living with his pregnant girlfriend in a different part of Houston. Although it was near the end of summer break, I realized I had not seen Zac, Butch or Caleb while back at home with my family. Caleb was still working as an assistant manager at his uncle's restaurant in southwest Houston.

Caleb's brother Kelvin, my former nemesis, was in prison for selling drugs to an undercover cop. Fortunately my siblings were faring better than other youngsters in the neighborhood. David was working for the city and Troy, even though he was a dropout, was working on his GED at Houston Community College. Fay was now a senior at Ross Sterling High School and a cheerleader. And Dee would be a junior in August at Texas Southern University, pursuing her bachelor's degree in social work.

As for my parents, mom and dad had buried Big Momma and were still struggling to make ends meet. They had a home mortgage, car note and a host of other bills. Yet they kept the family together.

I was working as a waiter at a popular eatery. With August and the new school semester fast approaching, I had to give notice of my impending departure. The Strawberry Patch was a reputable Houston restaurant, and I was one of its first black waiters.

Just before returning to campus, I got a surprise visit from Butch Webber, my former dorm mate and second-round draft-pick in the NFL.

I was flabbergasted.

"What's up, Buddy?" asked Butch, flashing his signature smile at my parents' front door.

"Man! I can't believe it. Look what the cat dragged in," I said. "Is that your black Jaguar in the driveway?"

"Yep. It was a gift from the alumni. You wanna go for a ride?" he asked, dangling his keys in my face.

"Hell, yeah!"

As we drove through the neighborhood toward Southpark Boulevard, I noticed a logo from the Los Angeles Rams swinging from the rear-view mirror in Butch's luxury sedan.

"Man, I thought I would never see you again."

"Why would you think that, Miguel? You thought I was like that, buddy? By the way, I had to pay you a visit after seeing you on television at the NCAAs in June."

"Yeah. That was kinda embarrassing getting last place and getting my ass kicked," I said. I was still slightly embarrassed.

"Miguel, what did I tell you about not giving up, man? You guys made history, and that's enough in itself.

"You're right, Butch. Anyway I hate that you're gone from campus, man. I still wish you were there."

"Miguel. Nothing stays the same, fella."

Changing the subject, he asked, "So, how is Zac doing, since I didn't see him on the tube?"

"Well, Zac flunked out of school, man!"

"What! Flunked out! I knew that guy was smoking too much of that shit. You're not still smoking that weed, are you?"

"Hell, no! After what it did to Zac!"

"Good, Miguel, because it's best that you don't, buddy. It can lead to other drugs and problems. I've stopped, too, because my career is more important than drugs, alcohol or a piece of ass."

"Yep. I hear ya. So, where are we headed?" I asked, enjoying the fresh smell of the leather seats in the cabin of Butch's sedan. I really didn't want to hear the part about giving up ass. I was hooked now, and he did it to me. Or did he?

"We're headed to a special place. I want to show you something before I leave for football camp in a few weeks."

The black Jaguar cruised down Southpark Boulevard, a black thriving neighborhood that led into a once-predominantly Jewish community known as South MacGregor. It was minutes from downtown, the Texas Medical Center, the Museum District and Houston's three major colleges – the University of Houston, Texas Southern University and Rice University.

When the Jewish community abandoned the fine homes and mansions, an influx of professional blacks moved in. It had become one of the premiere black neighborhoods.

So it wasn't a surprise when Butch pulled up to a huge piece of real estate property undergoing renovations.

"Man! That's a castle," I said, viewing the structure from the long curved driveway. "Is this your house?"

"Yep, so to speak. I bought it for my mom and family from this white doctor who moved to Seattle."

"Come see, Miguel. We're still renovating it to my mom's liking. Anything for momma, you know," Butch explained as I joined him on the grounds of the 18th-century cobblestone mansion. It was larger than anyplace I'd seen – even bigger than those in the city's wealthier neighborhoods.

"Now, this is what I've dreamed about having," I whispered softly. I was too proud of Butch to envy his success because he was doing what a responsible son should do: take care of family.

"Miguel. This is the payoff for those hard, brutal hours and years I've endured, so that my mom could live comfortably after all she's been through. This should be one of your goals, too – helping your family enjoy a better quality of life that many of us have been denied by our captors from the past. You feel me?"

"Yeah, I hear ya man. It's part of my goals – to excel and put my family in a nice home someday. All I need to do is stay focused. Right?"

"Right, Miguel. I see that you've been listening after all. Focus is the key. Focus, Focus, Focus."

I wondered if he thought much about our sexual encounter on campus last semester, which I often wanted to forget. I promised myself that it would be the last time I would ever sleep with a man. God knew I wanted to keep that promise, but like Butch often told me it's all about focusing on your priorities and not your desires and regrets.

Thinking he had taken advantage of me, he felt the need to apologize for our sexual encounter during the time I was bereaved after my grandmother had died. Hell, I wasn't mad at him, even though he did play me like a funky piano. But, all in all, he got what he wanted, and I suppose I did, too.

We both spent the rest of the day encouraging one another before departing into two different worlds and with apparently two entirely different philosophies about our future and sexual orientation.

Chapter 12
A Date With the SEC

December in Canyon, Texas, was snowy and bone-chilling. I stared silently out of the back window of the coach's canary yellow Cadillac during a slow, gloomy afternoon drive back to campus to begin another semester. All I could think about was breaking the news about my new college plans to my family and lady friend, Patsy. I wasn't sure how they'd take it.

Kevin and Kenny already were mad as hell that the coach was leaving for a job in the Deep South that, perhaps, was more racist than Canyon or Amarillo. Even so, I was certain that I was going to join him in Mississippi next semester to compete in the SEC (Southeastern Conference).

After returning to the dorm, I became worried because I hadn't received a phone call all weekend from Patsy. She had promised she would contact me. I wondered if she had been scared away by the same cowards who posted the racist note to my door last semester to protest our interracial relationship. Nevertheless, I decided to call her before going to bed early because classes were to start the following morning.

After a few short rings, someone answered.

"Hello," the raspy voice said.

"May I speak to Patsy?"

After a few moments of silence, I heard a yell in the background.

"Patsy. That damn boy is on the phone for you again!"

"Yes!" Patsy answered abruptly.

"Patsy. Miguel speaking."

"What do you want, Miguel?" she snapped.

"What do you mean what do I want? I've been waiting to hear from you. What's your problem?" I demanded.

"You're my problem, faggot!"

"What!" I asked, startled by her insult.

"You heard me, faggot! I know what you and the mothafucker Butch Webber did last semester when he was on campus. You bastard!"

"What in the fuck are you talking about girl?"

"Mothafucker! You know what I'm talking about. You and Butch in his dorm room with him half-naked, just wearing some red underwear with his dick on hard. You faggot!

"Bitch! Don't call me that again, dammit!" I demanded.

"Faggot!" Patsy repeated to torment me even further.

"Fuck you, bitch! You don't know what you're talking about."

"Yes I do, because Kevin saw you coming out of Butch's room that day when you told me you were drawing his picture. What did y'all do, play with each other?"

"That mothafucker! Kevin is a damn lie! Me and Butch are just friends. And I ain't no faggot, and neither is Butch. Ever since I met you that damn Kevin has been jealous of me."

"You're lying! I know Butch is gay because when we dated he told me he was interested in athletic guys. Damn you, Miguel!" Patsy screamed.

I was at a loss for words because Butch gave up the game.

"Why didn't you tell me, Miguel? Why didn't you tell me, motherfucker!" Her assault continued as she grilled me for being dishonest.

"Patsy. I'm not gay, dammit!"

"You're a lying bastard, Miguel! Stop lying to me. All I wanted was for you to be honest with me. Damn you, Miguel! Don't you ever call me again. You hear me, mothafucker?" she screamed hysterically.

The phone went silent for a moment.

"Listen hear, you damn nigger bastard. If you call my daughter again, I'll have the police on your black ass. You hear me!"

The phone then went dead after Patsy's mother slammed down the receiver, disconnecting us.

All I could think of at that moment was kicking Kevin's ass for fueling this anger. I marched down the hall to find him, but he wasn't in his room. Lucky bitch-ass punk!

Stomping back to my room, I knew it was time for a change. Time to dodge a minefield of gossip before rumors circulated about my sexuality.

Mississippi State University and the Southeastern Conference were looking better and better.

As far as I was concerned, it would be the start of a new opportunity and the last I would see of Canyon, Texas – its cowboy regalia, Patsy and that cock-blocking punk, Kevin.

*****

"This is an ABC news special report."

That was the announcement from the television inside the athletic dorm at Mississippi State.

Max Robinson, the first black news anchor for a major network, reported that Russia had invaded Afghanistan. The scene of Russian-made war tanks encroaching on foreign soil shook everyone's consciousness, including the school's many international athletes from Europe and Africa.

"Those bastards! How can they just invade a country that has little defense?" a West German tennis player asked in disgust.

"Those Russians are evil, and they have the distinction of hosting the Olympics this year," another observer noted.

It was my sophomore year at MSU. As I watched the televised message with keen interest, Herman, my new roommate, entered the dayroom and placed his right hand on my shoulder.

"What's up with the newscast, Morris?" Herman asked.

"Russia invaded Afghanistan, and things don't look too good," I said, still affixed to the television screen and to the sensation of Herman's touch.

"That's fucked up!" said Herman, who stood a bit taller than me.

He was a second-semester freshman from Atlanta, Georgia. Besides track, he played football. His evenly caramel skin attracted nearly every woman on campus. His deep voice gave him a huge sex appeal. He was good-looking, but he was also intimidating. Those who knew his character, though, also knew he wouldn't harm a fly. He was easy-going and calm – a gentle beast with a humble spirit, but with a hint of rough-ness.

"Ain't the Olympics in Moscow this summer?" Herman asked.

"Sure is. And I bet some stupid shit gonna happen. Just watch," I said, turning away to exit the room as Herman followed closely behind.

*****

After a few short weeks, my predictions rang true. My teammates and I were sitting in the dayroom watching *"The Young and the Restless"* when a special news report about the Soviet invasion interrupted the regular broadcast. The news broadcaster informed the nation that the White House was deeply troubled by Russia's aggression. Cameras showed the president declaring that America will boycott the 1980 Moscow Olympics in August.

Many athletes were unhappy with the decision by the commander in chief.

"Ain't that a bitch!" Terrance said, sitting upright in his oversized cushioned chair.

"Well, believe it, man!" I said.

"Damn! And here I am trying to make the Olympic trials in June. That's fucked up!" Terrance said angrily.

"There's always 1984," Chaz, a trash-talking track teammate who was a mediocre long jumper, said with a smirk.

Terrance, at 6 feet, stood eye level to me. He was a sophomore from Jacksonville, Florida, and one of the fastest quarter-milers recruited by Mississippi State in recent years. He was nearly as temperamental as Chaz.

Chaz, muscular and a light-skinned junior, hailed from Mobile, Alabama. He was the shortest member of the squad at 5 feet, 8 inches tall. He was an average long-jump competitor but one of the smartest athletes with a 3.5 GPA. Self-assured and brutally assertive, some fellow athletes considered him an arrogant asshole.

"Say, Morris. I'm going upstairs to listen to some music man. You coming?" asked Terrance, seeking escape from the disturbing news.

"Yeah, I'm right behind you!"

"Me, too," said Chaz, our interloper for the evening. We all rode the dorm elevator to the fourth floor of the 10-story athletic dormitory, better known as McArthur Hall.

Chapter 13
Striptease Act

After a few minor adjustments, I successfully glided through my first tour of duty at Mississippi State. But before heading home for the semester break, I decided to make yet another important change. I switched majors. Because I felt overburdened with design homework, I reluctantly ditched an architectural curriculum for Industrial Technology. I simply couldn't keep up with the workload. The lab times interfered with my track-and-field practice schedules, and math courses were grueling.

So, after taking care of my academic affairs, I boarded a flight en route to Houston on Friday morning. Upon arrival to my hometown I was elated to see mom and dad waiting to greet me at the terminal. Dad, as usual, was smoking and wearing his trademark straw hat with a dark blue ban around the base. No matter what the season, he wore the hat. Mom was decked out in calf-high boots, a blue-jean skirt and matching long-sleeved shirt.

They were brimming with pride to see me again.

After retrieving my heavy baggage, dad wondered why I didn't leave some of my belongings on campus. I assured him that my stereo, refrigerator and television were still in storage on campus.

Of course, the way he wobbled and struggled at getting my

trunk of goods inside the car, he would disagree that I left anything back in Starkville, Mississippi.

So, now it was back to my hometown. Let the good times roll.

A string of concerts, festivals and parties swamped the Houston area as summer got into full swing. The Budweiser Superfest brought an array of popular musicians to the Houston Summit. Groups such as Cameo, the Fatback Band, the Gap Band and Earth, Wind & Fire performed at the entertainment venue.

While back home from school, I returned to work at the popular Strawberry Patch restaurant, where I had befriended a 22-year-old blond co-worker. Smooth-talking Chuck, a party animal, was ruggedly handsome at 5-feet, 11-inches tall. He owned a Jeep and a super sport Honda motorcycle and would perform impressive daredevil stunts. He appeared to be shy at first but would loosen up quickly once he became comfortable.

During a break from work, he expressed interest in attending one of the evening concerts over the weekend.

He told me that he had already arranged our dates.

"I hope you got everything under control, man," I said.

"Damn skippy, dude! Check this out. You're gonna take this Spanish chick, and I got Miss Legs and Thighs," he said.

"Who in the hell is Miss Legs and Thighs?"

"She's this 5-foot, 10-inch tall black beauty who lives in my mom's complex in Uptown."

"Cool. I'm down with that idea."

"And after the concert, we're gonna drive to Galveston Island and spend the night at my uncle's beach house. That's when the real fun begins," he said.

Brilliant spotlights encircled the Houston Summit as the Budweiser Superfest got under way. Our group was ready to get its groove on as the Fatback Band performed one of its hits, *"I Like Girls."* The song was fitting because there were three girls to every male in the facility, and I was definitely into the girls, too.

My date was sexy and wild. I had never dated a Spanish girl before, but I wasn't tripping. And Chuck's black beauty was a Pam Grier look-alike. She was a well-endowed, ebony beauty.

The atmosphere became quite festive and intense for some patrons as the stench of smoke, including marijuana, consumed the entertainment hall. Titty-grabbing and ass-squeezing were conspicuous and frequent. Many of the young girls eagerly exposed their breasts as Chuck and I struggled to maintain our composure as we escorted our dates through the mass of madness.

"Damn, dude. This crap is wild, man!" Chuck bellowed with excitement over the loud instruments.

"No shit."

"You enjoying yourself?" asked my sexy Spanish date, whispering into my left ear with a cupped hand to amplify her voice.

I responded seductively: "Not as much as I'd like, too." I then firmly grabbed her waist and began to dance and gyrate on the floor. I was overdue for a good lay as I had not been with a female since Patsy.

Chuck, watching me get my groove on, followed suit. His date's cocoa skin gleamed under the floodlights, and the girl had some moves, too.

When the fest ended the four of us rushed out frolicking like teens – jostling, grabbing, squeezing and teasing each other lustfully. I knew I loved the intimate company of females, but I questioned if it were enough to completely satisfy my raging libido.

After we located Chuck's red topless Jeep after midnight, we rode into the breezy summer night, mesmerized by the brilliant glow cast by the full moon.

We were bound for Galveston, a 45-minute drive from

Houston.

Upon reaching Stewart Beach, Chuck partially disrobed by removing his nylon, white shirt, exposing his semi-muscular upper body. He covered his date with the shirt to protect her bare shoulders from the beachfront air.

When we finally reached our destination, Chuck – in another act of chivalry – quickly bailed first out of the jeep and ran around to open the passenger door for his dark and lovely date. He escorted her inside the beach home.

"C'mon, Miguel. Let's go, dude!" yelled Chuck, slowly reaching the top of the stairs.

My date and I joined them.

Once inside the massive structure, we were awestruck by its 20-foot vaulted ceiling surrounded by walnut-stained paneled walls adorned with a multitude of sliding glass-tinted windows.

"Wow! This place is amazing," Chuck's date said.

It was majestic. I noticed works by Andy Warhol and other artists, that included nude images, throughout the house.

My date asked the very question I was thinking. She wanted to know about Chuck's uncle and how he acquired his wealth. It appeared he was sitting on a load of money. Few people could afford such a lavish beachfront house and expensive artwork.

"He's got money, I suppose," Chuck answered modestly, as he shuffled through an album collection behind the mirrored bar.

"Girl, look at this. There's a huge pool down there on the back deck!" Chuck's date said as she peered through a glass door near the massive entertainment system.

Chuck then popped a bottle of Moet as music from the opera "*Madame Butterfly*" flowed through the spacious room.

That was my first exposure to opera.

Moments later a huge splash reverberated through the room. It was Chuck showing off as he leaped into the illuminated pool. Not to be outdone, I joined him to christen the pool for our next party. I stripped down to my boxer briefs. Just as I prepared to take a dive, Chuck's underwear became airborne. It hit the side of the pool where I stood.

Stopped cold in my tracks, I stared in amazement at Chuck but, again, I followed suit – more like birthday suit. Our own nudist camp was being formed when our female guests decided to bare all, too. The beautiful figure drawings on the walls inside the beachfront home quickly lost out to the poolside anatomy show outside.

After that night of revelry, Chuck and I became running buddies throughout the summer. He would often have access to large, immaculate homes that he claimed belonged to relatives or friends who were always out of town on business.

I became suspicious at one point. So early one Wednesday as we headed back to Galveston to the beach house, I decided to explore Chuck's secret world.

We spent the day playing touch football in the murky waters of Jamaica Beach. Chuck threw me a pass. I sped in his direction in an attempt to score but a surprise tackle forced me to fumble.

A proud Chuck celebrated by spiking the loose ball. He was feeling cocky now. With my back turned, he caught me off guard by pulling down my running shorts.

He ran back toward the beach house grinning and laughing as I chased his sneaky ass for baring mine.

"I'm gonna get you, Chuck!" I warned, as I struggled to run while pulling up my shorts at the same time.

By the time I made it to the house, Chuck was at the bar sipping on a glass of orange juice, with another glass of juice waiting nearby for me.

I asked him why he was so wild and unpredictable.

"Like I said before, Miguel, life is all about color, dude. Things are not just black and white, but full of variety. You get my drift?" Chuck asked.

"Variety, huh?" I asked, swallowing the last of my orange juice and trying to ignore Chuck's piercing stare into my curious eyes. "Speaking of variety. How many houses do you have access to, Chuck?" Even as I attempted to apply pressure, this dude was cool under fire.

"As many as I like, dude," Chuck said, grabbing two beach towels from behind the bar, tossing one to me. "You see, Miguel, I have access to a lot of things because of the kind of work I do. You dig?"

"Waiting tables?" I asked puzzled while wiping excess water from my body. But, in reality, I knew he must have been doing more than waiting tables.

"No, dude! Male stripping and escorting."

"Male stripping! You strip?" I asked incredulously.

"You damn skippy I do! I've made a lot of money doing it and met a lot of rich people, too," he said panning the inside of the house.

"Like who?"

"Like the person who owns this house and the townhouse in Tanglewood and elsewhere," said Chuck, facing me as he sat on the large wooden floor with his legs crossed.

"So, this is not your uncle's house?" The reality was that my friend was a hustler at heart.

"What uncle? I came up with that because I didn't know you then, and I was afraid I would run you off if I told you what I was doing to make extra money."

"Damn. Male dancing, huh? That's too deep for me, man."

"Miguel, people would go crazy over you, dude, if you decided to dance, man! You can be an independent. You could have all the things you dreamed of and more," Chuck said enthusiastically.

"People like who? Independent how?" I asked, entertaining the possibility.

"People who are moving things in this city," said Chuck, refusing to reveal his clients.

"Chuck, stop talking in riddles. Just say what you want to say. We're grown men, aren't we?"

"Well, Miguel, I do business with women and men. Like the man who owns this place."

"You strip for men, too?"

"Why not, dude? Money is green, regardless of where it comes from."

"Yeah, I suppose it is," I answered while looking out the glass bay windows at the rolling waves and the seagulls.

Then Grace Jones' *"Pull up to the Bumper"* played in the background. The powerful bass and symbols echoed from the stereo, and the ocean waves appeared to move in tandem with the instrumentals.

"Miguel!" Chuck shouted from behind the bar, "I'm gonna show you how it's done."

Chuck boldly displayed his skills as he moved rhythmically to the pulsating music. He began to slowly peel off his swimming shorts, exposing his pubic area. Then, strategically, he pulled them passed his knees, wearing only a G-string that covered his semi-hard sex.

By now, I couldn't believe my eyes as I watched the freaky side of my blond co-worker. I found myself in yet another sexual quagmire. My heart rate increased exponentially at the sight of Chuck's half-naked body and seductive moves. He was now inches within my reach, enticing me ever so boldly. He began turning his back to me, displaying his deep tan line that covered his muscular round buttocks. Even with my eyes tightly closed, I could feel my resistance failing, the lust too strong once again.

"You're not gay!" I chanted repeatedly to myself. I then opened my eyes to a full-naked Chuck. His sex was now even harder than before, and so was mine. Actually, I was tired of pretending I wasn't attracted to men. I just didn't want to be associated with the word "gay." But I didn't know what to do or how to handle my tendencies. I didn't want to continue denying myself.

Also, I'd never been with a white man before, so I was curious.

It seemed my road dawg, Chuck, and I had more in common than just our jobs and good tastes in women. And as Grace Jones's vocal pipes continued to blow, pulling up to the bumper defined the rest of the evening for the two of us.

Chapter 14
Loving Latisha

More than two years had passed since the invasion of Afghanistan and Chuck's striptease in Galveston. From that point I began keeping count of the number of guys I had slept with. I felt someday I would stop the wild acts, and the counting would eventually cease.

The amateur and professional athletic world had now turned its attention to the 1984 Los Angeles Olympics.

Track season was in full bloom and Coach Durham and our 1982 Southeastern Conference mile-relay champions had just completed our regular indoor season with a bang. Our award-winning squad consisted of Terrance, Charles, Kiel and me. We had posted records in the Kodak Invitational, the Indiana Invitational in Bloomington, and the SEC meet on the Louisiana State University campus. We had posted the No. 3 and No. 5 best times in the top 10 mile-relays in the country that winter, according to the February issue of Track and Field magazine.

Our next venture would be the Indoor NCAA meet outside Detroit in the spectacular Silver Dome in Pontiac, Michigan. Unfortunately, my roommate Herman didn't qualify for any event. So he would be going back home to Atlanta for the spring-break holiday.

*****

Beautiful thick snow covered Pontiac, Michigan, during the NCAA competition in March. Preliminaries of the 400-meter were a disaster for all three MSU quarter-milers. Terrance, Kiel and I struggled, producing a dismal non-qualifying effort that knocked us out of Saturday's finals. The small 176-yard track, with a new foundation and dangerous bank, deceived many runners at the NCAA competition. Despite the poor performance, our squad wasn't discouraged. There was still the prestigious mile-relay yet to come.

During my cool-down and recovery period, I noticed a beautiful Asian-African female with slanted light-brown eyes, lightly tanned skin and silky black hair observing me. She was a long-jumper and short-sprint specialist from the University of Florida. On previous meets, we would often exchange subtle stares.

Not being able to contain myself any longer, I slowly approached her from behind to congratulate her on advancing into Saturday's finals in the long jump and 60-meter sprint.

"Thank you. I didn't know you were watching since you were occupied with the 400," she said while stooping and avoiding much eye contact.

"Yeah. I've always noticed you when you jump. You're so perfect."

"You're full of crap!" she uttered with a smile. "What is your name?"

I introduced myself and extended my hand to hoist her from the ground where she sat.

"An aggressive man, huh? I like that. By the way, my name is Latisha. Latisha Okoee."

"O-Who?" I asked while stumbling to pronounce her last name and hoping my gaffe didn't offend her.

"O-ko-ee," Latisha repeated slowly.

She then asked me to simply call her Tish.

"Well if it means anything, Miguel, I was watching you, too, when you ran that quarter. Boy! The monkey really jumped on your back, huh?" she said, teasingly.

I expressed that it did but that the mile-relay was "gonna be a different story."

"*Going* to be," Tish said.

"What?" I asked puzzled about her statement.

"It is *going* to be a different story," she said, correcting my colloquial use of "gonna."

"An intellectual, huh? Yeah, I like that."

"Call me sometime," she said abruptly while handing me a card with her telephone number. "I'm living on campus."

I noticed the embroidered print on the card read the Atoms Track Club. I was impressed that she ran for such a prestigious organization, not to mention that she was beautiful, too.

It was time to break away from my chat when all the teams were alerted to report to the starting line.

"I'll look forward to hearing from you soon, Miguel," Tish said.

"You can count on that," I responded.

My past relationships with Tammy and Patsy were strictly about sex. But it appeared that this encounter could produce something more, and I aimed to find out.

I had felt that sex was threatening to ruin my life, and I hated myself for it. I was ready to be reprogrammed.

*****

My mom and dad sat in the doctor's office with older sister Dee, who had complained about being tired most of the time. As they waited patiently on the diagnosis early Saturday morning, they read the mail, including a postcard I sent from Michigan.

"Honey, here's a card from your son. And from the looks of this skyline, he's in Detroit," momma said.

"He's in Detroit, now?" asked Dee. "Don't he ever have time to study?" she asked, trying to allay her fears about her mysterious medical condition.

Dr. Jones, dressed in his white lab coat with a stethoscope around his neck, then entered the waiting area and sat in an empty chair next to Dee. He stared at all three as he carefully pondered his statement.

"Well. This is what we've found, Dee," Dr. Jones said meekly as he looked into her worried eyes. "We have reason to believe that you have multiple sclerosis, a chronic disease of the central nervous system."

"What!" momma said in panic.

"Yes. That seems to be the case," Dr. Jones said, holding Dee's sweaty palms as fear gripped her.

"Multiple sclerosis? How did this happen, doctor?" a stunned daddy asked.

"We really don't have the answers or a cure, Mr. Morris."

"Ohmigod!" mother cried. She was more emotional than Dee.

"I'm gonna be OK, momma," said Dee, unsure how to react or what to say about the debilitating disease. She promised that even if her physical condition was to become compromised that she was ready to fight for her life.

"Well, what about a prognosis?" mom asked.

The doctors said that over a period of time Dee could experience speech defects and loss of muscular coordination. He assured the family that medicine could help delay the disease's progression but reminded them again that there was no cure.

*****

It was now 11 o'clock the next morning in Michigan. The bright sun began to melt the snow that covered cars and other structures. Spectators began to fill the dome for the final day of NCAA track and field competition.

"Say, Miguel. Look over there," said Terrance, nodding in Tish's direction at the long-jump area.

"I'll be back, Terrance." I went toward her.

"Hi, Miguel. Are you following me?" she asked.

"Of course, I am," I said, smiling.

She then dropped her adidas bag to the wooden floor near her small feet as if I had frustrated her.

"Do I make you nervous, Tish?"

"Of course you do," she responded while adjusting her hair into a ball.

Surely, she couldn't be serious.

"Do I look nervous, Miguel?" asked Tish.

"I don't know, but I do know one thing. I want to date you. That's if you're not spoken for."

"What!" Tish exclaimed.

"You heard me. I want to date you."

"You are aggressive, aren't you?"

"No. Just lonely."

"Yeah, right. OK. Who is she? There has to be someone else in your life," she said, probing for an answer.

"She ... doesn't exist."

"Uh, huh. Whatever," she responded dubiously but still smiled, nonetheless. Her dazzling pearly-white teeth were awesome.

"I'm serious."

"I am, too, Miguel. I'm not buying that line of yours. Do you think I should?"

"So you don't believe me?"

"It's not a matter of belief; it's a matter of truth," she said, staring into my eyes. "So, again, are you telling me the truth, Miguel?"

"Yes, I am."

"Well, let's design the house before we build it, Miguel?"

Yes! I screamed internally, knowing that I had crossed first base. Now ... on to second.

"I can settle fur that."

"*For that*, Miguel. *For that!*" she replied, once again correcting my pronunciation.

"Maybe you should consider taking a diction course. It wouldn't hurt."

I told her I would consider the idea.

By the end of the day, Oklahoma went on to win the indoor nationals in the mile-relay. I figured its celebration, though, would be short-lived once the outdoor competitions began.

As for Tish, she failed to make it out of the long-jump semis but was pleased with her personal best of 21 feet, one-quarter inches.

Chapter 15
Trials and Tribulations

Spring break and the NCAA had ended and I was back on campus facing a rigorous semester. Physics, chemistry and business calculus threatened to kick my butt. The workload was as tough as solving a Rubik's Cube. It was all mentally exhausting. I was struggling to meet the semester grade requirements, and just maintaining a C-average was stressful.

After a disappointing day, I sat in my dorm room reminiscing about the failing mid-term scores from my physics and chemistry tests. This would certainly get the attention of Coach Durham. How much worse could it get? I decided to ease my mind and sort through my mail.

As I rifled through the stack, I ran across a perfumed letter from my mom. A few lines into the letter, my mother mentioned my sister's illness to me for the first time. I was slapped by the menacing words "multiple sclerosis," which seemed to leap off the pages of the letter like a cheetah attacking its prey. I knew this disease to be a thief, robbing its victims of their abilities to live normal lives or perform basic tasks.

Mom shared all the disturbing details about Dee and her condition. She assured me that my sister was still mobile but often tires easily after prolonged periods of standing and walking. I then immediately rushed to the lobby telephone to call home, forgetting that my parents hadn't arrived from work yet. I felt overwhelmed and helpless. I went back to my room and dropped to my knees screaming in silence, asking God to intervene.

"Oh, Lord! Where are you?"

*****

It was now April, a month after learning about Dee and her MS diagnosis. She was fine for now, so I decided to focus attention on my academic problems because I had been warned of severe consequences by Coach Durham and the dean of technology if I failed to meet the university grade requirements.

With track season in full swing and weekly trips out of town, a tutor was provided on many of our trips. Even with a tutor, the complex sciences baffled me.

For the rest of the semester, I continued to struggle. On a more positive note, I excelled in my advanced electronics and architectural classes, earning A-averages in each.

My drafting professor encouraged me to stay the course after he released me early to attend the SEC meet in Athens, Georgia.

I began to doubt myself. I even began to wonder how others viewed me. Was I attractive enough? Were my "hidden" behaviors actually visible? I felt that demons were haunting me as I became less confident in my abilities.

*****

May signaled the close of the semester and a heavy load of guilt and frustration. To try to lift my spirits, I headed toward the student union building. After sprinting up the stairs, I spotted my roommate, Herman, and his part-time girlfriend, Lenna, a member of Alpha Kappa Alpha sorority. They were conversing near the double doors at the entrance of the mess hall.

"What's up, Lenna, Herman?" I was direct and short.

"Nuttin' much," responded Lenna, noticing my dour

expression. "What's wrong with you?"

"Nothing," I said. I lied at first because I was embarrassed to face my failures. "Well, the truth is I flunked physics and chemistry this semester."

"Wow!" uttered Herman, shaking his head in disappointment.

"Yeah. I know Coach is going to flip his wig when he finds out," I said.

"Make it up next semester," Lenna suggested as she grabbed my hand in support. "It's not as bad as you're making it."

"Well, roomie, don't feel too bad because I flunked chemistry twice before I got it right," expressed Herman, trying to pull me out of my depression. "At least you're still running through the season because I'm through for the year. I didn't qualify for anything."

His downcast eyes summed up his own disappointment.

"Well, my last day for finals is tomorrow," said Lenna. "Perhaps we can do something tonight. Herman will fill you in on the details." She blew us a kiss for good measure and left.

"What is she talking about, Herman?"

"Well, it's like this," Herman explained, "A fraternity party is kicking off tonight on Frat Row."

Fraternity Row was a strip of huge, white colonial and Victorian-style mansions, occupied by white students. There were no black fraternity houses on campus at Mississippi State. Often, the Kappa Alphas would throw a Toga block party, inviting many athletes and some black frat organizations. Many of them were MSU athletes themselves.

When nightfall covered the campus Lenna, Herman, Tamela (my date) and I arrived at the party in our Toga regalia. I was actually enjoying myself until a fellow student from my dreadful physics class showed up. The idiot was drunk. God knew I wanted to forget about that course forever.

"Hey, man! Ain't you in my physics class?"

"Yeah, man. I was in that class. But now it's over," I said, turning away.

"I knew you was that Morris track fella when I saw you coming."

The country bumpkin, cowboy-boot wearing, tobacco-chewing menace stuffed his face with tap beer from a huge pitcher he'd been carrying all night as if it were a natural extremity, part of his anatomy. He and that beer jar appeared to be joined at the hip, and he didn't intend to let it go.

After acknowledging him politely again for the third time, I decided I had had enough. This dude was relentless, following me and talking incessantly about nothing. And since it was getting late I decided to bail out. My date indicated she was tired, too. I told Lenna and Herman I was ready to go. They agreed to leave with us.

Fortunately, both Lenna and my girl Tamela lived in the same dorm, only minutes away from McArthur Hall, where Herman and I lived. Once we dropped off our dates, Herman and I raced down the slanted street that led to the front entrance of our 10-story residence. He was a bit juiced like I was, but he could still drive.

After exiting Herman's convertible Mustang, I asked if he were going to raise the top, fearing vandalism. After all, we were in Mississippi.

"No! I know there's no one crazy enough to touch my baby."

I suppose he was right since everybody liked the guy. But still I couldn't figure him out though. He was odd, yet cool, in his own way.

With both of us intoxicated, Herman grabbed me around my waist to help balance me as we climbed the short flight of stairs.

After we reached the room, we collapsed on our beds and lie quietly there weighing our shower options.

After I mustered up the strength, I decided to freshen up.

"Say, I'm going to jump in the shower. You coming?"

"Right behind you," said Herman, jumping to his feet with surprising swiftness, tearing off his Toga outfit and standing in the room stark-naked.

What the hell!

I had seen him without clothes before, but not like this.

"Man, you were wearing nothing under that thing?"

"Nope."

"I felt a little freaky tonight, man. I'm a stone freak, I thought you knew that," Herman said smiling as he staggered off into the hallway butt-naked in the middle of the night, his towel dangling from his neck. Ass exposed, balls swinging. Yeah, he is a freak.

When I entered the shower area seconds behind him, I observed Herman under the warm pulsating water washing his hair. I noticed the symmetry of his back, buttocks and calves. They were so perfect. I had never looked at him like this before. I vowed to maintain control of my fetishes. But I couldn't deny that temptation and lust were eating at me, creating goose bumps and exciting my jimmy.

"Is that you, Miguel?" his deep voice asked. He turned, washing the shampoo from his hair, saluting me with a full erection.

My heartbeat raced as I honed in on Herman's eroticism.

"Are you coming in?" Herman asked.

"Yeah," I said, somewhat paranoid. Perhaps my old college buddy Butch Webber was right about me. I was a magnet to some people. Most people liked me, and I knew it – not just physically but socially, too. He helped me to realize my valuable assets – athleticism and magnetism.

"Well, jump on it, Miguel."

When I entered the shower my hardened sex began to throb immediately – overtaken by lust. And this time was no different than the others. I invited the intrusion with open arms. So with that, I had reasoned that I probably would start counting once again the number of men I had slept with.

It was now 2 a.m.

With the lights off and the curtains wide open, we let the moon illuminate the room. Herman and I were enthralled with each other. Our muscled bodies gave off heat like a fiery furnace as we explored each other from head to toe and performed every imaginable act – from his bed then from mine, a cyclical orgy of two.

This went on for what seemed like hours: firm grips to our hardened sex, locked tongues, oral and … anal sex.

To my surprise, Herman gently rolled over to his razor-cut abdomen and widened his massive quadriceps, as the moonlight highlighted his hairy buttocks.

"Take it, Miguel," Herman demanded.

So without argument, I did and began to explore my roommate's hot crater.

I had now crossed the threshold of a new beginning – sexual acts I had never considered before.

I was now defiant, wanting to rebel against morals and beliefs. I was in too deep to turn back now.

When I arose from bed the next morning Herman was nowhere to be found. I figured he had left to study at the library for his upcoming final exam before leaving town for the summer. Even so, I felt uneasy about our early-morning exploits. I dragged myself from bed and turned on the stereo. The bright sun from the East blinded me momentarily, so I closed the thick-white curtains. I pulled out an album to listen to Earth, Wind & Fire.

Suddenly, the song's lyrics caught my attention:

"Ain't it funny that the way you feel shows on your face. And no matter how you try to hide, it'll state your case." It was as if the words were tailored for me. It all hit me like a ton of bricks as I shamefully looked into the mirror and realized that I couldn't stand the sight of my own reflection. I was

disgraced, hit with failure and guilty for the umpteenth time.

"You damn FAGGOT!" The expression swirled in my head as I fell to my knees in perfect contrition.

Why, oh why, oh Lord, couldn't I conquer this behavior?

*****

When the team arrived at the track in Provo, Utah, for the Outdoor NCAAs – a week after my fling with Herman – the rain had not stopped. But we prepared for a showdown. Several rivals such as Howard University, the University of Alabama and Oklahoma State, which had battled us for supremacy all year, were marked for defeat. Mississippi State was determined to upstage any plans that the other schools had.

The rain-soaked track made conditions treacherous, but we were determined to accomplish our goals. And that was to win the championship. But when the rain worsened we altered our training. Our warm-up sprints were moved to the hallway of a Bringham Young University dormitory, where we had resided for the past few days. The floor was a bit hard for a running surface, but we still managed to train.

Coach Durham had always told us to use whatever resources were available.

So while it rained, we got as much practice in as we could.

Hours later, with the grueling 3000-meter steeplechase in its final laps, we prepared for the mile-relay.

Fortunately for us, the rain had cleared, and the sun was shinning. Now the showdown could begin. The clearing of the clouds allowed a ray of warmth to cover the cool outdoor arena. The sky unleashed its brilliant colors peeping from the mountains.

"Runners. On your mark! Set! … POW!"

The finals of the NCAA mile-relay were under way, minus Howard University, which pulled out due to an unfortunate groin injury to its anchor-leg runner. Not surprisingly, Oklahoma, the current NCAA indoor champs, was off to a superb start, and so was Alabama. MSU followed closely behind them. But by the time I received the baton, we were tightly trailing only the front-runner with almost less than 100-meters to go. With the final baton pass looming, Oklahoma was still on top when I handed off to Terrance, who scampered off at turbo force in the final stretch of the battle of the fittest. Lanes 1, 2 and 3 were occupied by MSU, Oklahoma and Alabama, respectively. Terrance, pushing all he had with fifty yards to go, muscled himself from the tight chain of runners to cross the finish line in superb fashion, earning an unprecedented first-place finish for Mississippi State. It was, indeed, a mighty display of power.

After he crossed the finish line waving the gold baton, Coach Durham and the rest of the relay squad charged toward Terrance as he gasped for air. We began to chant: "We're No. 1. We're No. 1."

Chapter 16
Wanna Be a Ditch Digger?

After the NCAAs, but before departing for Houston for the summer, I had to meet with the coach about my academic meltdown. This spelled trouble.

"Come in, Mr. Morris. Close the door."

I eased the door shut and took a seat to face judgment.

"Relax, Miguel. It's not brain surgery," said Coach Durham, trying to ease my anxiety. I cracked a smile at his attempt at humor, but the coach assured me that this was no laughing matter. "I want to start off by saying congratulations once again on your victory in Utah. As you can see, I have placed the team's time on the record board. Looks nice, doesn't it?"

"Yes, sir."

"Look at this, Miguel. The entire squad is ranked 17th in the nation. Now that's an accomplishment."

"Yes, sir," I responded, noticing our second- and fourth-place rankings in the mile-relay event in a magazine on his desk.

"Now, why couldn't you perform like this in your physics and chemistry classes, Morris?"

"I'm not sure, Coach!"

"You're not sure, Morris? Well, be sure of this. You are now on academic probation. And that's serious business!" Coach Durham said, pounding his fist on the desk. "You've never had problems with grades before, Miguel. And I know you can do the work. So, what's the problem? Girls? This is sad, Morris. Two 'As', a 'D' and two 'Fs.' You have a 1.97 GPA, Miguel. Not acceptable!"

"Well, Coach I … "

"You what?" he interrupted.

"I'm having personal problems."

"Like what, Morris?" Coach asked.

"Well, my oldest sister was diagnosed with MS," I said, trying to explain why my scholastic performance cratered.

"Multiple sclerosis?" asked Coach Durham, now sitting upright in his chair.

"Yes, sir. And I haven't been able to focus lately because of it and other matters." I tried to weasel out of the discussion by talking about my family problems while leaving out the dirty secrets about my sexual encounters with other athletes.

"Well, Miguel, I can sympathize with you, son, but you have to get yourself focused in a hurry. You only have this one chance to correct your grades, or else …"

"Or else I'm out?" I said, completing his sentence.

"Yes. Out!" he emphasized. "The university is very strict where academics are concerned. Star athlete or not, you must make the grade.

"Yes, sir."

"While on the subject of being strict, you now must report to the dean of technology before you leave campus tomorrow. Matter of fact, he's waiting on you now," said Coach Durham, glancing at his watch.

"Right now?" I asked, with wide eyes and a racing heartbeat.

"Yes. Now, Miguel."

I was petrified as I slowly left Coach Durham's office to visit the dean. I had heard rumors about him concerning black athletes. Many believed his policies were biased against minorities. Now it was my time to face truth and consequence before this alleged racist bastard.

During my walk to his office, I had a chance to think about my future at MSU and my true intentions with Tish. I really did like her, but could I actually fall in love with her? How could I even live with myself knowing that I might surrender to sexual temptations with other men? I knew I had to make a change or I was going to cause a lot of unnecessary pain and hateful feelings to women who I might get involved with in the future.

When I arrived at the entrance of the column structure, my knees began to buckle and my stomach churned. It seemed as if all energy had been zapped from my body, which wilted like a wet noodle.

As I inched closer to his door, I overheard Dean Kramer talking on the phone with Coach Durham about my future at MSU. I was about to face my executioner, a 250-pound tyrant.

The heavy-set Kramer wore wire-framed glasses that sat on the tip of his reddish thin nose, which appeared to be too thin for breathing because he often would wheeze between sentences. His thinning salt-and-pepper hair lay from one side to the other in an attempt to hide his baldness at the crown of his pale head.

He was still on the telephone with Coach Durham when he instructed me to enter and take a seat. He then abruptly ended the conversation with the coach, telling him he would call back with details about our meeting.

"So, Mr. Morris, how's your day been, son?"

"Not good, sir," I said, wanting to get out of there as quickly as possible.

"And why is that, Morris?"

"Because of my grades, Dean Kramer."

"Your grades, huh."

"Yes, sir. My grades."

"Well, Morris, how did we get to this point, son? Please explain that to me, boy."

"Boy!" How dare he call me "boy," I said under my breath as I tempered my anger. That reminded me of the time my high school coach used that word, which enraged Caleb during my first track practice.

"Well, Dean, it's like this," I said trying to explain, seething with anger.

"Excuse me?"

"I mean, sir. Somehow I got behind in my studies because of personal problems. I just lost focus and interest. That's all."

"Well, Morris, you cannot just give up, son, because of a few bumps in the road. You'll find that there are a lot of hurdles in life, and that's not an excuse for failure. Does that make sense, son?"

"Yes, sir, Dean Kramer."

"Good because we need you to pull your grades together and get back on track, so to speak. Keep in mind, Morris, you can be replaced; there are a lot of kids who would love to be in your shoes, boy. Do you understand me?"

"Yes, sir, I understand." But he better not call me boy again, I thought to myself. I swear I'll kick his ass.

"Perfect. Now this is the situation. You need a 3.0 to stay afloat here, Morris. Summer school is in your future. We will not settle for anything under a B-average from you this summer. So the ball's in your court. Can you make the grade?"

"Yes, sir, Dean Kramer."

"Just what I wanted to hear, because I know you don't wanna be a ditch digger like your daddy, Morris. Do you?"

"My father's not a ditch digger, sir!" I answered tersely. Now I was really pissed.

"That argument may constitute your belief, but the fact still remains he's supervising backhoe operators in the hot outdoors. Is that what you want to do?"

"No, sir," I said, masking my fury. What right did he have to insult my dad or me?

"Good. So get it together, Morris. Is there anything you

would like to ask me before I end this meeting?"

"No, sir. Not really." I answered. I was too hot under the collar to delay my exit from his office. I didn't need him to say another word, or I was going to be all over his white ass – school or no school.

"Well, just remember, Morris, a 3.0 is what you need."

I gathered my composure and made a quick exit.

*****

I regained confidence over the summer thanks in part to my elevated academic scores at the University of Houston and the receipt of a letter with ruby-red lipstick prints on its inside stationary. Tish had written from Florida. I resealed the letter to be read later.

For most of that hour I was afraid to reopen it because I wasn't sure of its contents. After class ended, I sat alone on a wooden bench near a wading pond of ducks and tadpoles. I reopened the letter, careful not to damage the lip prints. The scent of Tish was everywhere. It was just as intoxicating as a runner's high. The penmanship of the three-page correspondence was flawless, like its author.

"Hi, Miguel," the letter began. "I'm back at home anticipating your presence, which I hope I will be blessed with very soon before summer's over. When we talked last week over the phone nothing could have made me happier than the blessing of your voice."

I had not told Tish about my academic problems because of embarrassment. I knew now that I had to tell her.

As I got to the last page of the letter, I laughed when she reminded me of my past aggressiveness when we first met. She challenged me to use that same brashness in making my way to Florida.

It was great being wanted. As I sat on the bench alone, a firefly made me reminisce about West Texas State. I thought of Patsy, Kevin and, of course, Butch. The magnificent Butch Webber had become a guiding force in my life. He helped me identify my inner power. After the nostalgia, I finished the letter, now imagining myself on a Florida beach with my girl Tish and sharing with her my likes, dislikes and expectations. One thing for sure, I couldn't tell her about my sexual interest in men. Could she actually understand and accept me just as I am?

*****

A week later I was in Miami at a small beachfront bistro on South Beach. Not even the darkened sky or the tantalizing aroma of garlic grilled prawns with lemon butter could surpass my joy in seeing Tish. I still remember her soft cocoa butter hands and beautiful exotic face. The thought of her could make me melt to the point of sharing everything about my disappointing semester.

Over time she and I really grew to love each other. Beforehand, she seemed more concerned about obtaining U.S. citizenship. But beyond that, I managed to sweep her off her feet.

When she and I finally met up I told her I wanted to have a heart-to-heart conversation.

"There's something I hadn't told you about me," I said

"Something like what, Miguel?" she asked softly, but curiously.

"Well, I had problems last semester with grades, baby."

"What kind of problems?"

"I'm on academic probation."

"And what else is there? I can see it in your eyes," Tish asked.

She was right. They say eyes don't lie and are the mirror to the soul.

"I'm in love with you," I said, grabbing her hands. Actually, I wanted to distract her from the truth in my eyes because I knew what I was and had become over time.

"You are something else, Miguel. Don't try to get off the subject. There's more, and I want to hear it. So, what is it, baby?"

I had to think of something quickly, because she was no dummy and too damn inquisitive.

I reached into the pockets of my beach shorts and revealed a small document. It was a report of my summer grades from the University of Houston. I passed physics with a "C" and chemistry with a "B."

She then asked why I hadn't informed her about my academic problems.

"I didn't want you to worry," I said. I gazed into her eyes and also noticed the darkened sky began to clear. Whew! It seemed that explanation was enough to get her off my back. Her interrogation was getting the best of me.

"Miguel. If we're going to be lovers, I want to know as much about you as possible when it concerns issues that may affect us both. I want an unconditional relationship with the man I love. Does that make sense?" Tish asked as she lunged forward to plant a kiss on my lips.

"You love me?" I asked.

"Yes, baby, I love you!"

Damn! Was I really ready for this kind of affection? I could not turn back now because I had already opened the door. I expressed my love for her once more, not so much for *her* assurance as much as it was for mine. I wondered, though, if she could be there for me when *that* sick feeling comes over me – the feeling of wanting to be with a man instead of her. Could she tame the beast inside of me?

"I intend to make your every wish come true, Miguel. Just be truthful with me, OK? Don't ever cross me or you might see the Asian side of me erupt."

"Is that a promise?" I asked with a raised eyebrow. Her word was her bible.

Chapter 17
A Sexual Animal

The horn from a candy red corvette attracted my attention as I sat on the busy boulevard waiting on the 3:15 p.m. Metro bus. I was home in Houston for the summer and had just left work at the restaurant. A light brown brother with a close-cut beard offered me a ride home on a sunny, hot Friday evening in August. He had golden eyes and clear smooth skin like the picture-perfect male models in fashion magazines. His slender build supported his designer T-shirt even as it whipped in the wind from the open T-top of his sporty vehicle.

"Hey, guy, want a lift?" the stranger asked.

"No, I'm OK," I answered, peering into the open window of the sport car. The nerve of that bastard trying to pick me up.

"You're sure, guy? I don't mind dropping you off wherever you're going."

The horn from an impatient driver behind the stranger forced him to move on.

"I'll make the block," the persistent stranger said. "Think about that ride."

Actually, I did think about the heat beating down on me and the bus running late. I also had a few errands to run at the Galleria mall. I remembered seeing a black crocodile belt at the North Beach Leather store in Miami two weeks ago that I wanted but didn't purchase because I was short of cash and too proud to ask Tish for a loan. Anyway, I knew more money would become available soon because I had a few more weeks left to wait tables before heading back to school.

Vroom!

The sports car pulled up once again. I reasoned that if I accepted the offer it could net me a thrilling cruise in a cool car down the crowded Westheimer Boulevard much quicker.

Damn! Was I really a magnet?

"C'mon, guy. Get in," the stranger offered.

Reluctantly, I eased from the aluminum bench and carefully entered the stranger's car while watching his every move. The massive rear tires on the sports car screeched as it sped off.

"Hi. I'm Patrick Porter," said the stranger, staring intensely and offering a firm handshake.

"Yeah, I'm Miguel." I intentionally tried to sound hard and tough as if I were street savvy.

"Miguel, who?"

He wasn't buying that hard act.

"Miguel Morris, you dig."

"Well, Miguel, don't think that I do this sort of thing often."

"What sort of thing?" I asked curiously as I slightly raised my left eyebrow.

"Picking up strangers from bus stops."

"I didn't think that, man." I lied. It didn't take an expert to realize that he's been on the prowl before.

"Good because I know it's hot out there, and I just thought I would offer you a ride. I saw you come out of the Strawberry Patch restaurant earlier, but I didn't want to approach you because I didn't want you to get any bad ideas about me," Patrick said.

"Ideas like what?"

"Thoughts that I might be a murderer or rapist – something like that."

"Well, are you?"

"Of course not. I'm a lover not a villain, man."

"A lover, huh?" I replied. I wanted to ask if that meant he was gay. I could tell that he was, though. I could see it in his eyes, which were a dead giveaway.

"By the way, where are you headed?" Patrick asked.

"To the Galleria." The more I talked the more I shed the pretentious street-savvy role. It wasn't me anyway.

"That's where I'm headed, too," Patrick said. "Neiman Marcus has a sale this weekend, and there's this saleswoman I usually deal with. She puts things on hold for me the day before, so I can get first choice."

He wanted to sound privileged.

"That's good. I usually wait for sales, too. North Beach Leather is having a sale on men accessories," I said proudly as if I were balling. Even if I didn't have my own car, I knew how to play the part.

"You're into leather?" Patrick asked, excitedly.

"No, just leather accessories." I sensed he was attempting to go somewhere else with that comment.

Patrick laughed mischievously.

I complimented him on the leather seats in his corvette.

"They're expensive to maintain," Patrick said as we entered the Galleria's underground parking garage.

"Do you need a ride home?"

"Yeah, if you don't mind," I said, thinking it couldn't be that harmful.

After our purchases, we decided to become more acquainted and stopped by Bennigan's restaurant on the lower level of the mall for a quick cocktail.

It was about 5:30 p.m. The Chivas Regal and 7UP began to lower my defenses against Patrick, so he decided to ratchet up his attempts to explore my background and interests. Huey Lewis & The News' *"I Want a New Drug"* blared over the sound system, raising the evening's tempo. I didn't need any help with that since the liquor I consumed was working on me.

The Chivas Regal was bumpin'. Alcohol tends to make me say things I wouldn't express under normal conditions, particularly to strangers such as Patrick.

Moments later, a bartender offered another round of drinks.

"Sure. Why not?" Patrick eagerly answered.

I was down for another, too. But in reality, I wasn't sure if I desired more of the taste or whether the alcohol was merely influencing me to keep drinking. Nevertheless, I sipped the last of the Chivas and 7UP and prepared for the next round. We also ordered buffalo wings.

Displaying a little clout, Patrick raked through his pile of credit cards and pulled out a platinum American Express. If he were trying to impress me with his line of credit, I wasn't feeling it. Woozy was more like it. After his flashy display, I asked the burning question.

"So, are you gay?" I decided to ask after noticing earlier at the bar a rather feminine gesture with his wrist. That was strike one.

"Well, …"

He seemed a bit reluctant to answer.

The bartender interrupted, informing us that it would be a few more minutes on the buffalo wings.

"So, again, what is your answer?" I asked to restart the conversation.

"What was the question?"

"I asked if you are gay." He tried to play me again.

"I consider myself a sexual animal. Not straight or gay," Patrick said. "I don't like to be labeled. It's about a personal preference. You dig?"

After that answer, which made me choke slightly, I excused myself. This fool was full of crap, I thought. He must have thought I had just fallen off a watermelon truck or something. Maybe he thought I was just some naive kid who didn't recognize game.

"Are you all right?" he asked.

"Yeah, I'll be fine. I was just drinking too fast. What is a sexual animal anyway?" I asked.

"It's a person who loves exotic sex with both men and women with no limits or hang-ups. Do I make you uncomfortable, Miguel?"

"No. I'm fine. I just have to use the men's room. I'll be back," I said, leaving my barstool for a dash to the washroom, slightly tipsy and surprised at Patrick's response about his sexuality. He was no more a sexual animal than I was a straight male. We both were in denial about our sexual preferences and neither one of us wanted to admit it. Maybe it was best we left it alone, given the amount of alcohol we'd consumed. I didn't want alcohol to be a lame excuse for engaging in forbidden pleasures during my first meeting.

I began to wonder if Patrick were intentionally trying to get me cocktailed, so when I returned I decided I'd better lay off the drinking and prepare to sink my teeth into the mouthwatering, spicy buffalo wings that had finally arrived.

"You like the wings," I asked before taking my seat at the bar.

"They're good. Try some," he said, even while trying to push more alcohol on me. By now he appeared really dazed.

"You're not much of a drinker are you?" he asked.

"No. I'm not. I do it only on special occasions."

"Oh, is this special?" Patrick asked, looking at me much like a wolf's delight. His eyes said what was on his mind. Still, I wasn't down for that punk stuff.

"It is in a way. Here we are, two strangers enjoying each other's company, yet feeling comfortable with each other. I consider that special," I said, offering a bullshit response. I was more interested in the wings than the company.

"Has anyone told you that you're very attractive?" asked Patrick, seductively licking his right thumb and index finger as if to suggest he was wiping sauce from his digits.

"Yeah. I've heard that a few times before. And so are you," I said, returning the compliment.

After a few minutes of silence, Patrick besieged me with more questions.

"I'm curious. Have you ever been to a drag show?"

"No. I'm not into car racing," I answered.

"What!" I'm not talking about drag racing. A drag show is when a man impersonates a female for entertainment."

He laughed at my naivety.

"I didn't know. And no, I haven't been to no damn drag show." He was pissing me off now. I wasn't trying to pop it like that. Maybe I was being closed-minded, but I wasn't trying to hear no shit about watching a man parade around like a woman.

"Anyway, the reason I asked is because I'm going out tonight, and I'm riding alone. How about coming along with me and hit the town?"

"And go see men dress like women? No thanks!" I answered, shaking my head in disbelief. I needed some more of those chicken wings to calm my nerves – maybe even another drink.

"C'mon, it'll be fun. It's all fun and games. It's just something different to experience," Patrick explained.

"It's different all right."

"So, are you down?"

This dude was stressing me. I reminded myself that I still needed a ride home.

"Come on, Miguel. Nobody's gonna bite you."

He had no way of knowing that I was paranoid of drag queens and "femmes." I wasn't comfortable being in the company of female impersonators, let alone in a crowd of men who were obviously gay.

"What time are you talking about leaving for this "drag show?" I asked uneasily.

"Around 10 p.m. It usually starts about 11 p.m. with the first act kicking off."

"What the hell. I'll go. But don't expect anything, man!"

"I won't, Miguel. It's all for fun."

"Well, I don't want to have too much fun, considering I have to go back to school next weekend."

"I figured you were in college when I saw you with that MSU backpack."

Patrick then signaled for the check and asked about my major.

When the bartender arrived he plopped down an additional $10 tip.

"Big spender, huh?" I asked.

"No, not really. If the service is good, one should be compensated well. Wouldn't you agree?"

"Without a doubt," I said, smiling and pleased with his care for the wait staff, given that I had worked at the Strawberry Patch and relied on tips, too.

"You must play sports?" Patrick said. When I stood his eyes shifted down toward my crotch.

"I run track for Mississippi State."

"So that explains your huge legs and thighs, huh?"

"How did you know I have large legs?"

"One would have to be blind not to notice those tree trunks," Patrick said, poking me on my left thigh.

At that point I walked toward the door because he made me uncomfortable. One thing that irritated me the most was when someone touched me without permission in places I considered to be private.

*****

The smell of Polo cologne covered my body as I entered the doors of the Mid-Nite Sun bar on the lower Westheimer strip later that night. We heard the sounds of Diana Ross' *"I'm*

Coming Out." It was a fitting song for the occasion, I suppose. I was amazed at the large dance crowd that personified the musical "A Chorus Line." There was a lot of kicking, twirling and loud screams. The scene was almost riotous. But I tried to adjust.

I stood in awe, though, observing the electrifying crowd of men and women of various ethnicities indulging in a celebration of pride and freedom. I noticed a group of women standing near the bar, flaunting their hair and long nails. After studying them closely, I realized they were actually all men dressed as women. It was a first experience for me. I had heard about them through casual conversations, but I never had been in their presence so up close and personal. It was also my first experience being in a predominantly gay atmosphere. I was still uncomfortable about being here.

To my surprise, a lone hand grazed my ass. I angrily scoped the area for the rude intruder. My loose-fitting Levi jeans apparently didn't do much to ward off temptation. My athletic build was still noticeable and my heavily starched white button-down shirt showed only a bit of my hairless chest. Even so, it was a delight for Patrick, who had indicated he was attracted to my body.

I informed Patrick that somebody had just grabbed my ass. He only laughed.

"What's so damn funny?"

"Nothing, Miguel. Here, stand in front of me. I'll protect you," he said. "That way nobody can grab it." He was getting too much joy out of this.

"I really didn't come here for this, man. I don't think I wanna stay." I suddenly realized that Patrick was probably in his element here. He seemed to relish the idea of laying claim to me as his property.

"Don't trip! These guys are harmless. It was probably one of those white queens who couldn't resist touching your black ass. They do it all the time. Horny bastards."

"I don't care if he were white or black. I don't play that shit!"

After several minutes, he persuaded me to hold my ground when suddenly a high-pitched voice instructed the packed crowd to clear the dance floor.

"Good evening, everyone. Welcome to the Mid-nite Sun."

Spotlights flooded the far left corner of the bar as a full-figured female impersonator strolled with exaggerated grace onto the dance floors. The emcee resembled the Uncle Fester character from television's "The Addams Family."

He went by the name of Kiki and sat comfortably on a stool in the middle of the floor while slightly raising his sparkling champagne gown from the floor and belting out a yodel that humorously amused the rambunctious crowd.

"OK!" the emcee quipped, "Who's the grand girl with the little red corvette out front. Miss Thang, go move yo' car and turn off your lights because you know you don't have money for a tow if that battery croaks."

The crowd roared in laughter again.

"I don't know why these girls wanna be seen," the emcee cracked. "Don't they know I'm the shepherd of this flock."

I was not impressed with the emcee's comments about Patrick and his sports car. But when I turned toward Patrick he had practically keeled over in laughter. I had a lot to learn about gay culture.

Chapter 18
In the Spotlight

Academic probation was lifted in January. I had finally gotten myself together in time to enjoy my first Millrose Games at Madison Square Garden in New York. The city was full of athletes from around the world with the likes of Carl Lewis, Calvin Smith, Evelyn Ashford and other superstar standouts.

Not to be overshadowed by the parade of stars at the NCAA meet, our defending championship team flaunted our proud rings and apparel. We figured we had earned bragging rights after garnering our first contract with Nike USA, which had provided our crew with sponsorship, as long as we represented the Nike label at all meets. The generous contract included $250 weekly payments to Terrance and me.

The exclusive invitation to the Millrose Games attracted the world's top athletes, who were preparing themselves for the Olympic competitions in Los Angeles. This was also a tremendous opportunity for our mile-relay quartet to prove to the track-and-field world that we were serious contenders.

This was my first meet of the year and an opportunity to stand out for scouts and sponsors such as Nike, adidas, Asics Tiger and Puma. They would be looking for new talents to parade their latest sports gear and apparel.

Another scouted star gripped my attention: Tish!

I quickly separated from my teammates to approach her as she talked to Valerie Brisco-Hooks, another famous female quarter-miler. I caught her off guard with a pinch to her right side.

She quickly turned, wondering who would be so bold. Her anger was quickly replaced by a smile after she recognized me.

"Hey, baby!"

She bear-hugged me as her fellow athletes watched.

"When did you get here?"

"Oh," I said glancing at my watch, "about 3 o'clock yesterday."

She then introduced me to her fellow athlete as her "significant other."

"Say, girl," Valerie said, "I'll catch up with you later. I see someone I need to speak to."

"How long have y'all been friends?" I asked when Valerie left.

"We're just associates. It's all about mutual respect, Miguel. So, how's my baby doing?" Tish asked.

"I'm doing fine, baby." I still have to get used to calling her that. "What more can I ask for? I have you." I tried to be cool by grabbing her silky soft hands. But she busted my game as I tried to pour it on too thick.

"You could ask how I'm doing," she said.

As always I bowed to her suggestion. "I'm sorry, baby. You know I'm concerned about you. Things going OK with you and your family?"

"Yes, things are fine." She now appeared satisfied.

"By the way, how's your sister, Dee?" she asked as we walked toward the East corridor of the arena for a more intimate conversation.

I told her that Dee's condition with multiple sclerosis had worsened. She was now using a cane but otherwise in good spirits.

Lapsing into a daydream about my summer experience with Patrick, a foul sex scene entered my mind about a guy that Patrick had introduced me to. He appeared to have everything I sought in a man: ruggedness, intellect, athleticism and a basketball-shaped ass. At this stage, it was all about sex for me because it was the only affection I knew. I wondered if my disinterest in a relationship with men was due to a lack of a real relationship with my dad and male siblings. I felt that the men in my family never displayed affection, in part, because of homophobia. They thought that men shouldn't cry or express emotions because those were signs of weakness.

After my short mental vacation, I rejoined my teammates.

"So we gonna show Villanova and Baylor who rules the boards, right?" I bellowed, trying to rally my teammates and to get my mind off a piece of ass and back to the business at hand.

"Hell, yeah!" Jamal exclaimed. Then, Terrance and Kiel gave each other high-fives. The four of us walked off to a serene place to pray and prepare for battle.

*****

Our mile-relay team was now making a dash for the finish line to secure our top ranking.

During my baton swap, the spikes from my running shoes grabbed the wooden track and caused me to stumble and fall after I successfully passed the baton to Terrance. But I triggered a slight disruption when I inadvertently nudged him with my hand in his lower back as I attempted to regain my balance. The crowd gasped as I tumbled, forcing other athletes to leapfrog over me as I rolled toward the inner lane of the track.

My bruised body did not stop me from cheering on Terrance as he battled neck and neck with Villanova's fastest quarter-miler.

As I lie on the edge of the track, the shadowy image of Coach Durham approached me. He was concerned about me, one of his prized runners.

"Are you OK?" asked Coach Durham, kneeling to assist.

"Yeah, Coach. I'm OK." I kept my eyes affixed on Terrance as he maneuvered around the second far curve.

"You sure nothing's hurt?"

"Yeah, Coach. I just caught the tip of my spike on the track. That's all." His nurturing seemed strange but welcoming.

Oddly, I often had had recurring nightmares of being at a prestigious meet when the track suddenly would rotate and float, causing me to lose balance and fall into a lane of wooden needles and splinters. I never knew what it meant. But now I began to view this nightmare as perhaps an epiphany foretelling a bitter defeat.

As I attempted to lift my scraped body, I saw Tish striding swiftly toward me.

"Here, Coach, let me help him," she said as they lifted me from the surface.

Coach Durham thanked her.

I couldn't figure out what all the fuss over me was about. I was focused on rallying for Terrance. I watched him take charge of the race in its final lap.

"Is anything hurt?" Tish asked, holding me around my waist.

"No, baby. I'm fine. I'll be OK." The injury was to my ego.

"Tish, I think his pride is hurting more than his scrapes and bruises," said Coach Durham, reading me like a book.

I ignored the coach's comment and asked how he knew Tish.

He gave a slick answer.

"All coaches notice great athletes, Miguel."

He then focused on the final seconds of the race.

"And here we have it ladies and gentlemen, a race to the finish!" the announcer exclaimed.

"It's Mississippi State by a leg! And now it's Villanova with a slight edge! It's Villanova, ladies and gentlemen! It's Villanova

- our Millrose Games 1600-meter relay champions!" I grimaced in disappointment, feeling responsible for the second-place finish – all because of my clumsy feet.

It was also clear that my teammates were not happy with my slip.

Thirty minutes later I congratulated Tish in her flawless long-jump performance. I told her she was improving with age.

"Excuse me! Improving with age, huh! You are the one who's limping like a crippled man," she teased.

I should have known better than to mention age to a female. I still had a lot to learn about my estrogen counterparts.

As we passed a large crowd of young kids, Carl Lewis was trapped in a sea of fans, signing autographs for young fans. They surrounded him like ants attacking a lone piece of candy.

Somehow we got caught up in the wave, too, as kids flocked toward me and Tish seeking autographs from various athletes. We signed hats, cards, programs and torn sheets of paper. The excitement made me forget about my bruises and scrapes.

The feeling of being honored and idolized had taken me to newfound heights. Their cheers and adulation elevated me where I wanted to be all my life: in the spotlight.

Could I handle it? Had I finally arrived? And if so, am I ready for complete candor and giving up my privacy for public fame. I knew that I would no longer belong to myself and that scrutiny of my life would be fair game for anyone, including the media.

Chapter 19
Secret Lovers

On the eve of my 23rd birthday, Herman, his girlfriend Lenna and Tamela, my part-time girlfriend, were enjoying the Miss America pageant in the lobby of the athletic dorm. (Yeah, I was cheating on Tish, which in reality was nothing new.) Several couples filled the television room hoping an African-American woman would win the tiara for the first time. Miss New Jersey Suzette Charles and Miss New York Vanessa L. Williams were the two remaining black contestants among the 10 finalists.

Lenna, with ties to beauty competitions and the MSU fashion board, was excited about the possibility. She was gorgeous – beige complexion and thin facial features that gave her an edge over many competitors in the area. On occasions, she talked about wanting to go to New York and Chicago to model and perhaps start a scouting agency for inner-city youths. Even though I was not nearly as confident as Lenna, she convinced me to try out for the MSU modeling club.

Over time, she molded me. And we began modeling together as a couple, strolling the catwalks of Mississippi.

We continued to watch the telecast of the pageant. Suzette Charles and Vanessa Williams were now among the final five.

Silence gripped the room as the host began the elimination process. The final three contestants stood nervously as the host pulled the card for the second runner-up. The room roared, as the final two black contestants were left. The nation knew then that the winner would be of African descent.

The announcer raised the card, announcing New Jersey's Suzette Charles as the first runner-up, making Vanessa Williams of New York the winner.

Lenna jumped for joy, as well as many others watching in the lobby.

We then gathered outside for an impromptu parade of mostly black students.

"Can you believe this, man? Looks like the whole campus is out here."

Herman had broken away from the crowd but returned with his convertible. He signaled for Lenna, Tamela and me to join him on a late-night stroll down the strip to celebrate Vanessa's crowning moment.

*****

After we returned from the strip, we gathered in my room. To shield our nakedness, each couple was separated by a thick blanket that was used to form a makeshift partition. But still it didn't drown out the moans from Herman's side of the room, which caused Tamela to break out in laughter.

"Shhhh, Tamela!" I softly uttered, putting my right hand over her soft lips to quiet her.

"I'm sorry. But if my Delta sorors find out I did this, my ass is grass."

"Stop tripping. How would they find out? My roomie and his girl are cool. I ain't telling shit! Are you?"

"I don't trust those AKAs as far as I can throw them. But maybe you're right, Miguel, because she and I both have dirt on each other now, huh! "By the way, happy birthday!" Tamela loudly blurted out as she rose from the scented bed.

"Yeah, happy birthday, roomie. I heard y'all giggling over there," Herman said.

Moments later his girlfriend, Lenna, wished me happy

birthday, too.

Sneaking out of the back stairwell of the dorm, Herman and I safely returned our girlfriends to their dorm.

As Herman and I silently drove back to the dorm, I began to reminisce about our first sexual encounter with each other. It gave me an erection that was visible to him as he glanced toward my huge thighs. He gently grabbed my hard jimmy, suggesting that he knew Tamela hadn't completely satisfied me.

"So, you're down?" he asked.

"Yeah, I'm down."

Once in the room, we attacked each other, filling the room with more grunts and moans. With the curtains opened, we explored each other's bodies as the full moon cast its glare in the room. Herman selected an appropriate song by Diana Ross: "*I Want Muscles.*" There was no guessing now. I knew that I was attracted to the same sex. And, hell, I wanted muscles, too!

Herman then carefully rotated my warm body to an angle. He was overcome by my dark buttocks and could hardly wait to strategically deploy his tongue and throbbing sex into my hairy opening. I was now swept up in ecstasy, captivated by his scent.

Herman's powerful grip took command as he manhandled me in a way I've never experienced. His aggressiveness was not threatening, just surprising. But there was no sting or discomfort from the slapping of the buttocks and the widening of my cheeks. I simply relaxed and allowed him to slowly engage his hardened sex. The pleasure of his strong body helped to dull the pain from his penetrating strokes.

"Damn, so this is what I've been missing, huh?" he said.

This was only my second experience since Butch Webber.

I then returned the favor as Herman coaxed me to satisfy his wild desire, too, with the same pleasure he administered to me moments earlier. I did it with gladness.

I was enjoying every moment and everything about this dude. I had allowed him to be inside me because he didn't trip during our first encounter when I was the "top" dawg. He understood that it wasn't about playing a role, but satisfaction.

In this sense we became secret lovers, even developing a pact that would protect us from suspicion by our girlfriends and others. We vowed to not let selfishness and jealousy interfere with our lives.

For months, I had wondered what it felt like to have a male lover. The opportunity now presented itself. Herman and I secretly engaged in a relationship throughout college. We paraded around like regular men: playing sports, frequenting parties and dining with our girlfriends.

They didn't have a clue about us, even though there were red flags all over the place: unexplained whereabouts, late appointments.

Eventually, Herman went on to play for the Canadian Football League, showcasing his talents as a true-grit athlete. After graduation, Herman's girlfriend Lenna and my girl Tamela graduated and moved to New York. They became business partners at a fashion school.

Tish graduated from Florida State and landed a job in Miami as a transportation specialist. I was eager to see her again, but I couldn't risk her finding out about my secret. I would become a cooked goose for sure.

As for me, I did not graduate. I left campus because scholarship funds ran out. After all that talk about academic excellence by the dean of technology, he said he had no money in his budget to extend my scholarship for an extra semester. I realized I should have graduated on time, but shit happens. I had lost my focus.

With 12 more hours to complete, I decided to continue my schooling in Houston. Unfortunately, I didn't follow up on that goal either. I had wasted a lot of time polluting my mind with thoughts of sex with men and feeding my sinful nature. A degree was secondary.

But it wasn't all about sex. I merely wanted to experience life. I wanted a little danger in my mix. Just some damn adventure!

Chapter 20
Living On My Own

It was difficult for me to divorce myself from track and field. So I continued my quest for the sport after college. I was also on the verge of moving into my first apartment. I was ready to experience the privacy that Butch Webber had so often talked about when we were in college. I had about $10,000 saved from previous track meets, a gas card from Exxon and a Visa card from the Bank of New York. I decided to purchase my second car, a pre-owned Audi 4000. It was in good condition and bought from an elderly lady who had lost the zeal to drive.

But before I would move into my new place of residence, I had a score to settle at the Kodak Invitational in Johnson City, Tennessee in January.

Before leaving Houston, I treated myself to a fresh cut and facial. I was to meet in Tennessee with Tish, who was still working for Miami's Dade County. I had hoped that she would soon be joining me in Houston later in the year. It scared me to death every time I thought about marrying her. I wasn't sure what the hell I was thinking. It felt right, but all along I knew my intentions to exchange vows were wrong. I had agreed to help Tish gain U.S. citizenship by masquerading as a married couple.

Her sports career was over; she now wanted to focus on

maintaining an occupation in the States. I was surprised that she agreed to meet me in Tennessee. Her trip was two-fold: first, to support me in my endeavors, and second, to gather ideas and valuable experience from the transportation conference in nearby Atlanta in the coming days. I wasn't going to be in Atlanta with her because I had business to settle back in Houston after the Invitational.

After settling on the snowy campus of Tennessee State University early that evening, I searched for my personal day planner to find the phone number of the DoubleTree hotel where Tish was staying. Fortunately, she was staying only a few short minutes from campus and the track arena, which was blanketed by snow. I was anxious, not because of the upcoming competition, but due to the fact that I was finally about to see Tish for the first time in months.

The Austin Striders Track Club, which I was representing, paid for my travel expenses and room and board. Even so, the plush hotel room where Tish resided was more suited to my fancy. The built-in fireplace in the living area and bedroom set the tone. A walk-in kitchen and wet bar, surrounded with beveled mirrored walls, added to the ambiance.

Sitting on the tuxedo-back sofa and facing a brilliant fire from the glassed-in fireplace, Tish sat next to me and softly caressed my lips with the tip of her cool right index finger. My mouth slightly ajar, I quivered with passion as a rush of warm breath from Tish's mouth seduced me.

I then whispered, "Why did you touch me there? You know that's my weak spot." She then leaned toward me for a deep, intense kiss. I gently nibbled on her soft, voluptuous lips with my teeth.

Then she warned me.

"No, Miguel. We can't do this. We have to stand by our promise."

"Damn, Tish. Why are you doing me like this, getting me all excited and bothered? You know I'm weak for you."

"Let's just wait until our wedding night and not spoil things. It'll be the best decision of our lives. So, slow down, baby. Slow your roll. I'm not going anywhere."

"Are you proposing to me, girl?" I asked.

"Yes, baby. That's what I'm doing. I'm asking you to be with me for eternity. Can you handle it?"

So, is she suggesting that our marriage won't be bogus?

I had thought many times about marrying her, but I wasn't sure if I could handle the responsibility. That meant I had to give up a lot of behaviors that were causing me a great deal of pain. I wasn't sure if I would be able to keep things in perspective, like honesty, commitment, and, most of all, my attraction to men.

"Are you sure you want to marry me, Tish?"

"Yes, I'm sure," she said as she walked into the bedroom.

But when I looked inside the sleeping quarters I noticed two beds.

"Why not one bed," I asked.

"This way we don't have to worry about being tempted. I confess. I was wrong for teasing you earlier," she said.

I then rushed through the door and playfully teased her. I tackled her in her own bed and tickled her sides and belly. Before I realized what I had done, I said, "Yes, baby, I'll marry you."

I shocked myself. Strange thing was that I didn't feel any different than I did before the question was raised. I then gently covered Tish with my long body and spread her soft arms apart above her head, as she lie facing me without a clue about my warped past. All she knew was that I was the man she would be marrying and that she would soon become a legal resident of the United States.

*****

As for the track competition, I fared decently in the 200 meters, finishing fourth and earning a personal best. The Kodak Invitational was history.

I returned to the hotel room, and Tish had arranged an intimate night minus the sex. The sparkling chandelier provided a glow to the soft eggshell-colored walls. The dinette area was decorated in sterling silver and German crystal that sparkled along with the candle-lit table.

After a refreshing shower, we both enjoyed the silky feel of the Pierre Cardin full-length robes that Tish purchased at a downtown boutique in Atlanta. I danced with her near the crackling fireplace to the sounds of Angela Bofill, who serenaded us with "*I Tried.*" Although I was more horny than hungry, I turned my attention to the Alaskan king crab and lemon butter crustaceans.

To forget the ugly life I had been living, I showered her with praise and compliments, dodging my faults, lies and deceptions. How could I tell her that I was a male nymphomaniac who was chasing ass around the city and refusing to get help? At first, I thought I was simply going through a natural phase. But my sexual appetite was too extreme to be normal. I continued to feed the desire that was causing me so much pain.

Tish whispered softly into my ear. "This is all for you, baby."

That was before she carefully untied my silk robe, exposing my frontal nudity.

I returned the favor by exposing her perfect figure, too. This was a first.

She told me to stay focused on the night because it was still young. She then sat at the table with her robe still open, her perfectly rounded light-cocoa brown breasts on display. I wanted to dive in for the kill, but decided to oblige her request. This was tough to do since she was baring herself in front of me.

"No, not yet, baby," said Tish, reading my mind.

The candlelight enticed me even more as I took note of every curve and feature on her body that weren't obscured by the robe. Since she teased me, I opened my robe a little wider.

We both sat half-naked while devouring the king crab. Every move she made was calculated, graceful.

Do I really deserve her, God? I silently asked. Can I really satisfy her desires? A tear fell from my right cheek. What in hell am I doing?

"Miguel, what's wrong?" she asked, noticing my eyes welling with tears.

"Nothing's wrong." Again, I lied.

She asked if those were tears of joy.

Like a pathological liar I again answered "yes."

After a few more bites of dinner, we slow-danced. Our nearly naked bodies infused one another. After a short while, Tish released herself from my grip and led me into the dimmed bedroom. She gently eased me down on her bed and whispered in my ear.

"Lie back and relax. Keep your eyes closed," she ordered.

I obeyed.

Then the magic began, and my eyes reopened.

She stood at the foot of the bed, glowing from the fading fire of the fireplace. She looked like a mythical goddess, standing over me in a South American chinchilla coat that covered only the back portion of her body.

"Damn, girl. What are you trying to do to me?"

That's when I sat upright reaching toward the flesh in front of me.

"I'm seducing you; that's what I'm doing. Just remember our promise. No sex."

She made that point clear as she sat on my pelvis and lowered my silky robe to my buttocks.

This sophisticated woman was quite a vamp.

*****

"Somebody help me!"

I quickly raced toward Dee's room to investigate her distress call. When I entered I found her in a supine position on the carpeted floor. MS was becoming more crippling. Her fragile body appeared lifeless from the fall as David and I rushed to assist her. The disease had advanced to the point where her mobility was now greatly compromised. A wheelchair would eventually and permanently replace her cane.

Fortunately, on this day we had already celebrated a special occasion: her graduation from Texas Southern University. She became the first in the family to receive a college degree even though her battle with multiple sclerosis had delayed her graduation by a couple semesters.

I recalled her amazing feat earlier in the day as she strolled down the middle of the aisle in her wheelchair inside the Houston Coliseum. The crowd stood to applaud her as she accepted her bachelor's degree in social work. Even David was moved to tears by Dee's accomplishment.

Dee had inspired me to follow my dreams.

"If she can do it from a wheelchair, why couldn't I accomplish my educational goals?"

"Dee! You OK?" David asked, feeling for broken bones.

"Yeah. I'll be fine," Dee replied, straightening the gown she was trying so desperately to remove.

After further investigation we discovered that she was trying to retrieve her walking cane from the far end of her room. She was always independent, but her pride didn't stop her from asking for help when needed. Still, she refused to be treated as an invalid.

"I can walk with my cane," she would often say. And, like me, she was still planning to move out of the family home over the summer.

As David and I indulged in leftovers from Dee's graduation party, we engaged in small talk about our youngest brother, Troy, and his bad decision a few weeks ago that had landed him in the Harris County Jail, where he was awaiting sentencing for non-aggravated robbery after breaking and entering into a blind man's home and stealing his television.

Perhaps he thought a blind man had no use for a television, and it would be one less thing to trip over. Who knows? Nevertheless, the crime outraged me.

Even so, I tried to refrain from being judgmental. I had my own problems.

"Maybe it was the drugs and alcohol," David muttered.

"Drugs and alcohol?" This was the first I had heard about his alleged substance abuse.

"What drug?" I asked.

"The drugs they found in his system when he was arrested," David explained.

"Troy was on drugs?" I frowned.

"Yep. Crack."

"Crack. What the hell! Who gave him crack? Where did he get that shit from?" I was really angry. Had he become a drug addict?

"Man, I don't know!" David answered, even though I could tell he was withholding information.

"Are you smoking that shit, too, David?" I asked.

"Man, stop tripping!" said David, leaping to his feet for a quick exit.

I hated that mom had to deal with this matter. She was still coping with the death of Big Momma and the burden of Dee's battle with multiple sclerosis.

Crack cocaine was a mystery to many, including me. It had indiscriminately invaded our working-to-middle-class neighborhood of Southpark. Now it seemed to be taking its toll on my family at the worst possible time.

*****

Ahhh! A refreshing break from the summer. September signaled the arrival of beautiful foliage. The magnificent hues of white oak and cottonwood trees dotted the city. The colors might not have been as brilliant or plentiful as in New England, but Houstonians still celebrated a change in the season. The air was clear, the ozone alerts on the decline, and humidity low – a rare luxury in Houston.

I stood on the balcony admiring the aerial view from my Westwood apartment, delighting in the yellow, red and brown leaves that decorated trees and lined nearby lawns and gardens. I thought about the past and present, now living on my own. I had made decent money on the track-and-field circuit but nothing compared to megastars such as Carl Lewis and Edwin Moses.

But I was determined to make a difference with my life, perhaps even as a pioneer in some field. The realization of achieving a dream was inspired on this day in September 1985 as I watched a television network introduce Oprah Winfrey, who stormed onto the scene as the first black woman to host a nationally syndicated talk show. From humble beginnings in Mississippi to international icon, Oprah gave me reason to believe in myself.

As my attention was affixed on the screen in awe of Oprah, the telephone rang. It was Patrick. He wanted to invite himself over to see my new place. I gave him permission to come over and used the time it would take him to arrive to tidy up my place.

Seconds later, my mother called to find out how I was doing. I told her I was fine. But, once again, I lied. I was feeling like crap for keeping her in the dark about my February nuptial plans. I knew that my mother would never understand my reasoning for marrying a woman I didn't know from Joe's house cat. No family history. No background. No nothing.

To make matters worse, I questioned my own actions and wondered what I wanted from the relationship – perhaps just a cover-up for my alternative lifestyle. Tish had a plan, and I didn't. I was in a delusional state.

Chapter 21
Score: "40 to Love"

"**W**hat are you doing up there, man?" Patrick screamed from the bottom floor of my townhouse. I was upstairs sipping on vodka and orange juice that Patrick previously had given me. He would often store liquor in the back compartment of his red Corvette for after-club drinking.

In mid-November, he and I prepared to step out for the evening. We got dressed for success for a night at Club Echelons, an upscale adult facility on the southwest end of town where many of the city's athletic elite partied and flaunted their fancy cars, fabulous clothing and fine jewelry.

Patrick arrived at my house wearing designer wool slacks from Calvin Klein that matched a charcoal gray camel-hair blazer. His black slip-on Italian leather shoes complimented his crocodile belt.

I decided to wear a black pair of Perry Ellis wool-pleated trousers and a solid white crew neck sweater with a black calf-leather thigh-length jacket. My black Kenneth Cole dress shoes from Neiman's completed the ensemble.

Patrick told me I looked "wonderful."

I then cautioned him about using "gay" words that could draw negative attention. You wouldn't tell another man he looked "wonderful," I said. "Slamming" maybe, but not wonderful. Of course he ignored my criticism.

"The ladies are going to go crazy when they see that chest bulging from that white sweater!" Patrick said.

"Man, stop tripping!" I accepted the praise, though.

I then noticed that my NCAA championship ring was missing, so I retrieved it. I felt that my attire wasn't complete without it, thinking that every athlete who was somebody would be wearing theirs – if only for bragging rights, an ego thing.

So what if I were fronting and struggling financially? I craved attention, being in the spotlight. I knew that many people were fascinated with athletes – especially if they lived luxuriously. I wanted to be associated with that.

As Patrick and I exited my apartment and passed the courtyard, we noticed a young athletic dude volleying on the tennis court near the swimming pool. Despite the cool temperature outside, the tennis player trained relentlessly, hitting the small yellow ball with great force and power.

He was an attractive "youngblood," a word I used to refer to tough, streetwise, masculine guys with the potential to do freaky things.

My interest was piqued and so was Patrick's.

"I'm not sure who he is," I told Patrick. "But I can find out."

"Yeah, why don't you do that. See what he's all about because I know how you athletes operate behind closed doors. It's a secret thang," Patrick said facetiously. It appeared he was already drunk. We then entered his 'vette and drove off.

Patrick and I had become close within the past two years. Our non-sexual relationship had flourished to a point where we could talk about anything. I didn't like the fact that he was so judgmental of others, however. But I still trusted him. That trust eventually led us to a conversation about my upcoming marriage to Tish. The issue weighed heavily on my mind, and I began to second-guess my decision.

"You know, I'm not sure about this marriage."

"Oh, really," he said, being condescending.

"Yeah!" I snapped, knowing I was being toyed with.

"Well, what's the problem? You found out that you don't want fish now!" Patrick joked and snapped his fingers.

"Say man, I'm serious! And don't call her fish. What did I tell you about that femme-shit attitude? All that snapping and shit."

"And what did I tell you about being paranoid? Why would you put her through the headache, Miguel? I bet you haven't even told her you're gay, huh?"

"Gay! I'm not gay. I just have … I don't know, maybe I'm confused or crazy, but I'm not some faggot! And don't ever call me gay again. Respect me just as I respect you," I demanded.

In reality, I was tired of promising myself it would be the last time that I would engage in a same-sex act. I was constantly being defeated by lust.

"So if you're not gay, what are you?" Patrick asked throwing his right hand up out of frustration, while driving.

I paused then blurted out, "I'm a sexual animal. What else could I be? I'm like you. I'm not to be labeled." I played him with his own word game. "Look, Patrick. I love her, but I don't want to cheat on her."

"Well don't cheat. Walk away from this lifestyle and live a normal life. You can do that, can't you?"

"What if I can't?" I said.

"Well, you just do what you know is right. This thing is not about a feeling. It's about truth, man. Stop acting like you don't know the difference between right and wrong."

"You are no help, Patrick!" I shouted angrily. I knew he was telling me the truth. I just couldn't face reality.

"Well, don't get mad at the messenger because you're confused! Say you're a FAGGOT, Miguel! Say it! Say you're a FAGGOT!"

"FUCK YOU!" I shouted. "I AIN'T NO DAMN FAGGOT!" I

lashed out. I wanted to knock his teeth down his throat. I realized though that I wasn't really mad at him as much as I was upset at myself.

"Miguel, listen. Right now you're lost in fear. You're in de-ni-al! The best thing to do is to follow your heart. That's my suggestion, man. Do the right thang," Patrick said sincerely.

How could I follow my heart when I didn't know what direction it was taking me.

"Follow my heart, huh?" I gave it a brief thought.

"Look, Miguel. I love men, and there's not a woman who can make me feel any different. I would have to go to DA or something to cure my ills for the beef," Patrick said.

"What in the hell is DA?"

"Dick's Anonymous," he joked.

"See. That's what I'm talking about. You're sick man. Everything is sexual with you. Can you just be serious for a moment?" I was actually amused by his silliness. "Anyway, there's one more thing I need to get off my chest. That's if you're willing to take me seriously."

"OK. Confession is good for the soul."

"Yeah, you can say that," I said. "We're gonna elope to Jamaica in February."

There was a moment of silence, then a stormy response.

"Elope! Are you crazy? Miguel, what's going on with you? Have you lost your damn mind? How can you elope with someone you hardly know?"

"What do you mean?"

"What I mean is, why are you gonna elope and not tell your parents and siblings about such an important decision? You can't see the madness in that? It looks suspicious, man."

"It's my decision."

"So they don't know about this marriage? Whose idea is this? Yours or hers? Those bitches are dirty, Miguel. I'm telling you."

"Don't call her a bitch, Patrick. I've warned you about that once before. You watch yourself, dude."

"I'm not attacking her personally. I'm speaking in general."

"When you generalize women as bitches, you're attacking all females, including your mother and sisters."

Our heated exchange caused the windows to fog. I was seething.

"Do what you want to do. I don't want to talk about this anymore, Miguel. You gonna do things the way you wanna do things anyway," Patrick said. He turned up the volume on the car stereo to drown me out.

For the rest of the ride to Club Echelons, Patrick and I did not say anything to each other.

I was still miffed about his attitude toward women, and he was irked over my naiveté about my impending marriage to Tish.

As we approached the club's covered valet entrance, we flashed our smiles and began our proud struts as if we were on top of the world.

It's showtime, baby!

Before entering, we looked at each other and decided to let bygones be bygones.

"Say, man, I'm sorry," we both said in unison.

"Let's try to have a good night tonight, OK!" I then shook his hand to seal my apology.

"Cool. Let's go check out the scene, man. Who knows, we might land the one that got away," said Patrick, who was now back at his usual game.

It was no secret that many "straight" clubs were hideouts for homosexuals who might otherwise be uncomfortable in a predominantly gay environment. This was a great place to camouflage.

*****

Before I drifted off to sleep on this cold December day, I paused to remember and pray for the family of an associate I learned had died recently of AIDS. This also gave me cause to rethink my promiscuous behavior, even though I knew this was not just a gay disease.

An hour or so after I had been asleep, Tish called with some breaking news, as she put it. I wondered if she were having second thoughts about marriage.

"I have something to confess about to you, baby. So please, please keep an open mind, OK?" She appeared nervous.

"OK. What's going on?"

"Well, you know that my parents are still living in Jamaica, right?"

"Yeah."

"Well, there's a problem with my visa and work permit. It will expire in January next year. I was reluctant to tell you earlier in our relationship because I … I was just scared, Miguel. Miguel, are you there?" Tish asked.

"Yeah, I'm here. You think I would hang up on you or turn on you?

"Yes and no, but …"

"But what?"

"I just wasn't sure until lately Miguel about your true feelings for me. I didn't want to hurt you, and I don't want to be hurt now. I know this union seems a bit odd, but I really do have strong feelings for you – so strong that I want to be with you for a lifetime. Therefore, we have to move the date up to January."

"You once said you loved me. Now you're saying you have strong feelings for me. Are we going to start this marriage with a lie? I don't have a problem with moving the date up, Tish." I knew I wasn't in a position to ridicule her or anyone, but I felt she was attempting to play me.

"I don't mean to deceive you nor devalue my love for you. I do love you, Miguel."

"Good. That's all I needed to know. I just want this marriage to work. You don't have to worry about your visa, baby, because you'll be my wife next year in January. So stop sweating things with the INS. It'll work out fine, OK." I began to wonder if her parents had been influencing her to find an American husband to gain citizenship.

"OK, I just can't wait to see you next week – a week before our big day," said Tish, worried about potential problems with the Immigration and Naturalization Service.

My other line then beeped, interrupting us. It was Peggy, my booking agent for a local modeling agency. I had signed with them to earn extra income to assist me with bills and other needs. I wasn't that serious about the gig, but I did get quite a few bookings based on my height, talent and physical appearance.

"I have an interview for you tomorrow at the agency," Peggy said. "It's for the GQ live show here next month. This is a special occasion due to the late winter season. It's also an opportunity to hobnob with some important movers and shakers. Are you interested?

"Sure. What time?" I asked anxiously, forgetting my January commitment to Tish.

"It's at 10 o'clock sharp. And, Miguel, please be on time," Peggy instructed.

"Aren't I always?"

"Yes you are, Miguel. You're one of the few. So, we'll see you at 10 o'clock sharp or before."

I then returned to my conversation.

"Tish, are you still there?"

"I am."

"That was Peggy from Intermedia Modeling. I have a cattle call tomorrow morning at 10."

"Really! With whom?"

"It's the GQ live audition for late winter."

"GQ, as in GQ magazine?"

"Yes. Gentlemen's Quarterly."

"The show is in January, which is our wedding month. I forgot to get a date. Your visa expires at the end of January, right?"

"Yeah, it does."

"Well, we should be OK. I'll call her back and make sure this doesn't clash with our plans. If it does, I'll cancel."

"I hope it doesn't come to that, baby, because that money would come in handy," Tish said.

*****

It was three days after Christmas and the eve of my departure to Jamaica. The warm winter day inspired me to pull out my tennis racket. I enjoyed the solitude as I practiced my volley and weak serve. I really just wanted to do something to get my mind off my departure and wedding. I just needed a diversion from the stress.

To my amazement, I got more than I bargained for. The "youngblood" Patrick and I had noticed practicing some weeks ago was making his way to the court. The stranger, watching me struggle, eagerly offered some expert advice.

"Say! If you put a little more height on the ball, your follow-through will connect," the husky voice instructed.

My heart fluttered at the sight of the attractive athlete, who stood nearby with folded arms. His light-brown wavy hair glowed in the brilliant sunlight. He had thick eyebrows and light-colored eyes.

As he cautiously approached me, I got a better picture of his chiseled face. Up close, I was able to scan his posture and athletic features.

"In order to put power and control on your serve, you've got to put some height on the ball and make sure you're vertical with your lead arm," he said.

He demonstrated with my graphite Prince racket.

"So, that's how you do it, huh?" I asked appreciatively.

"Yep. It's just that simple," he said, twirling the racket by the strings with his index finger. "Here's your racket, man."

I thanked him for the tip and formally introduced myself.

"I'm Curtis," he said, smiling and extending his hand, "but

they call me Sweat."

"Why do people call you Sweat?"

"Because when I play I play hard. And the sweat begins to soak everything on me and the things I touch."

"I take it that you're an athlete?" I asked.

"Yeah. You can say that. I play for Houston Baptist University on the varsity tennis team. "You want to volley a bit?" he asked, pulling his expensive rackets and balls from his Fila gym bag.

"I'm down for that."

I observed his form-fitting tennis shorts that highlighted his buttocks as he strolled toward the opposite end of the clay court.

My first swing was a charm, clearing the net and forcing a surprised Curtis to react defensively. He then returned one of my serves with a strong surge of power, forcing me to sprint across the court for the cotton missile that he launched on my side. We found a rhythm as the ball echoed from one end to the other. Then, suddenly, Curtis upped the ante by approaching the net and slamming the ball and my ego. I was defenseless, his aggressiveness overpowering. But like a highly testosterone fool, I challenged him to a match.

"Wanna play a game or two?" I asked.

"Let's go for it."

The first few moments of the set were pleasant and tactful as Curtis mildly connected his serve onto my side. Still convinced that I could handle his powerful blows, I sprinted from corner to corner trying to impress him.

Eventually, yellow missile after yellow missile swept past me at incredible speeds and sent me hopping like a jack rabbit. Boy, the things we do to attract someone's interest. Despite 40-Love, I still maintained my composure. I realize that this was not my element. I was definitely invading another man's territory. Now, I just needed to find a polite way to exit.

"You all right, man?" Curtis asked, smiling.

After his winning serve, we decided to call it quits and shook hands. He gave me another tip: Don't always try to kill the ball.

He did, however, compliment me on my physique.

"With those thighs and calves, you gotta play some kind of sports," he said, wiping sweat from his forehead.

"Yeah, I do a little something."

"So where are you from? Houston?"

"Yep. Born and raised. And you?" I asked.

"I'm from the Big Easy."

"New Orleans, huh. I've been there before. It's wild and all-out freaky."

"Freaky like how?" asked Curtis, probing for an answer.

"Freaky like … voodoo freaky." I lied, not wanting to share my true thoughts.

"Well, that's if you believe in superstition."

"Well I don't. Hey, you wanna go to my place for a drink or a beer or something?"

"That's cool."

After he entered my place, Curtis began to admire the décor of my home – a masculine touch of style with portraits of Olympic stars around the world. I also had collected several accessories from specialty furniture stores from throughout the country while traveling to track meets. Various pieces were positioned at the bar area, fireplace mantle and tables within the apartment. A large Persian rug covered the living room floor. I had an eggshell-white Tuxedo sofa, a set of oversized black chairs and large black Armoire cabinet that housed a 36-inch television and Bose stereo.

"You know Carl Lewis?" Curtis asked, staring at a picture over the fireplace of the legend's famous leap at the 1984 Olympic games.

"Sorta, kinda. He's good people. Would you like beer or juice?"

"Water is fine. Perrier is even better if you have it, man," Curtis said.

"You're a runner or a sprinter?"

A sprinter, I said.

Curtis then noticed the awards and trophies dotting my downstairs living area, a shrine to my athletic career.

"Would you like lime with your Perrier?"

"That's cool," he said, his attention still focused on my athletic regalia.

With thoughts of perversion at first, I began to focus on my commitment to Tish. That's when I noticed the blinking red light from my answering machine.

"So, you said you've been to the Big Easy a few times, huh? What clubs did you go to while you were there?"

"I didn't do the club scene. It was strictly business," I answered, avoiding the club-trap question. Curtis then made his way to the bar. I thought I detected him looking at my legs from the corner of his left eye.

I gave him his Perrier water and excused myself as I approached the answering machine to retrieve my messages.

One was from Peggy congratulating me on the GQ booking. I had made the cut. She repeated that the job paid $300 an hour and the date was the last weekend in January. She told me to enjoy my trip to Jamaica and call her upon my return.

The message grabbed the attention of Curtis, who was apparently ear-hustling. Anyway, I wanted him to hear the message. It seemed to validate my ego and status.

"So, you leaving for the islands, huh?" Curtis asked, removing himself from the leather barstool to admire the gold medals on the fireplace mantel.

"Yeah. Matter of fact, I'm leaving tomorrow morning."

"Oh, yeah. So you have a track meet there?"

"No, just a special engagement," I said, not wanting to offer too much information. I knew I had his interest now.

"So they pay you guys pretty good for running?"

"You can make a living off it if you're competitive enough, just like in tennis."

"Yeah, competitiveness is the key."

"Are you planning to go pro in tennis, Curtis?" I asked as I sat on the sofa to remove my damp shirt.

"Yeah, man, that's the backup plan if this college thing doesn't work for me." He fought to avoid eye contact with me after I took off my shirt. "Say, man, I don't wanna wet your chair. Do you have a dry T-shirt or something I can borrow?"

It seemed it was now time for Curtis to show off his goods.

"Sure, I'll get you one."

Although I found Curtis handsome, I was unsure of his sexuality. I wondered about that as I climbed the stairs to my open bedroom that featured an oversized, near-motionless waterbed with a large semi-nude portrait of myself hanging above it.

I pulled out a shirt from my walk-in closet. As I turned to exit, I was surprised to see that Curtis had followed me and was staring at my portrait that highlighted my chocolate-toned structure. I noticed that he had removed his shirt, displaying his ripped upper body. I also noticed how his tennis shorts exposed even more of his buttocks. Was this dude teasing me in my own place? Did he know I was capable of seducing him at the snap of a finger?

"I hope you don't mind me coming up here since I wasn't invited on a tour," Curtis said apologetically. He smiled as he turned his head toward me while still facing the picture on the wall.

"Nah, man. No problem. I should've given you a tour, huh?"

I handed him an Izod sport shirt.

"Who's the photographer?"

"An associate of mine. He can give you a good deal on personal portraits if you're ever in need."

"You think I can look like that, man?"

"Sweat. What are you talking about, man. You already have what it takes.

Curtis then deliberately turned and faced me a few feet away and flexed his large biceps.

"Feel that. You think that's hard enough?" asked Curtis, seeking approval. I gently reached at his bulging muscle.

"That's pretty hard." From that point on, I decided to play it cool. I didn't want to rush into anything. After all, we're neighbors and we just met.

Curtis then asked if he could sit on my heated waterbed.

After giving him permission, I quickly answered the ringing telephone near the bed, wondering who the intruder might be.

"Miguel, this is Patrick. Were you busy?"

"Only if you knew," I whispered as Curtis stood to put on the borrowed shirt.

"What's going on?" Patrick answered exuberantly.

Curtis dismissed himself, thinking I needed privacy.

"Say, Miguel. I'll be downstairs. Is it OK if I play some tunes?"

"Sure, Curtis. Go ahead."

"Who's Curtis?" Patrick asked as I fixed my eyes on Curtis' calves.

"The tennis player."

"The boy that was playing tennis that night we went to Echelons!"

"Yep."

"Miss Thang, how did you get him in your house so fast?"

"Look! What did I tell you about calling me that shit?" I said.

"Oh, I forgot how fragile you athletes are about y'all's sexuality. Excuse me!"

I ignored his sarcasm.

"Check this out. I was volleying this morning on the courts, and he was watching me on the sly, right? So he decided he wanted to help me with my serve. So he did and later whipped my ass all up and down that court."

"Is that all he whipped?"

"Wouldn't you like to know?" I said, pacing the upstairs floor.

"Yes, I would. So what happened?"

"Well, before the phone interrupted us, he was sitting on my bed with his shirt off."

"Miguel, STOP! What happened?" Patrick screamed excitedly.

I decided to cut the conversation short.

"Look, he's downstairs and I gotta go. But I'm kinda glad you called because you know I'm leaving tomorrow, right."

"I'm aware. I told you I don't wanna talk about your marriage, so I won't comment."

The sounds of Diana Ross filled the townhouse as she sang *"Upside Down."*

So he's a Ross fan, huh? That's very interesting, I thought.

"Miguel, please be careful with these boys. They're just for the moment. So don't get caught up. Have your fun with them and move on," Patrick said, pleading.

"I got you. But the boy is fine, though."

"Miguel, be careful. Look, let's do something today before you leave tomorrow. Is that possible?"

"What do you have in mind?"

"I'm glad you asked, child. There's this black filmmaker named Spike Lee who made a splash at the filmmakers' festival. He spent about $175,000 or more with borrowed money from credit card accounts and friends. Now he's earned that and more from his debut. The movie is called *'She's Gotta Have It.'* Do you want to go see it? It's playing in River Oaks among the elite crowd, which I know you like."

"You're always trying to read somebody on the sly, Patrick. Sure, I'll go."

"Well, good. It's 2 o'clock now. I'll be there around 5

because the movie starts at 7:45 p.m. We can stop for a drink or snack before, OK?"

"Cool. I'm down with that."

Chapter 22
All Cracked Up

Tish was happy with her new job as she sat in a board meeting at Houston's City Hall. She was the new transportation manager and was happy to continue her career in Houston which had elected its first woman mayor, who then subsequently appointed the city's first black police chief.

We'd been married only eight months, but I could tell that her job as a manager and role as a wife were stressful.

She called me as I prepared to take a short early afternoon shower before lunch and practice.

"Hey, baby, it's me."

I was glad to hear from Tish because I had a surprise for her.

"I was just thinking, maybe we can meet for lunch in an hour. I can cater, and we can have your favorite: grilled chicken with fettuccine Alfredo. We can sit in the mall at City Hall and enjoy the day. How does that sound, baby?" I asked.

"That sounds wonderful, baby, but I'm so tied up here Miguel that I can't even think straight. I have to meet with the Metro Transit Authority at 3 o'clock for a proposal on this rail issue and then I have a conference with the mayor. I'm sorry. I can't do it," Tish said apologetically.

I told her I understood and to try to relax.

"I'm going to get ready for practice, and I'll see you for dinner later, OK? By the way, I have some news I want to share with you." There was a silence. "Tish, are you there?"

"Yes, I'm here. Someone entered my office unannounced," she explained, unhappy with the intrusion.

"I was saying I'll see you for dinner at home later this evening."

"That's fine. I'll see you then, OK," she answered abruptly.

Time after time Tish had warned her husky colleague about entering her office without knocking, but T.J. continued to disrespect her. He worked across the street at the city annex building as a building permit manager. He considered himself a Cajun Romeo and thought he was God's gift to women because of his fine, wavy black hair and hazel eyes. He was flashy, tall with an athletic frame and had a charming face.

Unlike most women at city hall, Tish was unimpressed with the arrogant brute. He was a waste of time as far as she was concerned.

"Travis Jacobs. May I help you?" an annoyed Tish asked.

"Yes, Mrs. Okoee-Morris, you sure can. I have some concerns about the Sharpstown Transit Center proposal. Or should I say the transit center deal."

"What concerns? It's already been approved, T.J.," Tish explained.

"Well, isn't Metro also seeking a permit to expand the Bissonnet project right through the historical Bellaire district?

"True. So, what's the problem?"

"The problem is the Bellaire civic club. They are concerned about the increased traffic, which will include buses and transients that may double the crime rate in their community."

"T.J., what does the civic club have to do with this? Are you being threatened or bribed? Please, Mr. Jacobs, tell me this is not the case?"

"No, that is not the case," answered T.J., who was acting suspiciously.

"Are you sure, T.J.?"

"Yes. I'm sure!"

"Look. This is the deal. I'm meeting with Metro in about an hour. I will address this issue when the time presents itself. OK, T.J.? But if I find out you're giving me half-truths, you're going to fry at the stake," Tish threatened.

"That's all I'm asking, Tish. Just address the issue. Maybe the Fournace Street option would be more beneficial. It's industrial-oriented with booming commercial business, not residential like Bissonnet."

"Oh, and by the way, Mr. Jacobs, for the third time: Do not enter my office unannounced again."

*****

Wading in the outdoor spa to soothe and relax my aching muscles, I welcomed the 6 o'clock sunset. I thought about my marriage and my mom's distrust of Tish.

"Who in the hell is she," I remembered my mother asking. When I told her Tish was my wife and her daughter-in-law, my mother blew a gasket.

"Where did she come from? Does she have a degree? Who are her parents? Does she work? Is she a professional? Do you love her?" My mother asked simple questions, but the answers didn't come so easily.

When I blurted out that I was helping her obtain citizenship, my mother blew a second gasket and just walked away. I knew then that I had made yet another bad life decision.

But eight months later, my mother finally has gotten over her bitterness, though she's still skeptical of my relationship.

The decision was mine, and I had to live with it. Tish and I had come to enjoy each other's company, and sex was "dyna-mite," which is part of the reason I decided to pamper her as soon as she arrived home. A well-deserved foot massage would start the evening, followed by a warm-scented bath.

Following that would be dinner and wine and a cool glass of Johannisberg Riesling to soothe her sweet tooth. I had marinated veal chops and prepared pesto fettuccine.

A splash of water suddenly brought me out of my daze. I opened my eyes and discovered Curtis' muscular body standing over me. He was wearing all-white Speedo trunks that tightly hugged his butt. His physique was flawless and toned. He then lowered himself on the opposite side of the Jacuzzi.

"I see the water was putting you asleep," Curtis said.

"Yeah. It's relaxing, Sweat," calling him by his nickname, which was a turn-on because it sounded edgy, rough, hard. "I didn't hear you come up. So, what's happening with you?" I asked.

"Nothing really – school and all. Just trying to get myself prepared for this upcoming semester.

"So classes begin soon, huh?"

"Yep," said Curtis. "It's gonna be a tough semester for me."

"How so?"

"Just is, man. Money's short, and my girl is tripping and shit. She's screaming and shit about a job: more money, more money, more money."

Maybe his girl was right. I had gotten the impression that this guy was high maintenance and a smooth hustler. He was very discreet. Other than his sex appeal, there was no real connection between us.

"So where does she suppose this extra money is going to come from since you're not working?"

"I'm a hustler, dude. I know how to be resourceful when I need to be. You feel me?"

I then asked him what his plans were for that day, and he said "nothing." Of course I wasn't surprised. So he shot the same question to me.

"Tish and I have plans for the night. A little quiet time. I gotta take care of home tonight," I said, throwing him a subtle hint. When I stood to sit on the inner edge of the whirlpool to analyze his reaction, he took notice of my body.

"You're getting bigger man. You're not on the shit, huh?" he asked.

"Steroids? Hell, no! That shit is for losers, man! Why take drugs?"

"That shit can creep up on you like a thief in the night. Mark my word," he warned.

Thoughts of drug abuse reminded me of the fate met by former college buddy Zac, as well as my younger brother, Troy, who was now in prison because of crack cocaine. He blamed the drug for his crime. I vowed to never use any kind of mind-altering chemical that could destroy my life.

I began to wonder if drugs had impacted Curtis' life in the past.

Curtis, noticing me in a daze again, splashed warm water on me again.

"Snap out of it, man," a smiling Curtis ordered. "Where did you go?"

"I was in another world, man. I have some things coming up soon, and I have to make some decisions."

"I know the feeling, man. I'm kinda in the same situation, too. My girl isn't going to lighten up any time soon about that money issue." He then began playing foot tag with me from the other end of the hot tub.

I was surprised at his boldness. Strangely, he was feeling rather comfortable.

"So you wanna play, huh?" I asked, splashing water into his face. He giggled like a schoolboy and then suddenly submerged himself, pulling my left leg until I, too, became submerged.

I grabbed Curtis by his inner thighs while we were underwater. When he slipped, my hands inadvertently got caught underneath his shorts. As his round cheeks rested in my grip, he didn't flinch.

When I apologized, he said, "Man, I ain't tripping. Are you?

It's all about fun and games, huh?"

"You're wild, man," I said.

"I told you I like to play rough. I ain't no punk, but I can hold my own. It all comes with the hustle, man," Curtis said, letting me know that he was down for anything.

Not long after we finished horseplaying, we noticed Tish approaching. We pretended that we didn't see her. When she arrived she placed her hands over my eyes from behind.

"Guess who?" she asked.

"Hmmm. Let me see. Would this be the girl next door? Or would it be the one down the way who has a thing for me?" I said teasingly before she gently slapped me on the left side of my head. "Oh! Now I remember. It's Mrs. Okoee-Morris, my wife." The sweet scent of her Opium perfume was hard to overlook anyway.

"How's my man doing today?" she asked, planting a small kiss on my neck.

"Your man is doing fine, girl," I answered. I stood to embrace her and noticed Curtis' envy. After Tish and I left the pool area, Curtis gazed at us as if to suggest that he and I were not done yet.

After a bath, dinner and sex, I decided to share my goals with my wife.

"Honey. I'm … I'm gonna retire if I don't make the qualifying time for the trials for the '88 Olympics. I think it's time, don't you?"

At first she was quiet, then agreed.

"Yeah, I do. Not to say you're not producing. It's only that money is getting short, and I want to keep a handle on our bills."

"I agree. So if things don't go as planned, I'm considering going into restaurant management. There's this guy I ran track with at Mississippi State who's a regional manager with Al Copeland Enterprises. He said whenever I'm ready to get started to give him a call."

"That's great, baby. Will you enter at ground level or mid-management?"

"Perhaps middle management. General manager or something comparable is the goal. For starters, I'm looking at $35,000 a year."

"GM would be nice. By the way, what is Al Copeland Enterprises?"

"It's a chain of QSRs, quick service restaurants, such as Popeye's and Church's Fried Chicken. They're all over the South and Southwest portion of the country."

"So what are you going to do about the modeling gigs, baby?"

"I plan to keep them going on the side."

"Well, you seem to have this all figured out. Just remember I'm 100 percent behind you."

*****

Death threatened my family again. My dad, suffering emphysema and lung cancer, was getting weaker by the minute, resulting from years of smoking.

As I stared at my dad on this gloomy, rainy November day, I watched him struggle to breathe with help from his oxygen tank.

With everything going on around her, my mom, like many women facing difficulties, showed true strength and grit.

She knew that dad's days were numbered.

"Did you get enough gumbo?" she asked me. "You know that's your dad's favorite. He always loved seafood gumbo," she said as I sat at the table.

"Yes, ma'am, I did. Is he gonna be able to eat any? He's breathing pretty hard. I don't think he's going to be able to get anything down," I said.

"He will once I get him comfortable, baby. I sure hope this weather gets better; it looks like it's about to flood out there," she said, changing the subject.

"Yep, it looks pretty bad, but it should improve, according

to the weather report."

The good news was that Troy was now out of prison. I was still reluctant, though, to try to develop a healthy relationship with him because of his past mistakes. I was unwilling to forgive him – despite my own messed-up life.

*****

I pretended to watch football as I sat on the country-style sofa in Curtis' apartment as he fired up a marijuana cigarette. The scent forced my attention onto Curtis, who had been observing me.

"I didn't know you smoked *chronic*, Sweat," I said, using the street name for the cannabis.

"Only on occasions," he said coughing. "Here, you wanna hit? You ain't scared are you?"

Now, I remember specifically telling him that dope was for losers. What was his problem? "Nah, man. That's OK."

"Come on, man. It's just a little herb, dude. It won't bite."

Being overcome by lust, I began falling into Curtis' web. His playboy charm was irresistible. It wasn't as if I hadn't smoked weed before. I did in college. So what the hell, I thought. I reached for the joint and took a deep puff. I instantly felt an unfamiliar buzz that brought both fear and pleasure that I've never experienced with weed before. My heart began racing, and I felt sweaty, disoriented and my skull compressing.

The herb was like a rush from an amusement park roller-coaster reaching an unprecedented G-force. I actually thought I was going into cardiac arrest. I began coughing repeatedly and violently, hyperventilating and light-headed.

"Damn! What's in this stuff, man!"

"Just a little somethin', somethin'," Curtis said with an evil grin.

"A little something like what, Sweat?" I asked, feeling way too high to move. I gave the herb back. I had been duped.

"You ever tried premo?"

"Premo! Hell, no! What's that?" I asked angrily.

"Weed mixed with a little bit of crack rock."

"Crack!" This mothafucker has just played me for real. "Sweat, what the hell you trying to do, man? I don't smoke that shit man. You know that. Why you give me that shit?" I shouted. I wanted to give him a knuckle sandwich, but he bailed out of sight to answer the knock at the door.

"Who is it!" he yelled.

It was Ike, a friend of Curtis.

"What's up, Miguel? Damn I smell the chronic, man. Where's the lick, man?" Ike asked excitedly.

"Man, y'all trippin'. That shit is all cracked up, Ike. You smoke that shit, too?" I asked as Ike passed me a cool Budweiser from the plastic bag he was carrying.

"Yeah. Why not, man? It can't hurt you. Just don't start smoking that glass dick," Ike warned.

"Sit down, Miguel. You still hanging with us, huh?" Curtis asked.

"Man, I ain't doing no more smoking though!" But with me lusting over Sweat, it didn't take long for me to have a change of heart - even if it meant sacrificing my lungs. I didn't even think about my brain.

Chapter 23
Falling From Grace

Club Oasis was the new rage of super nightclubs in Houston that attracted young black professionals.

Every so often Tish and I would treat ourselves to a night of dancing and dining to break our routine that often consisted of work and watching home movies. We stood on the second-level of the nightclub balcony, gazing down upon the crowd of patrons swaying and grinding their bodies into one another to the beat of "*I Like Girls*" by the Fat Back Band. I immediately grabbed my wife from behind, caressing and kissing her smooth body.

As I scoped the place, my eyes saw a familiar face – Patrick. He had been observing me and my wife, who I didn't want him to meet. I was gripped by fear of being exposed. The thought of their meeting spooked me like the force of a poltergeist victimizing guests in a haunted house.

As he sipped on a drink and stared at Tish, Patrick seemed to be plotting his next move. Be that as it may, I decided to approach him at the bar with my wife in tow.

"What's up, Patrick?" I asked, greeting him as if everything were normal about our friendship. He played alone.

"What's up!" he said. "How's it going, man? I didn't see you come in. How long have you been here?"

It was evident that he was lying as his eyes zoomed in on

Tish.

"Oh, I've been here for about one-and-a-half hours." I figured this would be as good a time as any to finally introduce him to Tish. Perhaps now he would see the beauty I saw in her long ago. "Patrick, this is my wife, Tish." She checked him out carefully but not so suspiciously that it was obvious.

"Nice to meet you, Patrick," said Tish, giving him a firm handshake.

He returned the pleasantries and then commented: "If you don't mind me saying, Miguel, your wife is beautiful, man." He tried to use language that would keep her from suspecting he was gay. I had hoped he succeeded. All he had to do was to remain "butch" for a few minutes longer – at least until she and I left the building.

"Thank you, Patrick. If you don't mind me saying, you're quite a handsome man," said Tish, returning the compliment while noticeably absorbing his character.

Enough with the compliments, I thought. Then, Patrick invited us to join him.

"No thanks, Patrick. We're about to leave," Tish said. "We have church in the morning, right Miguel?" She then pulled me closer into her arms as if to say, "he's mine."

"Yeah. That's right. Church starts earlier tomorrow. Would you like to join us?" I knew I was really pushing my luck.

"Church? Thanks, but I'll pass. I have a busy day tomorrow as well."

That was my cue to exit before Patrick became too inebriated and messy. I was still hoping he didn't reveal any tell-tale signs of femininity around my wife.

As she and I prepared to leave I told him I would call him later within the week.

*****

My future in track was hanging in the balance as I competed in the June 1988 Mount Sac Invitational in sunny California. In the end, my fifth-place finish in the preliminaries did not qualify me for the finals. As a result, I blew my chance to qualify for the upcoming Track and Field Association (TFA/USA) meet a week later. My Olympic trial dreams were shattered, due in large part to a small hamstring strain that also affected my performance. I remembered my promise to Tish about giving up the sport if my performance faltered. The time had come for me to end my love affair with track and field. I would now be forced to face the real world and an 8 a.m.-5 p.m. workday.

Later in the day, I decided that I would break the news to my family and Tish before she left for a transportation conference in Chicago. My effort to reach my wife was futile. I was not sure if she had already left the office. I was, however, successful in reaching my mom.

She asked how long I was going to be in California. I told her I would be there only through the night.

"That's good," she said, "because I'm arranging the wake services for your father. It will be in three days," she said sadly.

My dad had died on the second day of my trip to California. Even though I was sad, I didn't mourn heavily. We really weren't that close.

"I'll see you all tomorrow, mom. Say hello to everybody for me, OK?"

****

Before she could leave the office for the Windy City, Tish's colleague T.J. called her on the telephone to nag her again about the expansion project.

"We have to talk, Tish," he said.

"In reference to what, T.J."

"The Bellaire project."

"You mean the expansion of Bissonnet Boulevard?" she said.

"Yes. That project."

"Well, T.J., that deal is out of my hands. It's a done deal. It's dead. Metro has given its approval." She was puzzled by T.J.'s persistence.

"Is Metro that powerful or influential?"

"T.J., power has nothing to do with it. The Fournace Street proposal does not have a median separating boulevards such as Bissonnet, which is ideal for expansion. Why is this such a big issue with you, Travis?"

"Tish, we had over a year and a half to implement other alternatives. There are a lot of unhappy people in that Bellaire community."

"Mr. Jacobs! This issue is closed. I have a plane to catch to Chicago in two hours. Is there something else I can assist you with, sir!" an irritated Tish asked.

"No! Not a thing. Goodbye!" T.J. said rudely.

Tish had no proof, but she suspected T.J. of being in cahoots with the Bellaire Civic Club – perhaps some under-handed activities.

*****

It's been three months since we buried my dad. Now, it was back to business as usual for Tish. I had entered into the QSR (quick-service restaurant) business as planned. Al Copeland Enterprises offered me a generous mid-level man-agement position to operate one of its many Popeye's units. My three-month probationary period was over. I was now fully insured and secured with stock-purchase options. My $35,000 a year salary would help ease some of our financial woes after the purchase of another expensive German vehi-cle.

Meanwhile, Tish was developing suspicions about my commitment to her. She said my character traits were deteri-orating and accused me of being less patient and non-respon-sive to her needs.

We were disagreeing much too often on such trivial mat-ters as food preparation and car swapping. As the issues intensified, we grew further apart; even sex was becoming less frequent and boring. The surprise lunches and gentle caresses all but ceased.

There were several reasons Tish became suspicious. Patrick was the main reason, and Curtis was second. Ever since I introduced her to Patrick at Club Oasis, she seemed uneasy. It was as if she sensed he was being fake around her. Was it his physical movements and gestures I'd warned him about that caught her attention?

At times, I wondered if Patrick intentionally was trying to expose his true identity to her.

Then there was Curtis. He was hanging around me much too often. As our friendship grew, he began touching me in places reserved for her. She would observe his horseplay but, of course, didn't say anything. I just played it off as if nothing were wrong.

To further raise her concerns, she found a suspicious matchbox cover in a pair of my favorite blue jeans. She confronted me about it, but I weaseled out of that, too. She claimed she was doing laundry when she found it, and I had no reason not to believe her since we often shared household duties. At any rate, the Uptown Downtown matchbox cover kept ringing in her head, but she couldn't quite make the connection.

Actually, the club was just a few blocks south of City Hall where she worked. It was inside a landmark building that had housed the defunct Woolworth's department store and was adjacent to the Southwestern Bell building where many Houstonians settled delinquent accounts.

Days later Tish still seemed disturbed as she tried to connect the name of the nightclub. But she had bigger work issues to deal with. The expansion of Westheimer Boulevard was waiting to be approved for funding and the controversial light-rail proposal was still being considered. Money was being blocked by foes from City Hall to Washington, D.C.

Tish sighed at the piles of documents flooding her desk. She was frustrated with the political bureaucracy.

The pressure of the workday provided a good reason to escape City Hall for an outdoor lunch. After all, her work was stymied until she could secure signatures from City Council and the mayor. Realizing that, she and co-worker Joyce Manning, a transportation analyst, planned a lunch date.

"What would you like to eat?" Joyce asked during their phone conversation.

"Something quick and non-fattening."

"Girl, please don't say salad. This is my meat day," said Joyce, craving soul food.

"What about Subway?"

"You're on. I'll meet you in the hallway. I really didn't need those oxtails anyway," said Joyce, a 125-pound former volleyball player and NCAA champion from the University of Florida.

"See you in a few," said Tish, grabbing her purse. She stuffed her cell phone and pager inside her handbag.

During lunch, Joyce said she had heard about Tish's inquiry about a particular midtown club. She had hoped Tish wasn't entertaining thoughts of a lesbian encounter. Anyway, the club she asked about was frequented mostly by male homosexuals.

"So why do you want to know about that place? It's a place for those with alternative lifestyles."

"Girl, I'm just curious. That's all. Not for me, though."

"So, why the curiosity?" Joyce asked. She was even more puzzled now.

Tish reached into her leather handbag to pull out a matchbox cover.

"I found this in Miguel's jean pocket last night. Are you sure this is a gay bar?" asked Tish, her heart beating rapidly.

Joyce was 100 percent positive. She explained that her older brother used to frequent the popular nightspot until he became ill and developed AIDS. The virus had severely attacked his immune system, damaging nerve tissues and leaving him in constant, excruciating pain. He lost his mobility, job and was ostracized by friends.

"My family stood by him even till death," said Joyce tearfully as she remembered him as a vibrant athlete in college.

"I'm sorry. I didn't know," Tish said, feeling uneasy.

"I'm fine," Joyce assured her. "Do you trust your husband, Tish? I mean do you really trust him?"

"He's not a bad spouse. He isn't abusive," Tish said. But she realized that wasn't the question. Did she really trust me? "I never had a reason not to trust him until now," she finally answered.

Even though there was no incriminating evidence, I had been unfaithful. In fact, I had hooked up with Curtis on several occasions right under Tish's nose. She didn't have a clue. And as long as he was high, the party was on. I had also engaged in sexual activities with a few other people I met at the clubs. I kept their names in my BBB (Boogie Boy Black) Pages. There was no attachment to any of the men. For the most part, it was strictly about sex. But whenever I was with Curtis, drugs did factor into our fling because that was the only way he would agree to get involved with me on that level.

"Maybe you should start re-evaluating some things," Joyce suggested. "Just because you found a matchbox cover from a gay establishment doesn't mean he's practicing the lifestyle. Was there any writing on the inside of the flap?"

"You mean a name or something?"

Tish opened the flap but saw nothing to implicate me.

Joyce knew the game so well because her late brother had been her best teacher.

"There's no name, nothing," Tish said.

"Then there's probably nothing much to worry about then, is there?"

Despite the lack of clear evidence, Joyce still sensed worry in Tish's eyes.

"I guess you're right, girlfriend. How about an ice cream cone from the Marble Slab Creamery in the underground tunnel? It's on me."

"Sure. I feel like having a banana split."

*****

After returning from Chicago, Tish had packed her bags for a short unscheduled vacation to Jamaica without me. Her surprise departure left me uncertain about our future and where to go from here.

I sat on the sofa in disbelief as I read her letter explaining her abrupt departure. It was heartbreaking; I fought back tears until I couldn't anymore. I was an emotional wreck, trying to avoid a breakdown.

Part of me wanted out of the relationship. But I decided it was best to try to salvage my marriage, even while continuing my secret escapades and flagrant behaviors. I refused to get rid of my BBB Pages. I had a lot of investments riding on that booty-call book.

While I pretended to be the man I wasn't, God knew otherwise. And I didn't deserve Tish. There was nothing normal about my life. I had become clinically dysfunctional.

*****

As lightning interrupted the weekend darkness and the roar of thunder sliced through my quiet bedroom, Curtis and I took advantage of the third day of Tish's absence. We dimmed the halogen lamp just enough to spotlight our bodies and for the occasional streaks of lightning to cast our naked silhouettes against the wall. We then lie exposed on the warm waterbed that I shared just days ago with my wife. I had been catapulted into space from the rushing high of crack cocaine. It seemed I went against all reason for the sake of a piece of ass. I didn't care about the consequences of my actions.

In a way, I wanted to avenge Curtis – to brutalize him for my worsening sick behavior and for hijacking what little morals I had left.

I experienced an indescribable euphoria after inhaling the smoky substance from the pipe Ike had warned me about and referred to as a glass dick. After passing the drug and apparatus to Curtis, I strategically crawled between his open legs as he got high. His muscular thighs and fat-ass cheeks begged to be assaulted, and I obliged. Curtis then repositioned himself on his knees, thrusting his ass in my face like a "hoe" as I drilled deeper and deeper as if prospecting for oil in hopes of ultimately stumbling onto a treasure like the blast of the famous Spindletop gusher that transformed the Texas economy in the early 20th century. In my case, I was plowing for the ultimate orgasm. Pounding Curtis was far from invading pristine or virgin territory because the ease of insertion did not suggest a passageway that had been untarnished, untouched or unspoiled. I showered after warm fluid flowed from my body and after noticing my muddied stick. I hadn't bothered to suggest an enema to Curtis before we got all hot and messy.

As the high began to fade, Curtis eagerly asked for more – not just for the drug but also my hard jimmy. In the beginning, he tried to give me that song and dance about me being the first man he'd slept with. Of course, I didn't buy that. I had heard that line a thousand times from others like him. Since he asked, I intensified my attack and supplied more crack. I stuffed his mouth with the glass pipe and his other end with a much different pipe.

The sad part was that not once did I use a condom. By not using protection in this age of AIDS, I was as sick as he. Sadly, the thought of satisfying my lust put a stranglehold on my sanity.

Even when a few hours had passed and I hadn't inhaled crack, it was the sex now that gripped and intoxicated me. I had discovered the key to having Curtis at will but didn't bother to consider that this could backfire. My thinking was warped; I was falling deep into a trap and didn't realize it.

*****

Most addictions slowly enter your life without warning. It had now been three months since I hadn't used crack cocaine. I had better control over the chemical abuse. However, I developed a stronger interest in the thug-life culture. My desire to live dangerously on the edge had grown exponentially. I was hanging out with full-time and part-time drug users. Their weaknesses and addictions made them easy prey, giving up the ass on demand.

Over time, I experienced a small victory as Tish slowly redeveloped trust in me. I realized I had a lot of work to do in order to maintain peace. I was lucky that she had not picked up on my little escapades before, like those evenings in the hot tub with Curtis. Perhaps our actions weren't so obvious since we kept our masculinity in check. Still there were other times when Curtis and I played a bit too rough with each other in her presence. But now he was history. I got what I wanted from him: revenge for getting me hooked on crack.

Then one night Tish and I had a heated argument, which was rare. I would yield to her to placate her Jamaican/Asian temper.

Interestingly, though, we never argued about money or household chores. This argument was about Patrick. She finally voiced her concerns, thinking that he was pulling our relationship apart. She wondered why I bothered hanging out with a person like him, saying we had nothing in common. But, in fact, we did – our attraction to athletic men. We both liked the arts, fine foods and elements of danger that I really grew to hate at times.

Days after our argument, we made up over a candle-lit dinner at one of our favorite restaurants. But I still sensed that Tish's patience was running out.

My credibility had come under attack twice in one month, first with Patrick and then my late-night outing on the town, without so much as a phone call to my wife about my where-abouts. I could not blame her if she left me because I was reckless and neglectful.

*****

Patrick and I cruised through the Museum District one weekend when I was off work and Tish was at an out-of-town conference again. We wanted to view a featured collection of Monet, Van Gogh and the ever-colorful works of Picasso. The museum was also a place where some of the city's elite gay men would congregate in hopes of finding a Romeo.

Later, Patrick suggested that we find real action by ventur-ing to the outer limits, the wild streets, for our daring hunt for a "homo-thug."

"What do you mean real action?" I asked, as we exited the east wing of the museum.

"Well, how about us looking for some ass-tion! 'Cause there is no ac-tion or flavor in there, meaning black men."

"What's wrong with kicking it with Latinos or white men, Patrick?"

"I'm all about the black man. Don't tell me you're turning into a snow queen?" Patrick asked.

"What's wrong with Latinos and white boys?"

"Child, please!" Patrick screamed.

"You're racist, Patrick?"

"No, I just don't do white boys. Latinos maybe, but defi-nitely not snow bunnies. The blacker the berry, the sweeter the juice."

"I'll take mixed fruit, any day," I said as we cruised in my deep red Audi that I had purchased recently.

"Have you ever been on the "Cut" off Main Street and Elgin?"

"No. What's the Cut?"

"Don't give me that 'I'm so innocent attitude.' "

"What are you talking about, man? I don't know what the hell you're talking about. But I'm quite sure you're gonna tell me."

"Make this right; school is now in session," Patrick ordered.

Under a harvest moon, a crowd of men was seen hustling all over the place. The thumping sound of rap music could be heard from a passing car. That's when Patrick informed me that the harder and louder the music the more comfortable hustlers become. So I found a CD by Houston rapper 8 Ball and cranked up the volume.

"There, Miguel, over there!" Patrick said excitedly, pointing out a high-yellow brother standing alone on a corner.

My heart was beating as fast as the pistons turning inside the engine of my Audi.

All the boys here are on a hustle, Patrick said.

"What kind of hustle?"

"Duhh! Prostitution, Miguel. Open your eyes." Patrick then lowered the stereo's volume as we pulled over to the curb to greet the stranger.

"Hey, boy!" Patrick shouted from the passenger side.

"What are you doing?" I asked Patrick.

"Sit back and take notes," he ordered. "Say you! What's up? Yeah, you with your cap to the side."

"What's up, y'all?" the yellow-toned hustler asked as he approached the car.

"You tell us, dude." Patrick was at his best. I never knew he could be so forward.

"It's all about the dollars with me. Anything goes if the green is right," the hustler said.

"We got fifty dollars, so what's up?" Patrick said as I watched for cops or a jack move.

"Y'all ain't police, huh?"

"No. We ain't no cops," assured Patrick, who then reached to unlock the rear passenger door for the stranger.

"Before we pull off, I wanna see the money," the thug demanded.

"Money ain't no problem," Patrick answered as he flashed

two $20 bills and a $10 bill.

"Good. Now let's go get my crack. I need it to mess around, OK."

I hadn't smoked that shit for months now, and I wasn't sure if I could handle being around it. Now, how was I to going to handle this?

Twisting and squirming in an Uptown hotel room, the handsome street hustler lie naked and high. He endured thrust after thrust from Patrick and me. We had scored another lay from another crack-smoking street hustler, who didn't seem to mind our brutal sexual assault. A strong sense of power engulfed me as Patrick waved a small pouch of crack rocks in the face of our hustler who still appeared to be drug-starved. He begged for more even as he lie naked with his legs wide open on the bedding soiled with human excrement. After I took a shower, the sex acts continued for a third, fourth and fifth time. It made for a tiring night and one of my sickest acts.

*****

After my wild adventure, I finally returned home. I listened to my messages:

"Hi, Miguel. This is Peggy. I've been trying to reach you for the past three days. I have a booking for you with Foley's, but if I don't hear from you by five this evening, you will be replaced. Bye."

"Miguel, this is Frank at work. I hope everything is OK, Morris. We have not heard from or seen you in three days. Please contact me ASAP."

As I gallivanted around town with Patrick, I had put the rest of my life on hold. When I did finally return to work I offered an explanation that had more holes than Swiss cheese.

I explained to Frank that I was in the Harris County Jail for three days on traffic ticket violations. He allowed me to return to work without repercussions. I was also able to dupe Tish for a few days because she was out of town on business. Little did she know I had problems bigger than the state of Texas.

I really did need to slow down, but I did not know how.

Patrick once told me that while I may be another man's blessing I was certainly a woman's curse.

Chapter 24
Zooming Into Dangerous Territory

Bright lights from oncoming cars nearly blinded Tish as she struggled to follow Patrick's red Corvette through a construction site on Westheimer Boulevard. She was proud of herself because her efforts and planning were finally coming to light. There were many warning signs that our relationship was melting down: my disheveled appearance, emotional imbalance, lack of communication, becoming distant, change of friends in our circle. Tish finally had had enough of my deceptions and lies. She decided to become a de facto sleuth.

On an unseasonably warm Saturday night, she started her fact-finding mission. She almost lost us as she careened through traffic, attempting to outrun red lights and elude slower-moving vehicles. Construction barricades threatened her pursuit. But she continued to push her Audi harder than normal, hoping not to attract police. She was actually enjoying the cat-and-mouse chase. It was like her very own buzz. Her eyes dilated and heart rate accelerated as she floored her sedan, putting pedal to metal. The roar from her engine and screeching tires entertained her.

"Why are some men so damn cocky and stupid?" she asked herself, questioning Patrick's and my ignorance about her intellect.

She kept tailing us as we crossed Kirby Drive going east, leaving the affluent River Oaks neighborhood. We then ended up in an area flooded with neon lights, heavy traffic, louder music and notorious streetwalkers. Montrose was like a mini SoHo District in New York City, a carnival-like atmosphere at every corner. Tish observed the bawdy behavior of the women in the crowd, which she later determined were drag queens. One in a tight-red dress even flashed her because she was staring his way.

She was annoyed by the freak show and blew her horn out of frustration at slowing-moving vehicles. She thought she had lost Patrick's red 'vette, which was only a few cars ahead. She still held out hope that she was wrong about me. Even so, this was an adventure that she was not going to miss for the world. She had made plans two nights ago to spy on us after I had called her while she visited a girlfriend and told her I would be hanging out with Patrick. She approved, not letting me know that she was unhappy about my plans. She went along with my male-bonding idea. Her plan was to leave the house around 10 p.m., minutes before Patrick arrived, and stake out our own home. She waited about two blocks away and began her jaunt after we – her unsuspecting "criminals" – led her to our nesting ground.

As she continued to trail us, she noticed Patrick's car pulling into a small, crowded parking lot. She made a mental note of the name of the club, while watching feminine men hit, chase and gossip like young schoolgirls. As we entered Studio 54, her stomach turned. We were the villains, but she still couldn't believe that I would enter such a hellish place.

"I ought to go and bust a cap in his ass right now," she screamed. She then gathered her composure and thoughts, even as her temper flared and her palms became sweaty.

After a while she finally drove away from Montrose Boulevard, tired of my lying and cheating and wondering if I ever thought of her safety. Was I even using condoms? These questions angered her even more.

There was no way I could lie my way out of this, she mused. She saw it for herself. I was frequenting gay bars and putting our lives in jeopardy.

*****

As I prepared to stroll in after 3 a.m., I knew it would be trouble. As usual, Tish would be sitting downstairs on the living room sofa sipping on a cup of hazelnut coffee, waiting to confront my sorry ass like many times before. I figured I'd tell her that Patrick and I stopped for a bite to eat. By now I'm sure she resented our marriage, despite her desire to obtain citizenship. I truly believed that she had grown to love me, but now I had made a mess of things. I should have known she would soon discover my game. The woman, with generally profound "gaydar" abilities, was from Miami and had become a pro at picking out men perpetrating and living double lives.

Because I did not fit into any of the "red-alert" categories, Tish never suspected anything when we first met. My persistent pursuit of her and alluring eyes impressed her.

I knew that when I entered the house she would be listening to Marvin Gaye or Phyllis Hyman.

It was now 3:27 a.m., time for some damage control.

Patrick dropped me off at the front security gate, babbling about some play at the Actors Workshop later in the day. I really wasn't feeling him or that play. Hell, I had to confront my wife, and evening plans were too far ahead for me to consider. I was about to face a storm. To get rid of Patrick's drunk ass, I nodded at him to hint that I was down for the play.

As I walked up to my home, I noticed through the mini-blinds that the living room lights were on. When I opened the door Tish was sitting exactly where I had predicted, drinking coffee and listening to Phyllis Hyman's "*Living All Alone.*" She turned and looked at me in disgust. I pretended to be surprised she was awake.

"What are you doing up at this hour of the night?" I asked rhetorically. When I approached the sofa to kiss her, she resisted. "C'mon, baby. What's up?"

"What do you mean what's up?" she said, frowning. "What does it look like?"

I sat calmly on the sofa several feet from her, trying not to further provoke her. "I'm sorry, baby, I got … " She stopped me in mid-sentence.

"Do you know what time it is?" she asked, purposely glancing at her watch. "Or maybe you don't care about the time or my worrying about you and your welfare. You said you would be home around midnight, not 3 in the morning, Miguel! You're not a single man anymore. Have you forgotten you have a wife and obligations? I've waited up for you for hours, Miguel, hoping you would come home at a reasonable hour. I shouldn't have to go through this mess with you time and time again. If you want to be treated like a man, you better start acting like one or else," she demanded.

I knew I was wrong, so I swallowed my pride and took my tongue-lashing like a man.

"Patrick and I stopped for a bite to eat at Denny's," I said as Tish, with arms folded, fumed.

"Denny's! You have food at home, Miguel. Why couldn't you call and tell me you were going to make a stop somewhere? You know how to multitask, don't you? Well maybe you can answer this question for me since you have so little to say. How was the party?"

What party? I never mentioned any party to her. She was picking.

"I had a decent time considering the circumstances. The crowd was a little out of my league," I said, forcing a grin.

"How so, Miguel?"

"This friend of Patrick's held a gig at a gay bar in the Montrose area. I was a bit uncomfortable at first, but I adjusted. Patrick knows my views about crap like that. But since the

gathering was for one of his co-workers who was being trans-
ferred and who happens to be gay, I didn't rock the boat."

"What do you mean rock the boat? If people are not comfortable in situations they shouldn't sacrifice their morals or
beliefs to validate others, Miguel. That shit is so weak, Miguel.
My father was never that weak."

"Listen, sometimes we have to make sacrifices Tish for
the sake of others," I attempted to explain.

"Legit sacrifices, Miguel! Going to gay bars and pretending
isn't a sacrifice. And if Patrick was a real friend, he should
have understood that places like that area were uncomfortable for you – if in fact you were uncomfortable at all."

"What do you mean by questioning if I was uncomfortable? Are you trying to accuse me of something?" I sat farther
back on the sofa attempting to keep my cool, yet sensing that
she was withholding information.

She reached into her silk robe pocket to show me a colorful matchbox cover then threw it at me.

"I found that crap in a pair of your jeans last week when I
did laundry, Miguel. Now, can you explain to me very slowly
how you feel about those places again?"

Tish had backtracked to the City Hall lunch spot where
she had originally disposed of the matchbox cover. After she
retrieved it, she kept it hidden just for this moment.

Silence gripped me.

"You must take me for a damn fool?" said Tish, who was
now actually laughing at me. "I ain't your fucking play toy, and
I damn sure not going to let you ease your way out of this
crap again."

I decided to stand, hoping that by towering over Tish she
would become intimidated and back down. When that didn't
work I tried raising my voice.

"What are you trying to do? Wake up the neighbors?" I
yelled.

"To hell with the neighbors! I don't give a damn! What I

want is the truth about you and that damn FAGGOT Patrick! Are you screwing him, Miguel?"

"What are you talking about woman? The man's a friend. What makes you think I'm sleeping with a man? Oh, I forgot, a matchbox cover."

"Why are you lying to me? I deserve better than this, Miguel!"

"I'm not hiding anything, Tish!" I didn't have the courage to tell her the truth. So I walked to the kitchen for an espresso, strong black Java.

"You're lying!"

"Woman, you approved of me going to that gig with Patrick. Now I come home a little late, and you're throwing a hissy fit, accusing me of sleeping with him. I don't pop it like that and neither does Patrick! I don't know what you have against him, but you need to figure that one out for yourself. Whatever your problem is you need to fix it."

"Right now, Miguel, you're my problem, and I do intend to fix it. I only asked you about that damn matchbox cover, and you're the one who flew off the handle. Matter of fact, you never gave me a straight answer. So how am I supposed to react or even feel when you evade my questions? I'm still your wife, remember?"

At least she still was acknowledging herself as my spouse. That was a positive sign. I wondered how I was going to get out of this mess. I started blaming Patrick, thinking maybe he was more trouble than he was worth.

"So, tell me, Miguel. How many gay friends do you have – not that it matters or anything?"

"None. Why?"

"You're sure?"

"Hell, yes I'm sure!"

"Who is this Nathan person and this Jamal fellow who left phone numbers on this piece of paper napkin I found in your pant pocket? By the way, it's from that same club, Uptown

Downtown, where that matchbox cover came from."

I was all out of excuses and verbal ammo. I was simply busted, feeling ambushed.

"They're running buddies of mine."

"As in track and field or club-hopping buddies?"

"Neither." My answer was dry and short.

"You know, I followed you tonight," she said.

Did she say what I thought she said. "You did what?" I asked.

"I followed you and Patrick all the way there, Miguel. I even enjoyed the short race down Westheimer with that Corvette."

She mocked me.

"Surprised?" She crumpled the napkins with the names on them and threw them at me like she did the matchbox cover earlier. "Save your lies for someone who cares, because I don't anymore. I know you're screwing around on me, and you know that I know it."

"Tish … " I tried to plead my case, but was unsuccessful.

"Don't even start!"

She then slapped the hell out of me, not once but twice. She was pushing her luck. I had never hit a woman before, but at that moment I was on the verge of knocking her on her ass. But I caught myself. I formed a fist to suggest I might retaliate and hoping that she would recoil. There was no way I was going to confess to her now. I knew that some things were better left unsaid.

"I want a divorce," she said in a surprisingly calm voice. "I've been tracking you for weeks now, and all I've heard and seen are lies, Miguel. You've been unfaithful. For all I care, you and that FAGGOT can have each other. You have never been uncomfortable around gays, and you know it. So, you can just kiss my black ass goodbye! I got what I needed from you anyway."

Shortly after she had made her way upstairs, I heard a loud

thump from the staircase. Tish had thrown down a suitcase and demanded that I get out or else I would be sorry.

Was she serious? This is my place, too. *Both* our names are on the lease.

Since I didn't know if she had recently purchased a gun, I quickly contemplated my next move. Anyway, my safety was more important.

I then grabbed the bag and my cell phone and called Patrick to ask if I could stay with him.

"Damn! Did she say that she got what she wanted from me anyway?"

Chapter 25
Partners in Crime

Forty minutes later, Patrick's Downtown apartment at the Rice Lofts was dimly lit when I entered. As I sought refuge on his long sectional calf-skin leather sofa, he had that "I told you so look" on his face.

I have always loved Patrick's place and his taste for art and furniture, which was comparable to mine. His taste for music was even better as opera great Jessye Norman, blowing her pipes when I entered, was singing one of those old Negro spirituals.

It was around 4:15 a.m. Sunday when I finally relaxed. Despite that, Patrick had the audacity to ask, "You want a drink?"

It seemed the party never stops as far as he was concerned. He was a drinker. I wasn't.

What I really wanted was a piece of ass to calm my current ills. I desired a rough, tough Negro who was down for the cause – a risk-taker willing for a few hours to be banged and humiliated for the sake of the dollar or even some dope of his choice. Mainly crack cocaine. Most of them were willing to be used and thrown out like week-old trash just for the sake of the rock.

Nonetheless, wanting to bang-up some knucklehead was the least of my problems. I had thornier issues. Damn, I was going to miss Tish's warm bowls of cow cod stew and the excitement of a football game as we lie on the sofa with her warm legs curled into mine during those intimate moments. Those times were history now.

Approaching his well-stocked wet bar, Patrick grabbed a pair of spotless highball glasses.

By now I had changed my mind and decided to have a drink after all. Patrick reached into the mini-fridge to honor my request. Upon meeting him for the first time, one would think that Patrick was nouveau-rich. Everything around him sparkled. Even the crystal sculptures and African oil paintings had unrestrained character. Patrick's taste was masculine despite his feminine behavior.

Then the big question came after he gained courage.

"So she threw you out, huh?" he asked, popping the top from a soda can that echoed over Jessye Norman's voice from the sound of his Bose speakers.

I was reluctant to answer even as I looked down at the leather bag next to my right foot. I still questioned why I let this fiasco go on for so long.

"It's only for one night," I said.

"You sure?" Patrick asked.

Actually, I wasn't sure about much at this instant, not even why I was there at his place since he was partially to blame for my marital strife.

"I need a place to lounge in case my home life isn't resolved quickly. Can you accommodate me?"

"That depends," Patrick said.

"Depends on what?" I asked, almost pissed at that point over his conditional attitude.

Patrick sat to the other end of the sofa pondering an answer.

"My privacy is precious, Miguel. You know me. I need my space and air. But, if she does not let you back in anytime soon, there's the extra bedroom."

I thanked him and assured him that I would be back in my place sooner than later, perhaps no later than Monday morning.

"That late?" Patrick teased.

"I got problems," I attempted to explain.

"Yeah, I know. It's your marriage. Or is it you or both?"

That painful question hit me harder than a ton of bricks.

Had he ever realized that he was at the heart of some of my problems? Yeah, my marriage was in trouble. I was in the shit house with Tish, but Patrick was partially to blame. Or was he? I didn't challenge him because I needed a place to stay.

"It's a little bit of everything, man," I said.

"Everything other than what you're calling it. Why can't you admit it, man? This is not about your marriage, sexuality or your independence. It's about your fears. You can't even surrender to your own terrors."

"I don't have any terrors." I lied. Oddly, I could spot the insecurities in others but as for recognizing my own faults I was blind.

"Admit that you made a mistake by marrying. You don't want a woman, Miguel. You want a man!"

"Niggah, please! What are you talking about?"

"I'm talking about your appetite for the male anatomy. Can you honestly say that you can function without a physical relationship with a man? Can you, Miguel?"

"I'm not like you, Patrick. I can control my fetishes." I lied once again.

"You're just like me. You're hopeless just like me and will never be able to completely stop your cravings for a man. Matter of fact, I don't even think you want to, do you?" He mocked me to a point that he laughed at me to my face.

I sat quietly for a moment, hating that Patrick was seeing me for what I was. He was right about us being alike. I never once even tried to stop denying myself. I was self-absorbed in the danger of the lifestyle. Even though I was hurting inside, I welcomed the pain as if it were a normal behavior – an act that I couldn't stop even if I tried. I had longed for the day when I could pass by an attractive man and not lust.

"You know she followed us last night."

Patrick didn't look surprised at all. Somehow he seemed to know all about it.

"I would have, too, if I were in her shoes. Do you think she's blind, Miguel?" Patrick asked. "Your wife clocked me a long time ago. It wasn't that I wanted her to. I saw her looking through me the first time we met at the club. Don't be an idiot, Miguel. She tagged me as a punk. I'm surprised that she hadn't confronted you before now."

All I could do was to shake my head in disgust at myself, yet I wanted to blame him. I had been so damn simple-minded.

"Why hadn't you mentioned this to me earlier?"

"For what? She had accepted the fact that I was in the life. It was you she was doubting, man. Women like her aren't dumb or stupid. That's why I don't bother with them. I don't play with their emotions. I have my hands full enough with these sorry-ass wannabe straight men."

I admit that I was a deceiver. Patrick, on the other hand, was true to his game. He allowed things to go only as far as he wanted.

"Take my advice and leave before something really bad comes out of this. She has what she wanted – citizenship into the U.S. If you ask me, I think she played you. So cut her loose."

"I don't have to. She asked for a divorce."

"There you go. She's even made it easier for both of you. It was probably her plan all along: to pussy whip you for a few months and dump you at the first opportunity. You should thank me for coming along and ending your misery."

"What makes you think I was miserable?"

"Most men are when they are trapped in a relationship between a man and woman. What makes you think you're different?"

"That's not me," I said. Yet I was already making plans to add a few more male prospects to my Boogie Boy Black pages that I kept hidden in the trunk of my Audi. It still had a few empty slots that needed to be filled.

"Miguel, I know you like a book. I know what you like in a man and when you like it."

Even though we were different in physical appearance and demeanor, Patrick and I always kept a guy tucked away for special occasions. I never inquired about his "piece of game," and he never inquired about mine.

I asked him what made him so sure that he knew my thoughts, and he said he was as sure about me as he was black and sexual. I then watched him approach the bar for more drinks. I insisted I had had enough, but he whipped up another Scotch and Seven for me and Absolut Vodka on the rocks for himself.

Moments later he picked up the stereo remote and entered a different selection. He took his place on the sofa and shouted, "You can come out now!"

My heart fluttered when I saw what entered the living room – a fine-ass boy wearing only a pair of white socks and matching boxers. His head was hairless like the rest of the body – just the way I liked.

The tall hustler and dancer was cut to the bone and just as dark as me. I had never gotten into dark-skinned men before, but the light-skinned Patrick loved them.

As he lap-danced between my opened legs, I grabbed a handful of his chocolate ass, and it sent chills throughout my body. This mocha colored niggah was working me.

"He's only for the moment, man," Patrick warned. He saw the lust in my eyes. My prejudice against the darker skin was now lifted.

Instantly, I knew I had to give Tish what she had asked for – a divorce. Patrick was right about me. I couldn't let go of what I was feeling. I did not want to give up sex with men.

Ultimately, Patrick had proved his point. We were "partners in crime." No matter how hard I tried to separate myself from that reality, I couldn't. Our demented behavior that led us to fulfill our sexual appetite by luring men with drugs and abusing them like slaves would have been enough to prosecute us had we been caught.

*****

Six months or so had passed. My divorce was finalized, and I was without money, hope or a job. I surveyed my empty townhouse. I had pawned my stereo, television, microwave and others goods. I had a terribly nasty drug habit, and I was three months behind on my car payments and fifteen days late with rent. As I held the eviction notice, I had no idea how I was going to get the money to pay my debts.

I was drowning in self-pity. Then a knock sounded at the front door. It was Patrick.

He must have known I was home because my Audi was parked out front with the windows slightly down. When he walked in, he was stunned at my untidy home and what was left of it.

"Ohmigod, Miguel! What happened, child?" asked Patrick as he looked in disbelief to find many furniture items missing.

"I'm in big trouble, man."

"What are you talking about? What's up, man?"

"My stuff was confiscated by the office."

"The office. For what?"

He had a hunch; I could see it in his eyes.

"I'm behind on rent."

"How did you get behind on rent with your salary? Miguel, what's really happening here?" Patrick asked.

"I lost my job," I said as I stared out of the huge glass window.

"How did you lose your job? I don't understand. And it looks like you're losing weight, too," Patrick said.

"Like I said earlier, Patrick, I'm in trouble."

"What are you talking about, trouble? I know you're not doing …"

"Doing what? Say it! Crack!" I screamed and turned toward him with fire in my eyes."

"Man, I told you not to get caught up with these damn boys. Miguel, they are only for the moment. Did that fuckin' Curtis turn you on to that shit?"

"Curtis had nothing to do with it!" I lied. "Then who?"

"I did it on my own free will. I …"

"I what, Miguel? I know you're not that damned weak. Who was it that turned you on to this crap?" Patrick demanded, as he approached me for an answer. "Answer me, child!"

"Goddamit! Stop questioning me motherfucker!" I lashed out at him. I was already disgusted with myself.

"You're a damn crack-head!" Patrick yelled.

His hurtful words caused me to snap and go ballistic as I lunged forward and grabbed Patrick by his neck, pinning him to the wall next to the brick fireplace and sending a glassed wall picture crashing to the floor. My strength surprised me as I lifted Patrick off his feet with both my hands wrapped around his neck. I watched the terror in his eyes as he squirmed to free himself from my potentially deadly grip.

"Let me go!" he tried to demand as I shut off his airflow. His strained, frightened, breathless voice and wide-opened eyes showed his horror.

After what seemed like minutes, I released him as he fell to his knees in a desperate bid to breathe.

My addiction had now triggered violence. I realized I was causing great harm to someone who was merely trying to help.

"I'm sorry man. I'm sorry." That was all I could utter as I covered my face in shame.

"You're sick, man. You need help! You're sick!" Patrick uttered, holding his bruised neck.

I then asked to be taken to a drug rehab, but he told me that I needed more than a rehab. I needed an "exorcism," he said.

I didn't know how I would pay for the services since I did not have a job anymore. But Patrick, realizing my sickness, softened a bit. He said he knew of a place that would take me in at taxpayers' expense.

I wondered how I was going to tell my mom that I was hooked on crack cocaine? How was I going to be looked at by my family now, especially now since I dismissed my youngest brother after he fell victim to the same illness a year ago.

The next 45 days of substance abuse treatment would be the beginning of what appeared to be a fresh start. All I had to do was work the program and admit some things about myself that I hadn't before. Of course, that was easier said than done because I had built up walls that were hard to penetrate.

*****

It was the first of winter, and I had been sober for six months and divorced for a year. I was in a new apartment, minus the Audi, but had a "hoopdee" that served its purpose. I was now an assistant general manager in training with Taco Bell. This was another career opportunity out of the many that I had squandered. I was grateful to God. I was now planning to travel to Inglewood, California, for a management-training class in a month or so, and I was determined not to blow this chance. I had gotten rid of my Boogie Boy Black Pages because it was a trigger. This was part of my effort to come clean. I had even given up mind-altering substances, including alcohol, mostly due to allergies, though, rather than AA classes.

I had obtained some knowledge about addictive behaviors

from a pharmacology course I attended while in rehab.

*****

After my shift had ended around 6 p.m., I received a call from Patrick. I hadn't heard from or seen him since the time he helped to get me admitted into rehab, but I wasn't tripping. I knew it was better to move on than to hold on to old baggage.

"Before we get off to a bad start, I was just calling you to apologize for not calling and visiting you while you were in treatment. I just didn't want to interrupt your progress. I know how hard it is for a person to recover from the stuff. My brother was on it, too," Patrick said.

"I'm the one who should be apologizing because of my stupidity, man. I was wrong, too. I never should have attacked you. I was out of line. Maybe God wanted me to meet a few wrong people before introducing me to the right ones so that when I finally meet the right people, I'll know how to be grateful for that gift."

"That's pretty good, man. You've learned a lot over the past months. I was just thinking maybe we could meet somewhere later, perhaps around 8 or 9 tonight."

"Somewhere like where?" I asked curiously, knowing that I had to disassociate myself from old people and places.

"You name the place. You're the expert in fine dining."

"Well, how about Carrabba's on Kirby Drive off U.S. 59 South?" I said. I was glad that he recognized that I could no longer visit bars, especially if alcohol was their main source of business. He agreed upon the location. Now the question is whether Patrick could be trusted. I wondered if it would be worth the risk of me embracing him as a friend again.

Chapter 26
Back in the Saddle

The astonishing Inglewood Hilton was like a beacon as it appeared atop the forested mountains of California. The Pepsico Inc. occupied several rooms on this March spring day as it trained 30 future store managers for positions throughout the United States for its franchises such as Taco Bell, California Pizza Kitchen, KFC and Pizza Hut restaurants.

I was undergoing a career change. Sitting at one of two oval mahogany boardroom-style tables, I reviewed policies, procedures and deployment strategies for successful leaders.

I was feeling mighty proud of myself even though I had not attended an AA meeting in months. I was well into my sobriety. I worked to apply the teachings of the acronym HALT – never get too *Hungry*, too *Angry*, too *Lonely* and too *Tired*. In fact, I was back in the saddle again.

As the final day of training drew to a close, a young, black instructor named Ken, oozing with machismo, presented his analysis of his most successful class to date.

He proudly heaped praises on all trainees for participating in role-playing and trouble-shooting techniques. As he moved around the room, I stared at his form-fitting slacks and huge buttocks. The intriguing 6-foot hunk was among a wave of young African-American professionals saturating America's executive ranks.

Surprisingly his final accolades were directed to me. I was voted the most charismatic student of the class for my knowledge and eagerness to learn protocol and dictate authority without controversy. I was the laureate of the day, receiving applause from my peers as they offered congratulations and prepared to bid farewell. We all would depart Inglewood later the next day.

After a long week of training, I relaxed in my room. As I napped, I began having a dream about crack cocaine. A drug counselor had warned me that this could occur because relapse haunts recovering addicts.

When I woke up, I was perspiring heavily all over – my neck, face and chest.

During nightfall, I had worked up an appetite and ventured downstairs where a moderate crowd had gathered in the atrium. As I entered a restaurant, a local pop band was playing Sade's *"Is it a Crime."*

I walked toward a mirrored bar occupied by well-groomed patrons and sat on one of the stools, where I admired the band, which featured a voluptuous black female.

"So, what you having tonight, sir?" the woman bartender asked, breaking my concentration.

"A Chivas and 7UP, little ice please." I had quickly forgotten about steering clear of alcohol during recovery. This was evident that I was not out of the woods yet.

As I turned to face the bar again, I recognized a familiar presence.

"Excuse me," I said, tapping the man on his shoulder. As he turned, he recognized me instantly.

"Miguel Morris! How are you doing?" asked Ken, my tipsy instructor – the one I had admired earlier and who heaped praises on me in class. He was dressed in semi-formal black attire.

"I'm doing fine," I said, admiring his style.

He and I then turned to listen to the jamming sounds of the band's saxophonist.

Then the bartender returned asking if we wanted to start a tab.

"No, put it on my account. The treat is on me."

I thanked Ken but told him I could take care of my own tab.

"I know Morris, but why waste money when there's a company account?"

He had a point.

"So, what did you think about the class?" Ken asked.

"I think it had structure and substance."

"In what way?" asked Ken, probing further to gauge my intelligence.

"It enhanced my leadership skills and deployment tactics, which will make me a more effective manager. And second, it focused on my ability to recognize others' lack of production. I strongly believe I now possess the motivational tools to help enhance employees' self-esteem and productivity."

"I agree. You don't have to sell me. That's why I approved when the class decided to vote you as its valedictorian," said Ken, loosening the top buttons on his shirt and revealing his Herculean hairless chest.

He was a far cry from the hustler type I was used to, but he certainly was no punk or femme.

The more we drank, the more we learned about each other. Eventually, we cut the evening short to get more acquainted.

I later found myself being absorbed by Ken's warm breath as he stroked my bare buttocks while lying in his hotel bed. As he moved down toward my hairless quads, his warm breath excited me even more. He continued with a moist kiss to the back of my knees, creating chills down my back. I moaned in ecstasy.

I wasn't down for being penetrated, so when I sensed Ken

wanted to take it up a notch, I turned on my back. We attacked each other's luscious lips.

For a moment, it seemed we struggled for dominance. The imbalance began to show as Ken refused to turn belly down for the anal attack I had planned. The tug of war began to sour our emotions. So I begrudgingly released my firm grip from his hard body. Ken, without notice, then eased from the bed and entered the darkened bathroom. I wondered if he were upset.

But after a few minutes, he reappeared and entered the warm bed and my arms. I was surprised. He then began to crawl his way down my chest, stomach and navel as his hot, wet tongue worked my body. New life was bred as our sexes hardened. That's when Ken dressed me with a lubricated condom. The macho man had skills, and a double life.

*****

For a moment, it seemed that Patrick had it all together. It seemed he had the finest of all things: a Natuzzi leather sofa, custom-designed chairs by Century furniture, an elaborate Bose high-tech stereo throughout his place and, of course, money. But all was not well in his wonderland as he paced the hardwood floors of his home, disheartened over the brutal fatal attack of his former part-time lover, Malcolm.

Malcolm was a struggling free-lance painter from Denver. He often frequented bars, bookstores and bathhouses in Houston's gay community. He and Patrick had ended their relationship years ago, but they still communicated and had mutual respect for each other.

Infidelity had sent their relationship on a downward spiral.

Once, after Patrick completed his nightshift and returned home at 2 a.m., he noticed his assigned parking space next to Malcolm's car was occupied. It wasn't unusual since many guests regularly parked in reserved areas. As he entered his home, Patrick's keen sense of smell picked up an unusual scent.

He quietly climbed the spiral staircase as the sounds of jazz gently rang from the bedroom. He opened the door and noticed a lone body resting peacefully. He moved closer to the edge of bed, stepping on a pile of unfamiliar clothes – dingy blue jeans and a sports jersey. As he reached down to retrieve them, the bathroom door suddenly opened and a stunned Malcolm stood naked and convicted as he peered into Patrick's angry eyes. That day changed the course of their relationship forever.

But now, Malcolm was dead, a victim of a grisly murder that apparently resulted from his fetish for bookstore boys and roughnecks. His case remains unsolved.

He was found by his parents in a sea of blood at his Westside apartment after their unsuccessful attempts to contact him. They had become concerned and went to check on him. That's when they found his decaying body brutally stabbed 25 times to his back, legs and chest. His living room and bedroom walls had been spray-painted in black letters with the words "faggot," "homo" and "nigger."

"Those homophobic bastards killed him, Miguel! They just left him there butt-naked on the living room floor bleeding like a dog in the street!" an aggrieved Patrick cried out. He wanted to avenge the attack. "I told him to stop picking up those damn boys off the streets! I told him, but he just didn't listen. Why? … I gotta have a drink," Patrick said.

"Me, too," I said as we approached the wet bar in his home. "Patrick, have you ever wished you weren't gay?" I asked, thinking we should stop our ugly behaviors.

"No! Why?"

"Because sometimes I just wish I wasn't. But at other times I love being masculine and gay. Am I twisted or what?"

"I don't know right now. Let me get a drink. You're talking too deep for me to think," said Patrick, sipping his Absolut Vodka.

"Malcolm was just so damn hard-headed. I told him to

leave those niggahs alone. They are just for the moment. God is not happy with us, Miguel. We are doomed like Sodom and Gomorrah. Doomed!" Patrick shouted.

"Stop trippin', man!"

"I'm serious! We're gonna burn in hell if we don't stop using these men for our sick pleasures."

"I'm not using men, Patrick!" I said defensively.

"Yes, we are! Why can't you see that?"

"What?"

"The lies we're living! Look what's happening with our black men: AIDS, drugs, prisons. All that crap is hitting us full force."

"I'm not responsible for anyone going to prison and using drugs or contracting AIDS, Patrick."

"Yes we are, because every time we buy them drugs and pay them for sex it leads them into some type of sin - an immoral act. And we are responsible for that behavior, man!"

Patrick continued to try to drink his depression and guilt away. It appeared his own nasty habits had finally gotten the best of him.

But I wasn't trying to hear his pain or his mad talk about burning in hell, because I knew as soon as he got his drink on he would be ready to go back to his old ways.

Chapter 27
Sizzling Social Settings

It was New Year's Eve as we entered First Colony Estates subdivision, a stone and wrought-iron gated community in west Houston.

Patrick and I had invitations to a party in this upscale suburb. After the valet took our keys, we walked up toward a home of splendor with gray granite columns surrounding its porch. Once inside, the foyer resembled a Roman-like assembly with a skylight-dome roof welcoming the December twilight.

A cool breeze whipped the black-and-white satin curtains on the two indoor granite columns in the large Great Room, which had a set of matching gray granite stairs. A Who's Who crowd blanketed the neo-Persian designed banquet hall, which echoed with the crooning sounds of Mariah Carey's *"Underneath the Stars."*

As we checked out the ambience, we were greeted by a sophisticated, immaculately clad woman.

"Welcome to our home. I'm Mrs. Webber," said the lovely and attractive hostess, wearing diamond-studded earrings and a necklace that accented her designer dress.

"I'm Shea," she said.

As we introduced ourselves, I began to wonder why her name seemed to ring a bell.

"So, who are you representing tonight?" she asked curiously.

"We're representing Dr. Jai Holmes. He's a close friend of ours," Patrick answered.

"Yes, he is a character. Not to mention he's a brilliant plastic surgeon.

Shea then told us to enjoy ourselves.

The sounds of popping champagne bottles, holiday toasts, laughter and music encircled the structure.

As Patrick and I made our way toward the illuminated pool, walking past a multitude of French doors and towering floor-to-ceiling windows, I asked about the Webber couple.

"Who are they? They're living large," I said.

"He's a local sports agent who's doing very well. The brother has dollars, thanks to his former professional football experience."

"Hmmm. This Webber guy wouldn't happen to be Butch Webber?" I asked.

"Yep. But don't get any ideas because the guy is as straight as a ruler," said Patrick, who left me to satisfy his thirst for a cocktail and to devour hors d'oeuvres.

He didn't know that Butch and I had a history, and I was not about to reveal that to anybody.

As I stood alone, I heard my name.

"Miguel! What the hell! Come here, man!" ordered Butch as he rushed toward me with a hug.

Butch was still fine as all outdoors, and handsome.

"Where in the world have you been? I've tried endlessly to contact you for months, buddy. And Lord, behold, here you are. Just a sight for starving eyes."

He then released his embrace so as not to draw attention.

I told him I had been to Florida, California and back to Texas in recent months, but I failed to tell him I had been in rehab for drug dependency, among other things.

"I see you found the woman of your dreams, huh?" I said.

"She's wonderful, man. Just what the doctor ordered. So how did you find out about this party?"

"Through Patrick, a friend of Dr. Holmes."

"Who's Patrick? Do I know him?" Butch asked, folding his muscular arms.

"He's a longtime friend, Butch. Nothing like what you're thinking though," I assured him.

"So, what do you think I'm thinking, Miguel? Lovers, partners or friends? Wait don't answer that. I'm violating."

"No you're not. He's a non-sexual friend. We've been through a lot of mess together. You know – the lifestyle and the bullshit that comes along with it."

"It's good having someone to confide in when trouble arises," Butch said as he refused to probe further. "So, what are you doing as far as work is concerned?"

"I've joined a team of managers with the Pepsico Inc. as a special projects coordinator and assistant general manager for the Taco Bell subsidiary."

"Are you serious? I've just recently purchased some stock with Taco Bell, and we are booming with profit and new stores throughout the southwest region."

"Exactly. That's the goal. We are looking to have 2,000 stores built and running throughout the world by the year 2000. We are expected by the end of the year to gross $4 billion in sales. We want to be accessible in every way possible. We are now experimenting with our new project, Taco Bell Express. They are located on some college campuses and service stations. It's all about one-stop shopping," I explained with confidence.

"Absolutely. Munch on a taco while you pump gas? I see you're doing your homework, Miguel," said Butch, placing his right hand on my shoulder. "Hey, follow me."

He led me through the crowd as he greeted guests.

Twisting and turning up the spiral staircase above the crowd, I looked down on the breathtaking view of the elaborate Great Room and foyer. I desired this kind of success. We reached the peak of the marble balcony and entered one of the three wings of the house. I observed Butch's every step as we went inside an elaborate double-door room that opened into a small theater.

"You still have it, don't you?" I asked, looking at the partially nude portrait of him that I drew many years ago. It hung over a marble fireplace near a Mediterranean and Egyptian-styled office desk.

"Where did you purchase the frame? It really makes the sketch look like a masterpiece."

"From a place called Noel's Furniture. Heard of it?"

"Yes. Located on Westheimer between Kirkwood and Wilcrest?"

"Actually there are several locations, but you hit it on the head. That's one of my favorite stores," Butch said.

He then asked if I had remembered what he had told me back on the West Texas State University campus years ago.

"Hmmm, let me see," I said, putting my right hand to my chin in thought. "That you would save my drawing and put it in your house when you went pro?" I asked. "You thought I forgot, didn't you?"

"To be honest, yes. I thought you forgot about a lot of things, man. The way we used to play. The way we used to hug and shit. The way we used to kiss."

He then strongly pulled me into his burning body, hugging me once more.

All sorts of warning signals went off in my head as I remembered that Butch was now a married man, and I could not feed my lust or desire.

Then Butch released his grip and stared into my eyes.

"It took me a long time to differentiate my feelings for male companionship, Miguel. There was a time in my life that I could not hug an attractive man such as you and not let my hormones speak for me. I guess you're wondering why all of a sudden I'm addressing this matter, right?" Butch asked.

"Somewhat," I answered.

"Well, it's like the carpenter and the nail," Butch explained. "The carpenter keeps his eye on the nail and not his thumb because if he doesn't he will miss the nail every time and wound the thumb. So, I've learned to concentrate on the nail. I've had enough wounds in my lifetime, Miguel. I've learned to concentrate on my marriage, regardless of the lust in me. I finally feel complete and content to a large degree, but I still struggle."

"I wish I could say the same, man, but I can't. I still let people and things clutter my mind. I'm still struggling with a lot of demons, especially this sex demon. It's consumed me, man. That's why I do what I do. Have you ever hated that you are gay? I mean sometimes you love it, and other times you can't stand yourself."

"Been there, done that, Miguel – a lot of times. I still long for the male touch, but I must stay committed to marriage," said Butch, as he sat next to me staring into the fiery furnace. "Say, Miguel, I have something to share with you that may help you understand yourself and actions better."

Butch approached his desk, retrieving a leather-covered bible. He focused on Roman 7:15-20, explaining that these passages talked about struggling with sins and covetous desires. He paraphrased the text:

*"I don't understand myself at all, for I really want to do what is right, but, instead, **what I hate I do**. I know perfectly well that what I am doing is wrong, and my bad conscience proves that I agree with these laws I am breaking. But I can't help myself, because I'm no longer doing it. It is sin inside me that is stronger than I am that makes me do these evil things."*

Of all the scriptures I had been exposed to, those seemed to have been tailored for me. Butch was the first male figure

I had been involved with sexually who had ever taken the time to read scriptures to me.

"Does that make sense?" Butch asked, staring into my eyes and soul.

"It does. Now I understand why it's been so hard for me to understand myself. I'm powerless," I said, knowing that most of my life I had been in situations with lonely, warped people. "The reason I was powerless was because sin had me in bondage."

"Powerless yes, but not defeated, Miguel. This walk in life reminds me of a Wet Paint sign. Even though I see the sign, the glossy surface tempts me. After looking around to see if anyone's watching I touch the paint to satisfy my curiosity. I discover it's wet. I might not have had the power to resist, Miguel, but I've learned not to act on emotions, but rather logic. And that is a blessing from the Father above, man. I'm not preaching to you. But always ask yourself if you will be happy with your actions. Oftentimes, if you have to ask, you know it's not pleasing," Butch said. "And that is my New Year's gift to you, buddy. Think before you act, Miguel. I know you're still struggling with this lifestyle, but stop beating yourself over it. Happy New Year."

*****

As time passed and we were well into the New Year, I had not heard a peep from Butch. But I wasn't tripping. His advice was still trapped in the depths of my mind like meat on bone.

As I ran in circles around the indoor track at the West End Bally Total Fitness health club, I reflected on my life and the upcoming week. I had plenty to accomplish so I decided to do a few more routines before wrapping up my workout. I went downstairs into the weight room for an upper body workout. Once there, I noticed the curl machine being occupied by several guys. So, I made my way over to the bench press area where I noticed a person wandering around in a world of his own.

After my run, my Nike T-shirts and shorts were drenched. So, I walked briskly in the direction of the loner who appeared to be in a trance.

I asked if he were working out at the bench that I had eyed from afar.

"Yeah, I only have one more to go, but you can work in if you like," the stranger offered.

I took him up on his offer and slyly glanced at his rear-end. I couldn't help myself. It was the dog, more like sin, in me. With that, I told myself that I really needed to stop and get control of myself. Anyway, I lowered my body to the bench to begin the workout. As the workout intensified, I could feel my chest muscles getting harder and bigger.

I then made my way over to the bicep machine. As I began my routine, my concentration was broken again as I noticed a medium brown attractive, athletic dude. He was wearing a black-and-white cotton half-body workout suit. His strong hands gripped the padded handles of the lifecycle. I was a hands freak, too.

I scanned his athletic figure. For the next few minutes, I pondered the "what ifs." My curiosity about the guy was getting the best of me. So, I made the bold move to speak to him.

"What's up?" I asked. His response was dry.

"Were you talking to me?" the stranger said.

"Yeah, sorry for disturbing your workout, but I think I know you from somewhere, huh?" I said, offering a weak line.

"Nah, considering I just moved here from Michigan," the stranger said as he continued cycling.

"You're from Michigan?" I asked.

"Yes, Detroit." His answer was short. I assumed that he did not want to be bothered.

"I guess I made a mistake. I thought for sure you were this guy I ran against in track a few short years ago. He ran for the University of Mississippi," I said.

"You ran for Ole Miss?" he asked.

"No, not Ole Miss, but for Mississippi State back in the day."

"That's interesting. While tracing my genealogy, I discovered that my great-great grandfather's offspring were from Mississippi. But I was born and raised in Michigan.

"Really." I had broken the ice between us. "I guess we do have something in common, huh. By the way, I'm Miguel. Miguel Morris."

"I'm Lazlo Veasey. It's great running into someone else who has similar ties. So, you ran track at MSU?"

"Yeah. Four good years. I was really surprised about the attitudes of many of the whites there, considering all the rumors about the Deep South and all."

"Yeah, most people haven't realized that the South has really changed. All of those cross-burnings and widespread racial tensions have ceased. I've been back to the state a few times over the years and really like it."

"I heard that," I said, amused by Lazlo's observations of the South. He also shared that he had received an academic scholarship from Michigan State, where he studied and received a degree in pharmacy. He said he was currently working for a downtown pharmaceutical company.

As we talked, our time wound down as the gym announcer indicated that the club would be closing in 15 minutes.

"Well, I see they're trying to get rid of us, huh?" I said smiling, hoping that I would get to see him again.

"Yeah. It's approaching 10 p.m. I need to get my things out of the locker. Perhaps we'll do lunch soon."

I didn't have a business card to offer, but I did provide my home number to Lazlo, who had suddenly become too loose, too friendly, too quickly. Was there something up with this dude?

As he prepared to leave, I looked downward at his feet and noticed his colorful Nike running shoes. One of them neatly and snuggly held a gold wedding band tied to its white shoestring.

I had to wonder why a married man would take off his wedding band just to exercise on a lifecycle. Was it to protect his finger from being pinched? I don't think so. Or maybe it was fitting a bit loose, and he didn't want to lose it. I figured that had to be the reason.

"So, you're married, huh?"

"How did you know?" he asked.

"I see the ring tied to your shoestring. So, how long have you been married?"

"Two years, two months, 27 days from today. And you? Have you ever been married?" he asked, his Nike bag hanging from his shoulder.

"Two years, four months and I've lost count of the days since my divorce," I explained.

"I'm sorry to hear that.

"It was difficult, but not disastrous," I said as we walked to our cars, exchanged numbers and departed.

I was looking forward to our next meeting.

*****

Weeks later, Lazlo and I finally hooked up to get more acquainted. He was more interested in being caressed than having sex during our first few encounters. And as we got to know each other better, I developed more respect for him because he was intent on not being considered an easy lay. As a result, I nurtured our friendship and didn't view him as just a piece of meat. Compared to the other men I had slept with, oftentimes on the first night, my encounters with Lazlo were more sterile because they didn't involve drugs or other sexual abuse that had become common.

Our experiences usually involved kissing, something that was rare for me, and gradually elevated to lovemaking as we eventually explored each other orally and sometimes engaged in anal sex. It lacked the intensity I was normally accustomed to. So, needless to say, I continued sleeping with other guys. But I felt that Lazlo would become an important factor in my life. Call it a sixth sense. He taught me compassion – at least toward him. So, I was happy to treat him differently because he seemed to actually care about my well-being. For him, sex was secondary.

And from that moment on, I vowed to protect him from the culture that had me all caught up. Even so, I was still having reservations about this new friendship. I knew I needed counseling. It even bothered me enough to distract my attention during a theatrical production.

"I can't believe I'm sleeping with this dude," I whispered to Patrick as we watched Tony-Award nominee Hope Clarke and crew in a touring version of "*Don't Bother Me, I Can't Cope*" at Houston's Jones Hall. "I did the very thing I said I wouldn't do – sleep with a married man."

"Married? You didn't tell me he was hitched," whispered Patrick, trying not to disturb our neighbors sitting on the rows near us. "Does he know you're a recovering addict?"

"Yes," I said, wondering why Patrick always brought up that subject. "That was the first thing I told him."

But, of course, Patrick appeared not to believe me since I had lied on other occasions.

"We'll talk about this later after the production. Shhhh."

*****

Three months had passed since I met Lazlo. We were stuck in a love triangle of sorts – he more so than me.

He and his wife were still strongly married, but that didn't help the situation between us because he was frustrated in the relationship and was no longer deeply in love. He said they were childhood sweethearts, which made it tough to separate. He said he stayed in the marriage hoping that he could still grow to love her as much as she loved him. Also, their families were very close, and he didn't want to cause any turmoil. He didn't think that either the families would accept his bisexuality. So, as a result, he stayed in his marriage and tried to suppress his fantasies about men.

If I felt uneasy about anything in life, it was my relationship with Lazlo. It was moving too fast and was developing into a love affair I didn't want.

After the play, Patrick and I decided to grab a bite to eat. We went to La Strada, an upscale Italian restaurant in the Montrose area. It was an eclectic place with elegant wooden walls and granite bars and tables. It was packed with an elite crowd.

"Now, would you like to continue the conversation you started in the theater?" Patrick asked.

"Not really. I was just tripping. That's all."

Suddenly someone caught my attention. "Isn't that the football star Warren Moon over there?" I asked.

"Yes. So what?" asked Patrick, rolling his eyes.

"Why are you tripping and shit?"

"Because I'm not a fan of those people; they think it's all about them."

"Man, I'm not even gonna entertain that crap tonight. I have problems of my own. But anyway, I was saying earlier that Lazlo and I are getting a little too deep."

"Don't you mean a lot? It's my understanding that's he's married, right?" Patrick reminded me, signaling the waiter from a nearby table.

"If you let me finish, I'll explain."

"What's there to explain? You're sleeping with a married man, and that's all to it."

"Wrong. It's deeper than that Patrick. And you can't talk, considering you're dating an engaged alcoholic. So, you're doing the same thing, man."

Patrick was at a loss for words.

"So, will you just be quiet for a minute and let me pluck this chicken!" I said, raising my voice and drawing unwanted attention nearby.

"Go ahead and explain this one," Patrick said.

"Everything's a joke with you, isn't it?"

"No, just this conversation. Look, Miguel, if you're not comfortable with this fling of yours, get out! You know right from wrong, don't you? So stop acting like you don't," said Patrick, popping his fingers as if he had lost his damn mind.

"You look like a real fag when you do that," I told him.

"Where's that damn waiter? I need a cocktail," demanded Patrick as two guys caught his attention. "That's Gill and his boy over there," Patrick said.

Gill was a longtime associate of Patrick's. They were once colleagues, working the graveyard shift at the downtown FED-EX. He signaled for the two to join us.

They arrived at our table just after we had finished ordering appetizers.

Gill introduced Eli as his best friend.

"Eli, are you from Texas?" Patrick asked.

"Yes, I am," he said in his baritone voice while offering a firm handshake.

"Well, Gill and Eli, this is my 'pardner,' Miguel," said Patrick, introducing me to his associates.

"Haven't I seen you somewhere before?" Gill asked me, shaking my hand.

"Maybe so. I'm not sure." I wasn't falling for that old line, I mused.

"It was at the GQ show years ago," Eli said.

His response surprised me.

"Where?" Gill asked.

"The GQ show. He was one of the models – one of only two black men in the show. Don't you remember?"

"Oh, yeah! Now I remember," responded Gill, watching curiously as Eli and I shook hands.

Patrick then interrupted the conversation by inviting them to sit and dine with us.

"Thanks, but no thanks. We have some unfinished business to complete," said Eli, who seemed to be running the show as he took charge of the conversation.

As they turned, I distinctly heard a faint comment from Eli, calling me an "an old track queen that ain't making it."

At that moment, I wanted to put my hands on that fool for disrespecting me.

"You OK?" asked Patrick, who didn't hear the derogatory comments but noticed the nasty expression on my face.

"That bastard referred to me as an 'old track queen that ain't makin' it.' "

"Huh!" Patrick laughed. "Get over it. It's not the end of the world. He has issues, too."

Chapter 28
True Lies

Payback is hell. Plant bad seeds and the harvest will never prosper. Those were the words of my late grandmother. And I was about to get a first-hand lesson.

On a quiet Saturday in December, I felt the world riding on my shoulders. I was looking for strength to express my dilemma to my mother, who was sitting at the kitchen table.

We started out with the usual: How was your day going? Is the job working out? Are you seeing anyone? Are you staying clean and sober?

"Yes, mom. I'm OK," I said. But she still sensed something was awry.

"What's wrong? You didn't relapse did you, Miguel?"

"No, momma. I didn't." That was the truth.

"So, why aren't you eating? Why the loss of appetite."

"It's nerves." I, of course, lied this time.

"Is it that bad?" she asked, grabbing my right hand to comfort me.

"It could be."

"So, what is it?" She was getting tired of the guessing game. I took a deep breath.

"You remember when I was admitted to Spring Shadows Glen Recovery Center months back?"

"Yeah."

"Well, they took all sorts of tests like psychoanalysis, IQ and general physicals. Some years ago, I knew a guy who was diagnosed with HIV, which can cause AIDS. The reason I know this is because he was my college roommate, and we shared some personal things with each other. But anyway, he was wondering how he was going to break the news to his parents. So I suggested that he should wait awhile until he was positively sure about his lab results."

"So, what happened?" she asked with a puzzled look.

"Well, his test was positive. I was scared for him because of misconceptions about the disease, the ignorance out there, the fear that some people have concerning the virus," I said, not looking her in the eyes.

"So, why are you telling me this? I don't understand," she said, obviously frightened. "What's wrong, honey? Can you answer me?"

"I don't know when I got it. It was months ago when I was diagnosed. This disease can lie dormant for years before it even reveals any symptoms or damage to the immune system," I said.

She was silent for a while and then had questions I didn't want to answer.

"Are you taking medicine?"

"No."

"Why not, Miguel?" she asked in a panicked state.

"Because I'm not feeling sick or anything," I said, realizing my ignorance.

"So, you're gonna wait until you start feeling sick to start taking medicine? What's wrong with you? Are you trying to kill yourself?" she asked angrily through her tears.

"I'm not trying to kill myself," I said, putting my elbows on the table as I freed my hands from hers and buried my sweaty palms into my face.

"Maybe not, but you have to start getting treatment. Use your insurance from your job and get tested again. Time is crucial. There is no excuse for ignorance, baby. You hear me? Now, get your hands out of your face and do something for yourself before it's too late," she instructed.

"You're right, I'm acting like a child, a fool," I said.

"I don't mean to pry, but I have to ask you this. I've noticed in the past that you spend a lot of time with men, Miguel. Are you gay? You can tell me. Are you?"

"I'm not gonna lie to you. I've been experimenting," I said, feeling uncomfortable answering the question.

"But why? You are such a handsome man. Any woman would love to be with you. Why men, Miguel? I don't understand. What is wrong with you?" she asked.

"I like women, too, momma. Sometimes my hormones just go crazy, and I can't resist the feeling."

"I don't understand, baby. I think you're just confused. That's all. I didn't raise any of my sons to believe that way. How did this happen?"

"It just did, momma. I didn't plan this behavior. I knew about these feelings for a long time. I just suppressed them so I could try to live normal. I'm tired of lying to myself. Maybe I'm suffering from neurosis or something."

"Nonsense. None of my children are neurotic. Stubborn maybe. So, don't talk like that ever again."

"Yes ma'am."

We then stood and embraced. I needed a hug like there was no tomorrow – a motherly hug.

"Get tested again," she whispered softly. "I love you."

She then walked off toward her bedroom, probably to pray and to soak in what she had just learned about me.

*****

Over time I had become comfortable enough with Lazlo to introduce him to the No. 1 woman in my life – my mother. She liked him so much that she invited him over for dinner on numerous occasions, especially during holidays. He was really the only guy I was comfortable with bringing to my house. What really floored me was that my two brothers – known for being judgmental – even embraced Lazlo. They went so far as to tell him that they liked him better than any of the few other guys I brought to the house. So, it was no surprise that Lazlo would receive a distress call from my mother.

A storm was brewing.

My mother had contacted him worried about me. She had not heard from me, and I hadn't shown up for work in days. So, when Lazlo couldn't reach me, he went on a hunting expedition, zooming down Interstate 45 in his Maxima to the devil's den of Third Ward. I had revealed this area to Lazlo during one of my sober moments when I thought I had kicked the habit. I wanted to come clean with him and restart our friendship right.

As Lazlo exited the Scott street ramp, he faded into the dark roads of the ward, dotted with dilapidated homes, street-walkers, mangy and stray dogs – some missing legs – and other undesirables, such as vagrants. Trash and debris strewn everywhere depicted a community in disarray.

After an hour's search, Lazlo focused on a well-known crack house that was one of my several hideouts. He began to roll the mental tape in his head of the many lies told to him by me, his beau. There were so many untruths that Lazlo lost count of the number of times I vowed to never go down this road again with crack. I was convincing. I shed crocodile tears, often conning him and telling him "I love you." Lazlo didn't smoke, drink or do drugs – not even marijuana during his college days when so many other students would. So, it was easy for him to fall for my lies. He didn't realize that crack cocaine could be such a beast to defeat. But he tried anyway, even jeopardizing his life.

As he cruised 10 mph in his search, he inadvertently passed through a stop sign that was obscured by weeds and overgrown trees. A cop lying in wait noticed the violation by Lazlo, who stuck out like a sore thumb in this wretched neighborhood. The officer checked for outstanding tickets and warrants but found no rap sheet or blemish of any kind. The straight-laced Lazlo never even had a speeding ticket. So after being ticketed, he was steamed.

When he finally reached his destination and noticed my parked car in the crack-infested area, he exited his car quickly and angrily. For him, fear was not an option. And he proved he could handle himself. He put on a tough act: a no-nonsense attitude, strutting confidently and looking threatening through his fiery eyes.

He walked gallantly up to the house as he knocked on the door with his fist, getting the attention of an unsightly woman who came outside and sat on broken stairs with her hands between her thin legs trying to keep warm.

"I'm Miguel's brother. Is he here?" Lazlo pointedly asked with both hands in the pockets of his trench coat.

"Who the fuck is Miguel? You mean D-Low?" asked the woman, who instantly had a flashback to the time she first met me and I had introduced myself by my real name then before adopting a new 'hood identity.

"Yeah, D-Low," Lazlo answered in a combative voice, not knowing for sure if I used a street name whenever I prowled the 'hood.

"Say, Pee-Wee! Go Tell D-Low his brotha Lazlo out here, man. Say, dude, you gotta dollar?" the woman asked while he waited.

"For what?" Lazlo asked.

"To buy me something to eat, hell!" she demanded. "Pee-Wee! What's taking your mothafuckin' ass so long?" she yelled, coughing slightly, then spitting.

"Here's five dollars. I just want my brother outta here."

"D-Low said he don't know nobody name Larry," the drunken Pee-Wee said.

"My name isn't Larry; it's Lazlo, man!"

"God–. Excuse me, Lord," said the woman, cutting off her

comment and apologizing to God for her profanity and using his name in vain.

Lazlo was surprised to see her correct her language. Perhaps God is in this house somewhere, he reasoned, even inside this crack-addicted woman.

"I'll go get him, damn!" she screamed. "Mothafucking Pee-Wee. Sit your ass down somewhere, or go the fuck home!" she ordered.

This was Lazlo's opportunity to probe Pee-Wee.

"So, Pee-Wee, how long has Miguel been coming here?"

"Hell, man, we ain't seen him in about two years," Pee-Wee said as Lazlo noticed large holes in his soiled tennis shoes.

Then the woman returned.

"Look, man, D-Low is busy. He's not coming out here, dawg!" she said, standing in the closed screened door.

"Well, can I come in?"

"Hell nawl, man! The niggah busy. You need to get from in front of my house, man."

"Look, you tell Miguel, I'm gonna expose his ass, you hear!" Lazlo threatened.

"I ain't telling him shit, niggah. You need to get outta here," she said as she opened the screen door to confront Lazlo with a dirty baseball bat.

But Lazlo didn't flinch, telling the woman, "I'll shut this damn house down if you ever try to threaten me again."

For the first time, Lazlo had experienced the attitude of other crack-heads besides me. He realized these people were delusional, unmerciful, intolerable and extremely reactive.

With the money Lazlo had given her, the woman ordered Pee-Wee to buy her a nickle-rock from Fatboy.

"Fuck that food shit," she said.

Lazlo walked away, sadly amazed at the inner-city destruction.

*****

On the fourth day after Lazlo's search for me, I finally resurfaced. I listened to my answering machine and noticed that besides Lazlo's messages, my mom, the modeling agency and employer had called.

I wasn't expecting company, but someone was banging on the door after I retrieved all my phone messages. It was Lazlo. I could see the disgust on his face but he tried to appear composed. I opened the door; he stepped inside.

"So, Miguel, what happened?" he asked calmly as he stood staring into my eyes.

"I was arrested and went to jail." I lied.

"Oh, yeah. What jail?"

"The city jail."

"I called the city jail, and they said there was no one who fit your description there. I also called the county jail, too."

"Well, I was there." I lied again, which was a normal thing for me these days.

"Miguel."

"What?" I shouted and went to the kitchen as Lazlo followed.

"You're lying. Why can't you tell me the truth, man? Be a man, dammit, and stop acting like a DAMN child!" he shouted.

I brushed by him leaving him in the kitchen.

"Excuse you," Lazlo said.

"Look, I'm tired. I don't want to talk about this right now," I insisted as I walked toward the back bedroom with a cold glass of water. There was nothing else in the 'fridge to eat.

"I guess you don't want to talk about missing work either? Your job is worried about you, too, Miguel. Don't you care, man?"

"Lazlo. Not now!" I shouted, gritting my teeth out of frustration and guilt.

"You're gonna talk to me dammit. You may not talk to those jerks on your job, but you're gonna talk to me!" Lazlo screamed at the top of his lungs.

"OK! OK! Just stop tripping man!"

"Look at you, Miguel. You're filthy, and you smell."

"Look! Do you wanna talk or not?"

"Man, I left my wife for you. I love you. But I can't go through this kind of shit with you or nobody. This hurts, man. How could you go back to crack? How?" asked Lazlo as he sat next to me on my bed.

I wasn't comfortable with him being here, so I sat on the floor staring at the swirling ceiling fan.

I told him I didn't know why I did what I had done. I just knew I was tired and lonely as hell.

"What do you mean you don't know, man?"

" I ... I ... just tripped out. That's all. From all the pressure from ..."

"All of what pressure, Miguel?"

"Work, this relationship, money and all the other shit that keeps creeping up on me!" It was no wonder I was suffering because I hadn't been to an AA meeting or church in months.

"What shit? And what about our relationship? Are you saying you want out after all we've been through?"

"I'm not sure what I want, man. But I know I'm tired of dealing with a lot of issues, man."

"Issues! What issues? Talk to me, Miguel. Please! You're not making sense."

"It's hard, man. I was going to tell you a long time ago, but I had to talk to my mom first."

"Tell me now, Miguel!" Lazlo ordered. "What is it?"

"I'm positive, man. HIV positive."

Silence filled the room. Lazlo was speechless.

I got back on the bed to lie down. I was emotionally, physically and spiritually depleted from the drug.

"You're positive? How long have you known this? No, better yet, why did it take you so long to tell me, DAMMIT!"

"I was afraid you wouldn't want to be with me anymore, man. That's why. Damn. I'm so tired."

"Whose fault is that? I can't believe you kept something

like this from me."

"I was afraid, man! Can't you understand that?"

"No! Why should I understand you putting my life in danger?" Lazlo screamed and stormed out of the room.

"I'm sorry, man."

"Sorry is not gonna save our lives, man. Sorry is as sorry does. Don't you know when you smoke that stuff it hurts your immune system? Do you know that?"

"Yeah. I know that."

"So why continue to do this stupid shit, huh? And I know by now those people at your job have decided to replace your sorry ass, considering they've called four or more times looking for you.

*****

Miraculously, I began pulling myself together, thanks to the financial support from Lazlo. I was without a car, but I was able to maintain my credit card and apartment. I was still employable and working as an assistant technical coordinator and membership sales rep with a vehicle maintenance corporation. Once again I had bounced back from cocaine. I was still feeling guilty for destroying Lazlo's marriage.

After my 10-hour workday ended during an early sunny evening, I decided to kick back. Lazlo was out of town on work-related business in Atlanta. He forgave me for my sins and trusted me with his car during his absence. I needed transportation for job-related needs and personal affairs.

While en route to Starbucks to order a café mocha, I noticed an intriguing-looking dude at a Metro bus stop staring at me through the windshield of Lazlo's vehicle as I passed by. I affixed my eyes on him, acknowledging his "what's up" gestures.

When I backtracked I pulled over and asked if he needed a ride. I knew this could be dangerous, but I was a tough "niggah" from Southpark in Houston. I had come to realize that most guys have a nexus and that no matter how tough we pretended to be we were alike in so many ways. But I still did not forget what had happened to Patrick's former lover, Malcolm, who was killed by an unknown assailant. I am a risk-taker and a rebel, but cautious, too.

"Yeah, man," said the stranger, accepting the offer for a ride. When he talked I noticed a gold tooth with a studded diamond in the middle. He then identified himself as Alex.

Instantly, I was attracted to him. He was rugged, but not raggedy, ignorant or belligerent. He was also good-looking. On the other hand, my impression of Lazlo when we first met was quite the opposite. Sure, he was athletic, handsome, refined and conservative, but his style was more akin to hand-made suits, fine leather goods and high-performance vehicles such as Mercedes Benz.

I wasn't ready to embrace the clean-cut type yet.

Instead, I wanted to settle with a dude who was more thuggish – the kind like this stranger who wore his pants sagging slightly down his ass just enough to show a little of what he was working with. But what I wasn't attracted to was his oversized polo apparel and high-dollar tennis shoes. Now if this dude owned an IQ the size of a piece of lint, he was good only for a lay. All brawn and no brains just didn't cut it, either. And at first, it seemed that Alex's IQ and that little piece of lint might have something in common.

After coffee and an uninspiring conversation at the café with this brother, who said he played football at Texas Southern University, we headed to my place to become more acquainted.

"So, how long have you played ball for TSU?" I asked as we sat on the living room sofa listening to a Tupac selection from Alex's portable CD player.

"It's my third year," he said. "But I'm on academic proba-tion."

"Oh, yeah. Sorry to hear that." I wanted to ask why, but I opted not to be intrusive. "So what's your major?"

"Physical education," he said, gulping down his Heineken. After hearing that, I couldn't resist the thought that came to my mind. This niggah is majoring in P.E. and is on academic probation? What in the hell is he flunking: kickball, badminton or dodge ball? One thing for sure, I won't have to worry about competing against him or losing a game of "mental gymnastics."

But instead of belittling him, I played along. "That field can be lucrative if you land a college or NFL position somewhere," I said. As I talked to him, I noticed some movement between his legs. Was this niggah teasing me?

"What's up for the day?" I asked. As I stood, I developed an erection, too.

"It's your call. I'm down for the cause," he said, grabbing his pipe between his large thighs.

"Oh, yeah?" I asked.

"Yeah. Anythang, dawg," he said, sucking his gold-studded tooth.

For a few short seconds, my heartbeat raced as I stood face to face in front of this Tyson Bedford look-alike in my living room. He then lowered his bottled beer to the floor and boldly reached in front below my belt. He then gripped my ass. After that he unzipped my pants and swallowed my jimmy.

"This tastes good, dawg," he said. He then helped me remove my pants.

He wasted no time in removing his polo jersey over his cut-up body, displaying his eight-pack. After he got butt-naked, I observed his physique – massive thighs and a pipe so large that you wondered if it were an industrial-sized mechanical tool or an anaconda. Seriously, though, this boy was hung with a capital "H." I wasn't a dick fanatic, but I was taken aback by the size of this dude. Surely, he didn't think he would be laying this pipe anywhere near my ass. He would be out of his damn mind.

He had some other ideas, though. He led me to my dining

area and stopped at my weight bench, where I had left 125 pounds of iron on the bar. Alex then eagerly got on the bench and began to lift the mass as his naked body and hard jimmy became even firmer.

As I watched him do his thang, I was on fire. He was working my nerves.

He then ordered me to join him.

"Say, man. Sit on the front edge of the bench. I wanna show you somethin." He opened his large thighs, teasing me.

He then straddled my body, slowly easing down and pushing his buttocks into my thighs. Pretty soon the sex act turned into a circus act when he lifted the mass of weight toward the ceiling as I gently entered his warm opening. This fool was lifting weights and taking my jimmy at the same time. Damn!

"Don't tease me like that," he said. "Put that dick all the way in my ass," ordered Alex, as he then returned the weight onto the shoulders of the bench.

"Hold up, man," I said as I rushed from the bench to the bathroom to get the lubricant and condoms. When I returned he had positioned himself on the bench, lying on his stomach. I saw his massive thighs that were gapped as wide as the Grand Canyon. His large arms gripped the padded bench.

This entire scene was phenomenal and had me slightly nervous, but my hesitancy quickly vanished. That's when he turned and noticed my dark, naked physique and ordered me to spank him. He then faced the iron bar with his ass and thighs still gapped.

"Put Tupac back on, dawg. I like to take it when my niggah is spitting tunes."

I couldn't get to the stereo quick enough before I noticed he was entering his sex with his fingers, applying the cool lubricant for easy entry.

Yeah, this niggah is a fuckin' freak. I was down for that.

For the next forty minutes or so, Alex and I got into positions I didn't even know existed. We went up and down, in and out on that damn bench.

And then it happened.

He reached for something in his baggy pants. It was crack cocaine concealed in a brown glass vile and a glass pipe that he had wrapped in tissue paper to protect it like fine crystal ware.

*****

"Bring me my damn car, you sorry bastard!"

The message rang out from my answering machine as I stood in the living room wondering why I had fallen victim to my own rebellion and crack cocaine once again.

"I can't believe you left me at the airport waiting for your sorry ass! You have 24 hours to return my … " The message ended abruptly.

I returned Lazlo's car within 24 hours but was back in his graces within 36. I needed help, and Lazlo knew it. His few friends who were aware of our relationship called him a fool for dealing with a person like me. I was unfaithful and sick. He had invested a lot in our relationship and wasn't about to throw in the towel so quickly like most people had already done with me.

I loved the dude, but not as much as he loved me. A testament to my friendship is that I never put him in harm's way and never introduced him to the crack cocaine culture. I was protective of him, never wanting anyone to hurt him, even though I unintentionally caused him pain. Deep in my heart, I felt that I would die for that niggah. But, for now, crack had gotten the best of me; it was practically my full-time lover.

I knew I wasn't finished being chastised by the drug or, for that matter, my own demons. I still desired to experiment with behaviors that continued to cause me drama and emotional pain.

Chapter 29
"Stinking Thinking"

TGIF. I was anxious to start my weekend, so I was upset when I ran into computer problems near the end of my shift at the vehicle maintenance facility where I was working. At CUC International, a deep-pocket corporation, I was working as an assistant technical coordinator and membership sales representative. I was experiencing a troubleshooting problem with several computer VAX systems that had crashed that day. I was bouncing back and forth from my desk to the control room in an effort to correct the computer crashes. I was left with only one option, which was to alert the support desk in Trumbull, Connecticut. I was stressing over the problem.

But after some lengthy technical aid, the situation was corrected. It seemed that a glitch in the main deck servers had oscillated rather swiftly away from the normal eight-second intervals.

We were now back online, and I had a small break from my hectic day. But then the receptionist informed me of a phone call. It was Pamela from customer service. She was a supervisor and had been with the company for some years. We had been having a fling from time to time. She was good in bed but wasn't ready for a commitment, which was fine by me. She was petite, attractive and book smart with only one flaw:

a double nipple on her left breast. At first, it scared the hell out of me. So much so that I dreamed of being haunted and chased by a throng of circus freaks and disfigured people, such as a three-breasted woman and a schizophrenic hermaphrodite – a person with sexual organs of both male and female.

"Can you spare a few minutes, please? Two of my reps are experiencing problems with hearing their clients on their headsets. I think their batteries are low," Pamela said.

I told her I would check out the problem, which seemed minor. After a few simple adjustments, something that Pamela could have handled, the devices were working properly. And after some thought, I realized that she probably called technical support only because she wanted to see me or arrange a time for us to sleep together again.

In general, I often thought that most people had ulterior motives, with sex being the biggest. Even if that were so, I often obliged. Of course, this thinking error had often landed me in trouble. My drug counselors referred to it as "stinking thinking" – a way to suggest that I wanted to be the center of everything – that it was, indeed, all about me.

*****

I went to bed early after Pamela and I had hooked up for dinner. Sex wasn't on our minds. We just decided to enjoy each other's company and conversation. After dinner I dropped her off and then went home.

Around midnight, the telephone rang. I thought it might be my mother. Instead, it was Lazlo.

"What's up?" he asked.

I hate when people do that crap. What could he possibly think is up at this hour of the night? Either I was sleep or deep in someone's guts. He then finally told me he missed me.

"Well, Lazlo, you were the one who wanted to end it all. Not me." I realize I was being manipulative. "Anyway, why are you up so late?" I asked, as I sat upright.

"I couldn't sleep from turning and tossing, thinking about you. You know I'm still hurting."

"You don't think I'm hurting, Lazlo?" I said, playing with his emotions.

"I never said you weren't."

"You implied it. Why do you always throw that guilt shit in my face?" I asked, pretending to be upset and intentionally trying to start an argument to end the drama.

"I'm not throwing anything in your face. Do you have a guilty conscious about something?" Lazlo asked.

"Hell, no!"

"I can't tell considering the way you're acting. And besides, I didn't call to argue with you, man. I was just concerned."

"Concerned about what? Who I might have in my bed or maybe if I'm here doing drugs? Yeah. That's it. You think I'm doing drugs, huh?"

"You're tripping. That's not what I'm thinking. Actually I was wondering how your sessions were going with the therapist at the clinic."

"Yeah, right," I said sarcastically.

"What do you mean 'yeah right'? How are your sessions, man?"

"They're coming along." I decided to give him a straight answer this time. At least I owed him that much.

"That's all you have to say? You are sad, Miguel. Sad," Lazlo said angrily.

"Who in the hell are you calling sad, bitch? Don't you call my house with that crap!"

"Who are you calling a bitch, Miguel? To hell with you! You haven't changed at all. Fuck you!" Lazlo shouted, slamming the telephone.

That was the first time ever that I had referred to him as a bitch. Maybe I should have said bitch-ass or something – as if that would have been better. Anyway he didn't deserve that kind of neglect from me after all he had sacrificed. I was wrong.

*****

On Saturday, I decided to do something rare and hit a club called Incognito, located in the city's warehouse district. Upon entering I noticed male dancers atop speakers and on private stages. I fantasized about what a night would be like with just one of them. I approached the bar and ordered a drink as the New York-style house music blared. I then zig-zagged through the crowd in search of a willing soul who was down for just about anything.

"Shhhh!" A hissing sound caught my attention.

"What up fool?" the voice said. It was Patrick. "I didn't know you were coming out tonight. Nuts must be on fire, huh?" he joked. "As for me, I'm in search of a Dick!"

"Yeah, I forgot. Dick Anonymous couldn't cure you. Having a relapse?" I joked.

"Don't be messy, niggah. It will cost you a lashing I know you can't take," Patrick warned.

"I was just joking, man. I don't want any trouble," I said, trying to maintain peace. "Let me get you a drink. I need one, too, because right about now I'm about to jump that dude's bones over there on that box."

"He's good in bed, but he has just one fault. He tried to throw that ass on me. I didn't want it, but I did get what I paid for," said Patrick, who is a dick queen and had never been with a woman and never will.

As we sipped on our beverages, Patrick greeted one of his friends.

"What's going on Laurel?" Patrick asked.

Laurel was a full-figured dude with arched eyebrows and severe razor rash. He made my skin crawl.

"Recruiting baby, just recruiting," Laurel said, checking me out.

"A girl's work is never done, huh," Patrick replied. "Oh, by the way. Let me introduce you to a friend of mine. This is Miguel."

We swapped pleasantries. But when Laurel reached out to greet me with a soft handshake I took control and grabbed his hand firmly, hoping I had cracked the punk's knuckles.

"Not so hard, baby. You got to handle me with care. I'm not as hard as you," Laurel joked.

For some reason, he thought I was Patrick's trade.

I corrected him on that. With all the finger snapping and queen talk, I prepared to leave. But before I could, Laurel reached into his front pocket and gave me a business card.

"Take this if you're interested, and give me a shout. It'll be well worth it. Ta-Ta!" said Laurel, who was looking for dancers for his Boogie Fever Production outfit.

Was this Negro serious?

******

When I got home shortly after midnight I parked and sat for a moment in my rental car at my complex, thinking how lonely I was and about the offer Laurel had tossed my way. It was tempting. I figured if I took the gig it would be more out of vanity than anything else. Since I was getting older, I wanted to feel attractive and desired. But I considered exotic dancing to be so superficial and full of game. I wasn't sure if I wanted to do that. I really didn't need the money because I was making a decent salary. I was also re-establishing my credit history after being off crack cocaine. I decided to put the matter on the back burner.

After exiting my car, my heart began to flutter after noticing a white document taped to my door. I was stunned and at a loss for words at the bold, 30-point type. The top of the message read "Public Notice. And at the bottom it said, "Sexual Predator Lives Here!"

Lazlo immediately came to mind. How long had this crap been taped to my door? Who had seen it? And what was this all about? I became furious. I ripped the computer-generated notice from its post. After entering, I noticed that the stereo was still playing just as I left it and that Lazlo's paper assault wasn't over. Notices were also posted on my two front windows outside. So, I stormed back out of the front door and snatched the second postings from the panes, still wondering if anyone had seen them. Lazlo was bent on assassinating my character, what was left of it anyway.

I re-entered my apartment, slamming the front door, securing it and reading the rest of the posted message: "Warning! The occupant of this residence should be avoided at all cost. He is a sexual predator stalking men and is known to carry the HIV virus, which causes AIDS."

I leaped from the sofa about fifteen minutes later and snatched the black cordless receiver from its resting place. Even the speed-dial function wasn't fast enough for me as it automatically dialed Lazlo's phone number. I realized that in my last conversation I had provoked him, but I didn't think he could do something so low like this. It was so out of character for him. He had always tried to protect me at all cost.

Lazlo answered in a sad tone, confirming my suspicions that he was the culprit. I wanted to show mercy, but I could not find any.

"What in the hell do you think you're doing, man?" I asked harshly, with the intent to manipulate once again.

"I … I tried to get back there after I posted them, man, but I saw that you had already taken them down. So, I turned back and flew home to catch your call. I didn't want to see you then," he explained sorrowfully.

You damn right I was going to call. "You really want to hurt me, don't you?" I asked.

"I was angry because of the way you had been treating me, Miguel. Love shouldn't have to feel this way, man!"

"No relationship is held together simply by only one person's love, man. It takes strong partnership. I'm not connected or committed to anyone, Lazlo. Not even you. I realized that I have too many unfaithful desires. I just haven't been ready, man," I explained, hoping he understood.

"Why couldn't you have told me that from the beginning? I would have understood. You've caused us both a lot of unnecessary pain, man. Do you realize how much pain you've caused the people in your life who love you?"

"Yes, I do." But actually I had not realized it until this instant.

"When we first met I was attracted to your honesty, but right now it hurts to know that you've sacrificed truth, honor and friendship for a life of confusion. I guess we should stop the hurt, huh?" he asked, feeling somewhat at ease now.

"I guess you can put it that way. It sounds like a beginning of a redefined friendship. I'm willing to let bygones be bygones. I'm not mad at you just a bit disappointed and stunned. I suppose I did push you to the edge." It was hard for me to admit my wrongs, but I was learning. "My bad, Lazlo. I'm the one with the problem, not you."

For one of the first times in a long while, I had finally accepted responsibility for my actions.

Lazlo apologized for posting the notes and told me that it was out of spite. Of course I forgave him. I then sat on the floor and shredded the notices.

Chapter 30
Money and Power

Comedian Bill Cosby once said if given 200 active 2 year olds he could conquer the world.

There's truth to that statement because kids have a thirst for knowledge and are willing to take risks. And for years I have been acting like a rebellious big "kid" living on the edge and thinking life is all about me. If I would have channeled that energy into something positive, I could have been occupying a company's boardroom rather than a backroom, where I sat through another therapy session trying to learn how to improve my selfish behavior.

Observing the eyes and body gestures of my therapist, I sat and wondered if the blue-eyed, blonde yuppie really could help me. She wasn't an addict and had never used drugs. She was a recent college grad with a degree in social work and a certification in chemical dependency and counseling from Lamar State College.

"Miguel, are you still with me?" she asked, catching me day-dreaming.

"Yeah, I'm with you," I said, snapping out of my trance.

"I was asking if there was a reason for your guilt about your sexuality."

"It's the comfort factor, I guess. I'm not interested in revealing my sex life to strangers or even to some of my family members."

"That's understandable, but you have to deal with the fact that you are homosexual."

"I hate that word," I said in frustration.

"Why?"

"Because it doesn't describe me. I don't like labels. I'm human. I can't accept being labeled. I'm not an object."

"That's true. It doesn't describe you, only your sexuality, Miguel." She paused with a penetrating stare. "So that's the real issue. You are afraid of being labeled, correct?" she said.

"I guess that's true, counselor."

"Not counselor, just call me Jane," she insisted.

"OK, Jane," I said, smiling as she attempted to put me at ease.

"Now, we're getting somewhere. But keep this in mind, OK. Remember that your own insecurities and doubts will translate directly into the attitudes of your peers if you're not sure of yourself and goals. That includes your purpose."

As the session drew to a close, Jane gave me final instructions.

"Next week we will talk about resentments," she said. "So, be prepared. This was a good session today. I look forward to our next meeting."

*****

The following weekend Patrick and I had hooked up at my place to attend the Jones Hall Theater production of *"Le Ballet National du Senegal,"* an African show of music and dancing, storytelling, drum rituals. It also included partial nudity.

As I shaved in front of the mirror in my master bathroom, I listened to Patrick on the telephone venting and spewing expletives to someone about one of his female co-workers.

"I told you those bitches are no good!" Patrick said. "She knows the boy is an alcoholic."

He was speaking about his current male partner who

drinks rather heavily.

"But what does she do? She gets him drunk, sits on his dick and cries she's pregnant. That bitch is trying to take a niggah's trade," an angry Patrick said.

After he got off the phone, I chimed in.

"He was hers before you stepped in, right?" I asked.

"The boy approached me! I can't help it if he wanted some boy pussy," said Patrick, snapping his fingers.

"You're a sick puppy, man," I said, walking to my closet to find something to wear.

"She just couldn't stand the fact that the niggah is bisexual."

"I thought we agreed to stop using that word?" I asked.

"Excuse me. Is Negro more politically correct?"

I ignored him, realizing that he was being sarcastic as usual. "All men don't mess around, Patrick."

"I don't want to hear that! Give them a drink and a joint, and it's on. Besides, I'm not concerned with other men, only mine that that bitch tricked into bed."

"Stop calling women bitches, man!"

"When did you … well, just forget about it. Can I get a drink?" Patrick asked.

"You know where it is."

I was happy when the telephone rang. To quiet Patrick, I asked him to get the call for me.

DAMN! What a mistake.

"One Whore Productions!" Patrick said, answering my phone.

My mouth fell to my chest after hearing this fool answer my phone like that. I rushed out into the living room and grabbed it from him. What in the fuck was he doing answering my phone like that?

"Who is it, man?" I asked. I was hotter than a Latin plate lunch.

"It's your pimp, Laurel, from Boogie Fever Productions," he

said, laughing. "I saw the name on the Caller ID."

It was, indeed, Laurel. And Patrick, again, was in rare form.

I was now performing for Laurel's production company as an exotic male performer, but only on weekends and when time permitted.

Laurel had a gig for me. It wasn't one of those last-minute gigs. He needed someone for a gig that paid $250 an hour. It was for Alpha Kappa Alpha Sorority at Texas Southern University, and they wanted a dark, handsome type with a hint of sophistication.

"I'm down with the AKAs," I said. This would be my first official stripping gig.

"Great! I'll give you all the details later in the week. Ta-Ta!" Laurel said.

He was a real punk.

"You're hustling, now?" Patrick asked. He loved being a jackass.

"No, dancing. There's a difference," I said.

"You gonna do the private shows, huh?" Patrick asked, standing and leaning on the frame of the bedroom door doubting all my intentions.

"What private shows?"

"I'll set one up for us, and then tell me if it's dancing or hustling," he said, walking to the stereo. He flipped on some music featuring the heavy bass and voice of Scarface from the Geto Boys, singing *"Money and the Power."* Was he attempting to tell me something on the cool through music?

*****

The August heat was draining at Jamaica Beach. I had finally gotten over my fears about dancing and was anticipating my photo shoot. I was also ready for Patrick to differentiate between dancing and hustling. For the shoot, arranged by Laurel, I posed in tiny swimwear that was pasted to my body like a tight pair of shoes. Me and two other dancers were picked to pose for next season's calendar, "The Men of Texas

Uncensored." The other two dancers were from the Houston-based "Boogie Fever Productions." The sun was absolutely unbearable as the heat from the sandy beach scorched the bottom of my feet as I waited for the photographer to reload his camera.

The calming waves and breeze, however, brought some relief as I ventured out into the waters for another shoot and to cool off my body.

"Yeah, that's it. Just like that. Get that body wet," the photographer instructed. "Yes! Now kneel down and let the waves roll up behind you. Yeah! That's perfect."

I was no stranger to the camera, so I played the lens. I then seductively lowered my swimwear, slightly exposing the pubic area. Before long I was butt-naked, walking the beach, although concealing my front side with my trunks and catching the eyes of the two other dancers.

I was done. Now, it was time to see what my competition was packing. They were as fine as wine, but one of them had a grill so in need of repair.

Without a doubt, they were amateurs in front of the camera. But they were photogenic, light-skinned, muscular and willing to do what it took to get the job done. There was no way they were going to let me outdo them. They courageously disrobed, taking camera shots in every provocative position possible.

*****

A few hours later, I was back at my place. The phone rang disturbing my rest.

It was my mom calling, wondering if I were OK. I told her I was fine. She said she was going on a cruise next weekend for three days to the Bahamas and Nassau. She then asked about my health, sobriety, my medicines and my T-cell count, which had risen to 487 with an undetectable viral load. I told her those were good indicators, considering a T-cell count below 200 was considered to be critical.

I was taking a cocktail of AZT, 3TC and D4T, all of which were improving the lives of a lot of people.

*****

Hard Knocks Enterprises was a new player in the entertainment world of male exotic dancing in the Houston area. It was a creation of a former dancer from Boogie Fever Productions.

That same evening, hours after mom called, Patrick had hired one of Hard Knocks' dancers to prove his point of distinguishing dancing from hustling. I waited at my apartment patiently for his arrival. Patrick described him as a strong brother with urban flair. He also said he had nipples the size of dimes.

When the phone rang again it was Patrick asking me to buzz him.

I jumped from the sofa, dashed to the bedroom and gathered my $50 in ones and fives. If the dancer were as Patrick claimed, the fives were going to be placed in areas I wouldn't even let a niggah approach me when I'm performing.

I decided to relocate my jewelry since I didn't know my guest. Could he be a thief? I wasn't taking any chances. With the jewels safely secured, I dashed back into the living area, put in my After 7 CD and turned up the stereo. I immediately tracked to the first selection, *"Ready or Not,"* then heard a knock on the door. And surely, the song fit the occasion.

My guests arrived on time. I composed myself but was a little nervous about the evening.

I opened the door to let Patrick and his guest inside. He was a tough athletic type with familiar facial features that were mostly concealed by a baseball cap.

"What's up?" I said.

"I need a drink," said Patrick, making his way toward my bedroom instead of the bar. He was up to something. As he dismissed himself, he told the visitor and me to get acquainted. So we did.

"You don't remember me, do you?" the dancer said.

"No, not really. Have we met?" I asked, puzzled.

"La Strada's in River Oaks, a year or so ago?" He then lifted his cap from his smooth-shaven head.

"Eli?"

"In the flesh, dawg. Thought you would never see me again, huh?" He was an arrogant asshole just like the first time I met him.

Patrick, standing in the bedroom doorway clearing his throat, said, "I'll take that drink now."

When he returned to the bar area, he asked, "You remember Eli, don't you?" He knew damn well I did. Patrick could be very messy at times.

Eli rested his leather bag on the living room floor next to the sofa. Yeah, I remember the bastard, I said to myself. He was the one who said I was an old track queen that wasn't making it. Maybe he was right at that time, but this night he was in my domain and I was the one in control of the ship and its rudder. So, I ordered him to put his bag in the bedroom until we were ready for him. He was just another "hoe" who thought just because he was fine and good-looking he had it going on. He was a dime a dozen. Dispensable.

We have him all night," Patrick said. "Teach this 'hoe' a lesson. Let's show him how it feels to be pimped. He's dumb as donkey dung and will do anything for that green money, man. I mean anything," Patrick said.

Eli entered the room and sat on the sofa.

Yeah mothafucker enjoy yourself while you can, because in a few more minutes you're mine, I told myself.

"You want a drink?" Patrick asked Eli.

"Yeah, I'll have some of that Chivas Regal. I understand it's Miguel's favorite," he said.

It was obvious that Patrick had been running his big mouth and perhaps coached him on my likes and dislikes. I wasn't tripping because actually I found it funny.

"So you like money and power, huh?" I asked.

"What else is there, dawg?"

"How about some peace of mind," Patrick said.

"I'm down for that one," I said. But what I really wanted to say was that I was down for a piece of that ass.

Nearly two hours had passed and Eli was lying on my living room floor next to the Bose stereo, preparing his music. He was right where Patrick wanted him to be, inebriated and gullible.

"So, you fellows ready for a show?" asked Eli, somewhat sluggish.

"Been ready," answered Patrick as he pulled out a roll of bills.

The Tommy Hilfiger briefs peeping from Eli's baggy jeans showed a chunk of ass so fine that I knew it was going to be a long night. Patrick had already told me that he could take dick from the back like a champ, better than any female.

I moved the coffee table and prepared for the show. I was a bit smashed, too, from the liquor.

Eli then stood, stared and patted my hard abs. He then asked me to crank up the CD player on his cue.

After a few minutes, I dimmed the fluorescent lamp next to the sofa. Patrick reminded me again that he was going to prove the difference between dancing and hustling. Actually, I didn't give a crap. All I wanted was a chance to get into Eli's guts and tame his arrogant ass. He needed to be humbled, and I had the remedy. Hopefully when he meets another stranger he'll know when to keep his big mouth shut.

The knock on the door sounded, and he entered. Patrick and I were about to be entertained.

I muted the television, but Patrick asked that it be turned off. I pressed play on the CD and took my seat.

The voice from the Bose speakers flooded the room.

"*Don't Worrrr-y!*" The lyrics dragged. *'I-Won't-Hurt-You.'*
Eli then slowly entered the living room dressed in pure white

as if he were an angel. He wore a set of white wings that dangled toward the floor and covered his frontal area.

"Pegasus!" the demonic voice called out as Prince's *"International Lover"* cast a spell over us and Eli triggered our hormones.

He then seductively spread his wings, revealing a form-fitting one-piece white body suit. Eli, aka Pegasus, stood with his huge thighs tightly closed. His hardened sex leaped through the white outfit. He began to grind and twist. Damn, the boy was good.

"Take your time, child," screamed Patrick, as he removed the rubber band from his roll of bills and pulled a twenty from its stack. He then trapped the money into the zipper of his 501 jeans.

That's when Eli released his wings, made a 360 degree turn and displayed his tight buttocks. He teased us with his muscles, thighs, calves and his irresistible ass cheeks.

Damn! I couldn't help but scream. I reached into my pocket placed a $5 bill behind my right ear and then my left, watching Eli's every move.

He first approached Patrick, who grabbed Eli's ass just like I would have done.

Eli then slowly kneeled between Patrick's legs and scooped up the $20 bill from Patrick's zipper with his teeth and lips. He grabbed my hard jimmy as I sat there excitedly watching his skills.

Patrick leaned over toward me and whispered, "dancing or hustling?"

He made his point. I then reached over and rubbed Eli's bald head as he came up for air and crawled over to my end of the sofa, where my legs were spread wide.

He began to lower the top of his body suit, exposing his large chest and huge hard nipples that Patrick had advertised.

"Damn!" I shouted, excited by Eli's chest and nipples. Patrick was right. I'd never seen a man or woman with nipples so large. I touched them. "Good gobbledygook," I said.

As Eli disrobed, Patrick urged me to "suck 'em." And like a starved pit bull, I attacked ferociously.

After I finished feeding on his hard mammary glands, Eli stood to his feet with his body suit down to his ankles. He wore a strapless dick sock, or G-string, as it was called.

"So, what do you think of the private dance so far?" Patrick asked.

"What dance?" I asked, watching Eli untangle his suit from around his ankles to get on with the show. By the time he had ditched his bodysuit to reveal his goods, Prince's song ended.

I couldn't contain myself and leaped off the sofa with a hard-on. I placed two $5 bills between my teeth and brushed the opening of Eli's ass with the tip of the green money.

Patrick then placed four $20 bills down Eli's spine as he remained kneeled and lowered to the floor. He surprised me when he assaulted Eli's lips with his wad of cash.

"Money and the power, child," Patrick said as he snapped his fingers and grabbed Eli's' hard sex. He then urged me to "slap that ass."

"He loves it, Miguel. He's a freak. Go ahead. Slap it."

"Whack! Whack! Whack!" I was turned on by the spanking.

Then to my surprise Eli gave meaning to sadomasochism by punishing his own cheeks.

Patrick looked at me again.

"Dancing or hustling? Which is it?" he asked.

As more music played and the slapping continued, Eli proved that he was a hustler. And he was in for a long and bumpy night.

Chapter 31
All Caught Up

The cool September air blowing outside on the back atrium of the tinted blue-glass, 10-story building was a perfect location for a lunch break at CUC International, where I had been working for a while now.

I noticed Ruth Spears, a co-worker, outside smoking a cigarette. She was still fuming about having been demoted. She had been ordered back to the sales phones because as a consultant supervisor she didn't net the results the company expected. Many of the consultants she supervised and trained were ill-prepared. They didn't know proper data coding for computer software, had difficulty accessing client data on their computers in a proper time frame and provided misinformation. Also, several of her workers lacked knowledge of products and services used by the company's clients.

Ruth's anger spread to me.

"Look at him," she would say. "He thinks he's big shit because he's off the phones now. He'll be next to go. Just wait and see."

Since I knew she had a vendetta against me, I went back inside the building and watched as her eyes followed my every move. I went to the employee cafeteria and took a seat next to Belinda, a rotund sister, who was also attracted to me. Like Pamela, my occasional hookup, Belinda also worked in customer service. She was sitting in the room waiting on her microwave popcorn. Her thickness attracted me, and she was fun to be around. We had fun in the past teasing one another from time to time.

"How are things in customer service?" I asked.

"You know the routine. Call after call after call," she said avoiding my eyes, giving more attention to the candy bar on the table.

"I want to tell you something, so please take it to heart, OK?"

"Sure," I said.

"Watch your back. Be on alert for Ruth. She's jealous of the fact that you're progressing in the company, and she's back on the telephones. So, watch out."

"I'm on to her, but thanks. I've noticed that all Ruth's responses to my questions are always dry and rude."

"You're good people, Miguel. I don't want to see you caught up in any mess with Ruth. She'll bite you like a snake. Her venom is lethal. You hear me?" Belinda warned. "I gotta go. Call me later." She winked and then left.

Since I had left work earlier than normal, heading into downtown, I decided to surprise Lazlo with a late lunch.

He and I still remained friends despite the ugliness of our past relationship. Much of the anger had subsided. I still feel, though, that he had allowed fears and doubts to stunt his progress in some areas.

Nevertheless he didn't look back as much as I did.

He was elated to see me when I reached the lobby of his office. When we dated I used to bring him lunch periodically. It was my way of showing appreciation.

I invited him to join me for lunch at the City Hall mall, but his schedule wouldn't allow him to join me. He was working hard on some deadline projects, so he took a rain check.

*****

As I made my way up the stretch of Interstate 45 toward

Dallas for a night at football star Deion Sanders' club, Prime Time, my heart was heavy because the most unimaginable thing had happened. I was accused of verbally abusing co-worker Ruth. She was the same woman I had been warned about. She was now more determined as ever to have me dismissed by falsely claiming she feared for her safety.

I objected to her bogus claims because she provided no concrete proof of a dangerous confrontation. We had exchanged some words weeks before, but nothing profane or threatening. The dispute never escalated to a physical altercation, but apparently she exaggerated the story. As a result, Human Resources informed me that in order to maintain the safety and integrity of the company it was in their best interest to terminate my employment. They feared the possibility of a harassment lawsuit and negative publicity. I didn't contest the decision by threatening legal actions because I thought the allegation was a crock of shit in the first place.

Ruth had concocted an evil plan and prevailed. While I had focused on ignoring her, she was busy strategizing. She definitely outwitted me. For a brief moment, I let my temper override my self-control and it cost me my job.

*****

Dallas' Prime Time club was a classy place and host to the city's elite and athletic professionals. It was hopping. A sign in Deion's club warned that G-strings were prohibited. Only full or athletic-cut swimwear was allowed during rare performances by male and female dancers.

Some of the regulars had their favorite dancers, who showcased their skills one by one. Several of our New York-based male dancers were not pleased with the restrictions on G-strings and "tie-ups" by management at Prime Time. They were used to stripping down to the 'G' and then to the bare.

"Sorry, no hard dicks here," the dressing room coordinator told the two New York dancers. "Dancers don't strap or tie up here at Prime Time. We try to keep it as legal as possible, fellas," he said staring at their sizes.

"You guys are slow in Texas," said Intrepid, repositioning his chunk of meat.

"We're not slow. It's the law in Texas. Blame the law, dawg – not the player," the coordinator said. "By the way guys, the finale is after the next act. So, be ready. And no straps."

A whacking sound echoed through the room as a rebellious Intrepid flapped his hard jimmy from side to side at the coordinator. This caught everyone by surprise.

"See, no strap here. I'll be natural," Intrepid said.

"Sure, Intrepid. Please be natural, Girl. Maybe one of those Dallas Cowboys will give you what you want … a dick! Oh! I meant money. Or did I?" The coordinator then popped his fingers and exited the room, leaving Intrepid embarrassed.

"Faggot!" Intrepid shouted.

"Man, stop trippin'! He's only doing his job," I said. One thing I had learned about dancers: Attack their masculinity and ego, and they are crushed.

*****

"Nice show," said a female patron, observing me closely as I stood close by brushing away lint off the left sleeve of my Yves Saint Laurent Royal blue, Italian wool jacket.

I also noticed her looking at my stainless steel Raymond Weil Allegro watch.

"Yeah, thanks. I'm glad you enjoyed it?" I said, looking at the stranger as she sipped her cocktail, displaying a stunning yellow-gold diamond bracelet and matching Cartier watch.

"To the fullest," she winked. "What are you drinking?" she asked softly.

"Chivas and Seven, little ice," I said, smiling brightly and wondering how old she was. The beautiful perfectly attired Cappuccino-color woman in a black, strapless dress appeared to be in her 30s or early 40s. After I introduced myself to her as Miguel Morris, instead of using my stage name, she felt more comfortable and told me to call her Monica.

I wondered why she was here and whether her jewels were real.

Instantly, she signaled the bartender, and in a flash he arrived.

"Chivas and Seven. Little ice, baby," she requested seductively, then winked at me again.

"More Cardon Negro?" the handsome bartender asked her. She nodded yes, drank the remainder of her champagne and got back to business.

"So, M&M is your stage name, right?"

"Yes."

"How old are you, baby?"

"Old enough. I'm a big boy. Don't worry," I said proudly, staring into her dazzling mouth of white teeth.

"Let me see your ID?" she asked, reaching out with her right hand.

"Sure. But I'm warning you. I look younger than my age. I hope that's not a problem," I said, reaching into my jacket pocket.

"Hmmm! 1959. So you're not lying. That's a brownie point in your favor. Hooray for you," she said, returning my wallet.

After we got our drinks, our conversation continued.

"So, how did you get the stage name M&M? No, let me guess," she pleaded. Miguel Morris is your name. So, that must be the obvious combination."

"That's a brownie point for you. I like a woman who's attentive and astute, not to mention beautiful."

"Now, it's my turn again. Since we're here attempting to get acquainted, I was just wondering M&M. Are you plain or peanuts?"

She then reached into her small shoulder Gucci leather black purse, then applied a peach-color lip balm to her full lips.

"Nuts, of course," I answered, taking a sip of my cocktail.

"Do you like surprises?" she asked.

"Of course," I said.

"Good! Five hundred dollars and no questions, deal?" she said, signaling the bartender. "Are you really Mr. M&M with nuts, baby?"

"Are you married?"

"Remember, I said no questions. Shhh! It's a secret." She whispered a few words and then signed the credit voucher. "Oh, and that Intrepid dancer ... I wonder if he's bold and courageous? Bring him along with you. Remember, no questions. Shhh!" She warned once more, waiting for me to make things happen.

It was finally my opportunity to see what Intrepid was really made of because I was really curious about this New York "trash-talking hustler." Now I would have a chance to witness if he would display femininity or masculinity. He talked tough. Now was his chance to prove it when he's not around his "dawgs."

*****

The sounds of *"If You Really Wanna Party With Me"* by Buster Rhymes pumped from the lavish North Dallas home in an upper bedroom of our mysterious hostess. Even Intrepid was a bit amazed by her craftiness as she rested on a queen-size carved cherry poster bed undressing and revealing her coal black Victoria Secrets bra, panties and garter belts that gripped her voluptuous thighs. Surprisingly Ol' Girl didn't have any imperfections such as spider veins, cellulite and sagging breasts like some older women. There was a hidden agenda here, and I sensed it would be revealed soon. Minutes after she stood butt-naked in front of us, we noticed her big dick "husband," who appeared to be about 10 years younger, rolling a camcorder.

For 20 minutes she seduced the camera and then joined in with Intrepid as her partner recorded our orgy. I wasn't tripping, and I wasn't asking any questions, even as her man's Texas-size cock saluted us.

"Damn!" he shouted. "You guys look edible behind those disguises." The couple, wearing black Mardi Gras-style masks, had asked Intrepid and me to wear Long Ranger silk masks. It was a good idea I thought, because it's better to protect identities and reputations.

There was no question this guy was an athlete.

After a few more minutes of foreplay with his video camera, 'Ol' Girl' ordered her endowed "Hangman," as I called him, to put down the camera and join the action.

"Bold and Courageous and Full of Nuts, huh?" she said, describing Intrepid and me to her "husband" as he entered the pillow-filled area attacking her breasts with his tongue. "Take those "Gs" off and get in the bed!" she ordered.

I didn't care much for her tone, but Ol' Girl was paying us well to do our thing. So, I kept my big mouth shut and followed along. My heart skipped beats as I watched Intrepid peel off his "G" from his hairy body and entered the bed with a full hard sex. I was a little uneasy, so my nerves killed my sexual desire when I peeled my "G" and entered the right side of the bed next to our host and hostess.

"Where's your nuts, M&M?" she said, teasing.

At that point I knew I had to prove myself. So I watched Intrepid and then her "husband" attack her soft breasts and calves as she lie moaning. That was the act that caused my jimmy to grow. Now let's see who can really hang.

"Ooooh! Aaaah!" she wailed.

Without notice, her sexy light-skinned beau grabbed my hard jimmy and placed his warm mouth over it, swallowing it whole and mumbling incoherently. Maybe he had indulged in more than he could handle.

With Intrepid's cherry Popsicle ass saluting me and ready for entry, I grabbed it like a fox in a henhouse as he sucked Ol' Girl's toes. Mr. Hangman released his lips from my hard sex and immediately attacked the hairy opening of Intrepid with his tongue. Yeah, Intrepid was all game. He was lying there with legs wide open and still sucking Ol' Girl's toes while being primed for a sticking by Mr. Hangman, whose features became more apparent after he exited the bed to check the video camera. He then grabbed a fist full of condoms and lubrication from the cherry-wood dresser nearby.

Without a doubt he was a professional football player here in Dallas. His profile and mannerisms became more apparent as I observed his movements. I just couldn't place his name. I had hoped that his mask would fall off during his "gymnastics" in bed, but he made sure it stayed securely fit on his face.

"Now the fun begins, boys," Ol' Girl whispered through the slow sounds of the music. She then reached into the right nightstand putting several $100 bills atop the drawer, placing the money next to the condoms.

A *grand* in cash sure looked good at that moment.

"OK, who's first?" she asked.

"The hairy one first," Mr. Hangman suggested. He applied the sticky gel to his mass.

I could almost hear Patrick's voice: "Dancing or Hustling, Miguel?" he would ask. The voice taunted me for a while as I watched the familiar-faced brute slowly approach a submissive Intrepid. Hmmm, the coordinator back at the club was right about him. Well, I wasn't tripping. I wanted some of those beefcakes myself. I was caught up once again in the madness of my behavior as I watched the masked, massive booty bandit place Intrepid on his knees and eased himself closer into Intrepid's warm opening. That's when 'Ol' Girl' pulled a silver platter from beneath the poster bed and revealed a substance that kicked me straight in the stomach.

I watched her put that crap on that "glass dick" and inhale. I was speechless. I simply followed the flow, even if it meant inhaling that poison again, which I wanted to do anyway.

When she passed the pipe to Intrepid, I was surprised that he hit it like a pro. He was definitely versatile in at least two things – taking dick from the back and smoking crack. But there was one thing I was sure about. It would soon be my turn to hit that crap and satisfy Mr. Hangman. There was no way he was going to take no for an answer. He had the best of both worlds: his female protégé and two hot male dancers not afraid of the camera and willing to endure his oversized jimmy.

And as my time approached to be stuck, I finally realized just how hung the niggah was. Damn him!

Woe is me!

Chapter 32
The Devil Made Me Do It

When a demon is cast out of a man, it goes to the deserts, searching there for rest; but finding none, it returns to the person it left, and finds that its former home is all swept and clean. Then it goes and gets seven other demons more evil than itself, and they all enter the man. And so the poor fellow is seven times worse off than he was before. (Luke 11:24-26)

*****

October was still hurricane season in Houston, and I was experiencing my own violent whirlwind. My life had deteriorated miserably. I was in full-blown denial about my addiction, and still hadn't recovered from last month's Dallas fling, which became a regular gig. Apparently, Intrepid and I had become Mr. Hangman's favorite exotic performers. I began to feel like a whore. I was so deep into the game again that I was not sure if recovery were possible.

My money was funny. I was down to my last thousand. Bills were due, and rent was going to take half of that. I needed a hit. Not a $20 rock, but an ounce. It would take at least that much to satisfy my craving and reach a high. And that would cost me at least $600. With that amount, I wouldn't indulge alone. I would seek out the likes of Intrepid or Alex, the TSU student athlete.

The amusing thing I discovered about Alex was that he liked to take the jimmy from the back while performing oral sex on a female. I had done that with him once but was uncomfortable with a woman being in my mix. That's the reason I had refused to go back to Dallas to hook up with Ol' Girl and Mr. Hangman. I grew disinterested after a few trips and decided to cancel future invitations.

With little money, no job or dancing gigs scheduled, my problems magnified. I needed a quick cash flow.

When I heard the telephone ringing Tuesday afternoon I was in no hurry to answer. So, I first slowly walked across the room to return a self-empowerment book onto the shelf between two keepsake novels, Nathan McCall's "*What's Going On*" and E. Lynn Harris' "*And This Too Shall Pass.*" After a few more rings, I reached for the cordless phone and answered.

It was Patrick. I hadn't heard from him in a minute. I had been trying to put distance between us. So, if he weren't talking money, I didn't need him. I answered to see what he wanted.

"What's up, Patrick?" I said dryly.

"Just checking on you. Where have you been, and what have you been up to?"

"Surviving. So, what's up?"

"How was Dallas?"

"I don't want to talk about Dallas."

"Is there a reason why you don't want to talk about Dallas? What happened up there?"

"I don't want to talk about Dallas, Patrick!" I said with a hint of anger.

"Are you all right?"

"I'm fine, man," I said lying. "I'm just a little frustrated right now. I need time alone for a while to sort out some things. You know how I am when I'm out of work. I need to work, dawg. Things aren't happening quick enough."

"Are you sure that's all there is?"

"Yes, I'm sure, man! What else could there be?"

"I'm gonna say this, and I'll let you go. Get yourself under control, please! Regardless of what has gone on between us in the past, you have to deal with it and move on, man. You're not the only man out there who's going through hell over your sexuality."

"I ain't tripping man about no sex. I just need time alone, OK?"

"Sure, Miguel. Hating yourself for enjoying sex with a man is going to destroy you. You can have both, you know. Talk to somebody if you can't talk to me. Anyway, I love you, man," Patrick said, surprising me. He'd never said that to me before. But if he really loved me he wouldn't take me out there on those sexual expeditions - even if it were my choice. He never tried to discourage me.

Truth is, I almost felt hatred toward Patrick as much as I hated myself for my failures.

I quickly ended the call.

*****

Not surprisingly, I found myself on the "Cut" again - the back alleys of Third Ward. This was the devil's playground, and I was seeking my next prey. Soon, my first victim appeared. The bold, muscular dude from TSU trudged down a crack alley.

I got his attention by blowing my horn from a rental car that was long overdue. I needed the transportation. When I finally got Alex's attention he ignored me. It was obvious he didn't recognize the car, so I caught up to him. It was amazing how he still managed to keep up his appearance despite hanging out on the streets so often. He was clean, had a fresh cut and a bright smile.

"Say, dawg! What's up?" I said.

"Long time no see, my niggah," he said, approaching the white Buick Regal.

I unlocked the door for him to enter. We both agreed that we were in no hurry. I always wondered why he never tried to get into the modeling business, but I realized, he probably didn't have a good support network. We were both down for whatever, but we first stopped at Popeye's Fried Chicken for a three-piece dinner with red beans and rice. And afterward, we shot by Starbucks to chill before the start of our freak show later.

The Montrose-area Starbucks was busy on this Halloween night as Alex and I waited patiently to order my favorite, Café Mocho. I suggested a Café Latte with a double shot of Irish crème for ol' boy since it had a slight kick to it.

We settled at a table by a window to view the traffic and action on the boulevard and to engage in a rare conversation. I really thought I had nothing in common with him, but I was wrong. Neither one of us had significant income, although my finances were better than his. We both were non-heterosexual crack addicts. But Alex was different than other men I'd hustled. He was masculine, handsome, raw in nature and just all-out fine. He didn't talk much, but that was fine with me.

We sipped coffee and enjoyed a box of chocolate-covered coffee beans and almonds. The issue of sex kept surfacing, but I made it clear to Alex I was in no hurry.

"Check this out, my niggah. When was the last time you had some pussy?" he asked.

Alex was one of those guys who loved to talk about having sex with a female just to validate himself. He was trapped like me in a life that was full of pain and self-hatred.

"Just last month," I said, referring to my trip to Dallas. "Why?"

"Just wondering, dawg."

"When was your last time?" I asked.

"You mean some good pussy?"

"Yeah."

"About three months ago from this Delta honey on campus."

"Yeah. So what makes pussy so good, Alex?"

"The three T's, dawg!"

"The three T's? What's that?" I wondered.

"The touch, the texture and the taste of it. See, it's like this," he said, leaning toward me. "When you first caress that monkey and the hairs are soft and silky, that's the touch. First base. Then when it's plump and full of texture, moist and wet, that's second base. And then comes third base. The taste of it must be like pure spring water, no preservatives or additives. You know what I mean? That's good pussy – sweet pussy, my niggah. Three-T pussy," he explained. He then leaned back and resumed his regular posture while taking another sip of coffee.

The fool was turning me on right then and there. A piece of "monkey" sounded just about right at that moment. But my interests were elsewhere. "So, that Delta girl had some good monkey, huh?"

"The best monkey I ever had."

"So, tell me. What makes the ass so good?" Male or female?" he asked, sucking his gold tooth.

"Male, of course."

"Why don't you tell me, dawg. What makes that ass so good?" Alex asked, touching his crotch.

He wanted to do the word game, so I played along.

"Let's go, and I'll show you how I rate good ass," I said, grabbing my cell.

"That's a bet, dawg."

*****

"Good morning, Miguel Morris, this is Clare Pecacello of Home Entertainment from the human resources department in Houston. I received your resume by fax, and I would like to speak to you concerning an interview. Call me at 281-555-8900. Goodbye."

The next message played.

"Hi. This is Wendy Elterman of Circuit City. I'm trying to reach Miguel Morris, please have him contact my office concerning his resume. My phone number is 713-555-2222. Thank you."

After listening to my automated answering service, I rested flat on my warm bed in torment and guilt from my drug-induced mess the night before. Alex was in the bathroom washing up, and I was still trying to think of a quick way to make cash, aside from the job prospects.

The first of November was cool and pleasant, but my finances were a hot mess. I had lost my appetite and suffered weight loss from heavy drug use. Anxiety didn't help either. The thought of money consumed me. I called my bank's automated teller and discovered just how much my life was in disarray. I learned that I had numerous overdrafts. I slammed the receiver after hearing about insufficient funds.

Checks for the rent and telephone had bounced. My Providian credit card only had $75 in available credit, and the next payment was already due. My debt had compounded. I needed money.

"Shit!" I shouted. "No fuckin' money!" That's when Alex exited the bathroom, apparently hearing me grouse. With all that was going on, I got temporary relief from his presence. It helped that he was fully nude. Sex would be good right about now, I thought.

*****

On a rainy November 15, a bank robbery occurred as a black Nissan Maxima flew past several vehicles on the far West Houston beltway.

As the suspect fled, a rap song called *"The Hands of the Devil"* by 8 Ball played on the stereo. Fortunately for the bandit, the moneybag from the heist didn't appear to have transmitters or dye packs. So, he managed to get away.

The cool and rainy weather made conditions ideal for the caper he pulled during the heavy-traffic lunch hour. Efforts by law enforcement officials to foil this robbery were futile.

The assailant then entered a members-only health club after his card was scanned, then proceeded to a back dressing room. He checked the money once more for transmitters. Seeing there was none, he stuffed the athletic bag into a long locker and secured it.

Still wearing the same gear worn during the robbery, he exited the dressing room and entered the workout area, where he then took off his Nike rain suit that protected his Spandex tights and long-sleeved cotton top. To calm his nerves and ease his mind, the assailant ran around the padded track as if all were normal. But there was a noticeable guilt.

"How could you rob a bank, Miguel?" I asked myself when I passed my mirrored image. Lap after lap, it was getting harder to look at myself.

Days later, I used the lame excuse that the devil made me do it. I was still caught up in unlawfulness and found myself back in the ghetto of Third Ward.

This time my boy, Alex, was missing when I sat in a back room of a wood-frame crack house. I had also rejected all job offers from the previous days, except for one, the Gourmet Coffee Café. It was a part-time managerial position.

While in the 'hood, I sensed an omen in the kitchen of the crack house, where me and several other users indulged in a masochistic act of smoking crack cocaine like there was no end. A spooky fellow, tall and dark – who resembled a Louisiana witch doctor – stood behind a well-worn stove stirring a strange concoction of smelly broth. He placed a Corona bottle filled with clear liquid in the middle of a steel pot that simmered over a fiery flame.

He stared at me and asked, "What's up?" Oddly, he called me by my name, and I didn't remember revealing my identity.

I said nothing; he just grinned and continued his work. Whatever he was brewing I didn't want any part of it. I had

had my share of crack and was already suffering hallucina-
tions. But out of curiosity, I asked him what was brewing.

"A little somethin' somethin'," he said, grinning again and
shaking the Corona bottle. "There, it's ready."

After he raised the bottle from the steel pot, the clear liquid turned royal blue.

This "witch doctor," or whatever he was, puzzled me. I was
very uncomfortable. I tried to relax by engaging in small talk
with him. I wondered if he practiced voodoo.

"How long have you been cooking, dawg?" I asked.

"Long enough, dawg," he answered. Then he blew steam
from the long-necked Corona bottle in my direction.

An awkward feeling came over me, so I walked to the front
half of the wooden house to get some air. I was becoming
faint. I didn't know if I were just imagining things or if he
were hexing me.

"Where you going, dawg?" he asked with a sinister laugh.

I lied and said it was hot, and I needed some air. I didn't
want him to think that I'd been spooked. I didn't believe in
spells and crap, but his brewing was making me nervous. I
stood and stared into the heavens from the front porch. I was
desperate to find release, but instead I was ushered back into
the house by an unknown force for another hit of crack.

*****

Thanksgiving had passed and I had managed to pull myself
together for that day and spend time with my family and
some true friends such as Lazlo. He noticed my weight loss
immediately. Mom, too, but she remained silent. I guess she
had hoped that her suspicions about my continued drug use
weren't true, despite the "white elephant in the living room"
syndrome.

Anyway, I was off work this particular evening and had
taken a shower. I got a haircut and facial. I actually began feeling better about myself. I had paid my bills, had food in the
fridge and a new job – even if it were part-time. I still hadn't

dealt with my addictions, though.

During another cool and rainy day, I strolled into the breezy downtown tunnel used by patrons for underground shopping and eating. I was dressed in a fashionable thigh-length black leather Italian jacket and matching baseball cap, with a caramel crewneck sweater that highlighted my black corduroy pants. Even though I was hit with hunger pangs after skipping breakfast, I continued on my venture and walked past several eateries and coffee shops. I wanted to meet my scheduled deadline. With only minutes away, I began fumbling in my black leather business tote to retrieve my checkbook and day planner. I stood at one of the bank's two kiosks, where deposits and withdrawal slips were kept. I signed one of the documents and waited patiently in line for the teller to call me.

"Good morning," she greeted.

"Morning. How are you?" I asked, somewhat in a trance. I then presented her with my withdrawal slip. She read the warning on the document indicating this was a bank robbery: "You have forty-five seconds. Hundreds and Fifties only," I said softly, not wanting to draw attention.

"Yes, sir," she replied nervously, filling piles and piles of wrapped large bills on top of the granite counter.

The robbery note scared us both. I then stared once again at the note, the money and camera, which filmed my half-hidden face from underneath the black leather baseball cap I wore as camouflage. I broke the seals from the hundreds and fifties, making sure the money was free of transmitters or dye packs.

Seconds later I made a fast exit on a nearby escalator with an undetermined amount of cash. I swooped out of the building onto the wet street. I quickly ditched my hat, jacket and black leather tote that had concealed a much smaller brown tote that I kept. I tossed the other stuff onto the back of a truck in a parking lot. A waiting Metro bus became my getaway vehicle.

Oddly, I was the only passenger aboard that early morning. The driver pulled off after I paid my dollar fare. I avoided the back seat so as not to raise suspicion. I checked one of the stacks of money again and discovered the teller had inserted a bundle of $1 bills covered with $20 bills on each individual stack. I also noticed a transmitter in the middle of the pack. To avoid being apprehended, I stuffed the whole damn thing in the crease of the seat and rang the bell to get the hell out of dodge before "5-0" made a visit. When I exited the bus I noticed a series of sirens. I maintained my cool, waited for the light to change and then crossed the street with the brown tote over my shoulder.

Within the hour, I was back in Third Ward at the motel where I had rented a room for three hours. I got in my rental car and headed back to West Houston, avoiding capture for the second time. This time I didn't feel as guilty. I was getting better at this. I changed clothes once more when I arrived home.

Minutes later I headed to Bank One, made a deposit and then went to the mall, where I purchased a pair of Nike shoes, a leather bomber jacket and a watch. I still had $4,000, but I was certain that I would need more dollars soon.

In the midst of a crumbling world, I could not even remember the last time I had been to church or called out to God for help. I knew that I needed Him, yet I felt He was allowing me to suffer until I was ready to make a conscious effort to change my wicked ways.

With only 20 days until Christmas, I decided that I wanted a steady man in my life. I realized that only after I had left work and entered another bank. I had eluded authorities for the sixth time in less than two months. But this time was different than the others. An Asian teller from the bank followed me out to my car. Since I wasn't sure if she had written down the license plate on the Honda Accord I was driving, I decided to kill time by hanging out at the Fine Arts Museum instead of going home. I had planned an escape route via the high-occupancy vehicle lanes since it was a straight shot back to far West Houston where I lived.

As I drove home, my nerves got the best of me. I was extremely paranoid, feeling sick to my stomach. I probably needed something to eat, but I was afraid that if I had committed my crime on a full stomach I might vomit.

When I arrived home I called Alex. I also noticed a message on my answering machine from a drug dealer named Oz.

Oz was someone I had been kicking it with for a minute. He was curious about my sexuality, but I refused to introduce him to much because I didn't want to threaten our business relationship. Besides, sex was no longer a priority. I was focusing on drugs and money.

"What's up, dawg?" asked Oz in his sexy voice on the telephone.

I told him I was just chilling. In fact, I was counting up the spoil I had taken earlier from a suburban bank. Oz had called to confirm my appearance at the gig he was throwing later that evening. Normally, drug dealers don't invite their customers to their events, but Oz claimed that I was a horse of a different breed since I was able to handle my business and still get high. But that wasn't always the case. He just never saw that other part of me. As long as I kept the money flowing and rented him a car, he was happy.

"Check game, dawg." He spit those words out as if he were running things. "That niggah, Alex. Don't bring him tagging along cause that niggah owe me money for my cheese," said Oz, referring to cocaine.

"Don't sweat that man. It's on me." Now all of a sudden I'm a big baller.

"Nawl, dawg. Don't pay that niggah's debt. That mothafucker's grown. He better sell some ass or something. I want my money from that fool tonight."

"I got it," I said, counting $7,000 and then some.

"Oh, it's like that huh, niggah. Aiight. Aiight. I feel you. I'll squash that shit. Bring that niggah along – only because you said so," said Oz, failing to manipulate the situation. "You don't pay me shit. Just show up tonight with that niggah. That's a bet?"

"Bet that," I responded.

"You always been a real niggah, Miguel. You never know what might materialize between us, if that's worth anything to ya," Oz said flirtatiously.

He was a rough, tough-talking drug dealer with three gold teeth on the top portion of his mouth but a gentle bear at heart. That's not to say he couldn't turn into a ferocious beast. Even so, he was a slender but cut brother with an average-looking face.

"Yeah? So what is it you're offering?" I asked.

"I just might show you tonight, niggah. But check this out," he said, changing the subject. "The gig starts around 9 p.m. I'm gonna wear some of that DK shit we shopped for last time and the leather goods. What about you?"

"I'll try to match you man with some black DK and leather, too." I said feeling like a kid again, yet wondering if this niggah was serious.

"That's a bet, dawg. Later."

*****

As darkness settled over the city, Alex and I sped off in my rental car toward the party in Third Ward. I dressed him in a heavy, golden brown crewneck sweater and a handsome pair of Ralph Lauren deep lavender corduroys. His deep brown footwear was the envy of the house. They were Adolfo crocodiles with a double bronze buckle. He looked good for a dope addict.

When Oz saw him he was pathetically jealous.

"So, you dressing these niggahs now, huh?" an envious Oz asked.

"What's up with you, man? He needed an outfit for the party. He needed something fly, so I provided," I said not really feeling the need to explain my actions. "Don't get too comfortable in my shit, niggah," I warned Alex. I wanted to rid the N-word from my vocabulary, but I felt the need to fit it in.

"Niggahs! Always want to be ballers. But it's all good though. At the strike of 12, game over, niggah!" said Oz, looking at Alex's feet from across the room as the heavy thump of bass from the rap music shook the small wood-frame house.

I wasn't sure who his comment was meant for, so I ignored it.

"Yo, that bass is hitting hard tonight," I said, attempting to soothe Oz, who eventually lightened up a bit and flashed a smile – his gold teeth shining.

Later in the evening, Oz approached me and said, "Get your boy and meet me in the far back bedroom 'cause I know he wanna get his smoke on, if not his freak first," he said before walking away and shoving off his female companion.

Oz, Alex and I sat in the guarded backroom testing a sample of his latest purchase. I felt like a sucker, because that was the first time I had witnessed Oz take a puff from the glass dick. He sat there calmly at first and then became the freak he was all along. It then became obvious that he and Alex had a history. It appeared that this whole thing had been planned. While inhaling, Oz joined lips with Alex to give him a charge from the crack. Oz was a crack monster just like us, and all that hard play was nothing but a front.

He then looked toward me.

"Yeah, niggah, you thought I was bullshitting when I told you I might just show you something, huh?" he bragged as he kicked off his Italian-made half-cut boots.

"Nah, man, I believed you," I said as I picked up a pair of dice and rolled them on the dresser. They landed on a pair of treys – two 3s, equaling the number "6."

"Snap!"

The sound of my fingers echoed as I rolled again and watched a double "6" glow through the soft light.

"Taste this shit, man," Alex said, passing the glass and drug to me to test its potency.

"What you know about the craps?" asked Oz, pulling his DK sweater from his sleek upper body.

"Nothing man, just bullshitting with them." I actually was lying.

"Don't play with fire, dawg," Oz uttered as he led Alex to strip down to his Joe Boxer briefs.

At that moment, more rumbling sounds of rap filled the entire house. The lyrics were quite eerie: *"The devil made me do it, the devil made me do it ... It was the hand of the devil!"*

The walls reverberated from the heavy bass.

With that, I joined my two party partners as we stripped out of our clothes. I placed my Raymond Weil watch next to the dice on the dresser.

A knock sounded at the door.

"Who is it," shouted Oz, lying naked on his back across an antique bed as Alex, kneeling between Oz legs, swallowed his hard sex while I slapped Alex's ass.

"Come move your car, dawg!" a voice ordered from outside the door. The command was directed at me. Apparently, I was blocking someone in the driveway.

"Yeah, he'll be out!" shouted Oz, enjoying every minute of Alex's lip service.

I then greased up Alex's ass and put on a rubber, only because Oz was there. Typically, Alex and I didn't practice safe sex. But with Oz in the room, I changed course.

I then entered Alex and quickly climaxed. I then got dressed and promised to return after moving the car. As I left, I remembered that I forgot to remove my watch from the dresser. I hoped it would still be there when I returned. As I entered my car and was pulling out of the narrow driveway to allow another person to park in front of me I began to think that this request was rather strange. Was this other driver expecting me to leave before him?

Just as I prepared to pull back into the narrow driveway, a sea of blue lights swarmed my Honda Accord, blinding me.

What the Hell … !!!

"Put your hands on your head," the law enforcement authorities ordered as guns were trained toward my head. "Do it now!"

I was completely surrounded and was careful not to make any sudden moves. I didn't want to provoke a trigger-happy cop.

As police closed in on me, they pulled me from the car and slammed my face to the hood. As I was being cuffed, dope addicts on the street watched as my designer-wearing ass got busted.

I should have known that my luck would finally run out. As the handcuffs chewed into my skin and bones, I realized this was perhaps my ultimate embarrassment.

When they put me in the back seat of a cruiser I noticed it was 12:06 a.m. This can't be happening, I told myself. As I thought back, I remembered Oz mentioning something happening around midnight, but I couldn't piece it together then. I tried to convince the cops that they had the wrong guy, but they were not hearing it. I then watched them search the rental for cash and dope. There was none, just $300 that I had in my wallet, which was in my back pocket.

It was my dream to one day earn millions and have my own driver carrying me around town, not necessarily downtown. So, I never imagined being chauffeured in a squad car with blue lights mounted atop the roof and subdued with my arms behind my back. This was a scary moment.

I wasn't superstitious, but during my ride to the police station, I began to piece together all the odd events before my arrest. I recalled the double "6" roll of the dice (an earlier roll had resulted in a pair of 3s that equaled "6"); my six bank robberies; and today's arrest date, the 6th day of December. Thus, my unfortunate situation seemed to be linked to the prophecy of 666 (viewed as the mark of the beast in the book of Revelation).

Oz had already warned me not to play with fire, but I did not take him seriously. It would appear that this party was a setup and that he and Alex had gotten wind of my crimes and were in cahoots with the devil – or at least law enforcement. Was there a reward? If so, they must be laughing at my disgrace.

And looking back over the years, I realized the evil of my ways. I had crushed the hearts of the weak and victimized the willing. I even sensed that the Destroyer (the prince of darkness) was constantly lurking and gnawing at me, even encouraging my destruction.

So, as I prepare to spend time in a 6-foot by 9-foot cell, I'll take you to prison with me in the sequel to this story. Hopefully, we'll learn together whether divine intervention led to my arrest so that I might possibly escape the netherworld and enter into a new covenant with God that says: "For what I hate, **don't** do."

Character Profiles:
(Alphabetical order)

("pg." indicates the start of the page where each character is introduced)

Protagonist: Miguel Morris – Misguided track star seeking fame; befriends ruthless individuals

1. Alex – Texas Southern Univ. football player; rugged, attractive hustler; crack cocaine addict (pg. 251)

2. Belinda – Miguel's rotund co-worker; cautions him about envious colleague (pg. 272)

3. Big Momma – Ailing, sage grandmother; urges Miguel to seek goals (pg. 13)

4. Butch Webber – West Texas State Univ. star college football player turns pro; Miguel's idol (pg. 57)

5. Caleb Thibodeaux – Temperamental high school best friend; introduces Miguel to bisexuality (pg. 3)

6. Chaz – Brutally assertive but intelligent long jumper (pg. 111)

7. Chuck – Blond Houston restaurant waiter; introduces co-worker Miguel to gigolo lifestyle (pg. 113)

8. Coach Bill Turney – Sterling High School track coach; helps expose Miguel's talent (pg. 6)

9. Coach Joseph Durham – West Texas State, Mississippi State Univ. track coach; trains Miguel for pro circuit (pg. 55)

10. Curtis (aka Sweat) – Houston Baptist University tennis player; introduces Miguel to crack cocaine (pg. 175)

11. David Morris – Eldest brother; he and sibling Troy ridicule Miguel (pg. 13)

12. Dean Kramer – Mississippi State Univ. administrator; dislikes athletes; trashes Miguel, father (pg. 136)

13. Dee – Miguel's eldest sister; first in family to graduate from college; suffers multiple sclerosis (pg. 2)

14. Dr. Jai Holmes – Plastic surgeon; invites Miguel to Who's

Who party where he reconnects with idol Butch (pg. 230)

15. Eli – Muscular, bald stripper hired for night of revelry; friend of Patrick's (Miguel's partner in crime) (pg. 240)

16. Fay – Miguel's youngest sister (pg. 20)

17. Gil – Longtime associate of Miguel's club-hopping buddy Patrick (pg. 240)

18. Herman – Mississippi State Univ. track teammate; double-dating partner who secretly sleeps with Miguel (pg. 110)

19. Intrepid – New York stripper/hustler; joins Miguel as hired performers for prominent Dallas couple (pg. 275)

20. Joyce Manning – Trish's co-worker; helps Trish deal with husband Miguel's alleged double life (pg. 197)

21. Kelvin Thibodeaux – Caleb's brother; had incestuous relationship with cousin Tammy; vendetta against Miguel (pg. 25)

22. Ken – Six-foot hunk corporate manager; exposes his own double life to Miguel (pg. 223)

23. Kevin Knight – Teammate at West Texas State Univ.; becomes Miguel's nemesis; "cock-blocker" (pg.67)

24. Kiki – Houston club's drag queen emcee; delights in ridiculing patrons (pg. 149)

25. Latisha (Tish) – Asian-African track athlete; elopes, becomes Miguel's wife (pg. 121)

26. Laurel – Manager of Boogie Fever Productions (male exotic dancers); hires Miguel to join roster (pg. 258)

27. Lazlo Veasey – Handsome pharmacist; love for Miguel fails to save him from underworld (pg. 236)

28. Lenna – Alpha Kappa Alpha who dates Miguel's roommate Herman; encourages Miguel to model (pg. 127)

29. Malcolm – Former lover of Patrick (Miguel's partner in crime); killed by homophobic assailants (pg. 226)

30. Mattie Morris – Miguel's strong-willed mother; tries to cope with Miguel's turbulent life (pg. 13)

31. Mr. Hangman – Dallas pro athlete; wife hired Miguel, stripper Intrepid for sex with couple (pg. 278)

32. Mr. Morris – Miguel's father; provides for family but rarely home (pg. 19)

33. Mr. Weatherbee - Miguel's flamboyant high school teacher; killed execution-style in gay hate crime (pg. 3)

34. Ol' Girl - Wife of Dallas pro athlete hired Miguel, stripper Intrepid for sex with couple; smokes crack (pg. 277)

35. Oz - Tough-talking drug dealer with shady past, secret life (pg. 291)

36. Pamela - Job supervisor; double nipple on one breast; fling with co-worker Miguel (pg. 255)

37. Patrick Porter - Misogynist; influences friend Miguel to hire, take advantage of male prostitutes (pg. 142)

38. Pee-Wee - Crack house addict; allows himself to be belittled (pg. 246)

39. Tammy - Had incestuous affair with cousin Kelvin, bore child; briefly dated Miguel (pg. 15)

40. Patsy Pollard - Tutor, Miguel's girlfriend at West Texas State University; disastrous breakup (pg. 60)

41. Roland - Track teammate; competed with Caleb for high school homecoming king (pg. 35)

42. Ruth - Miguel's vindictive co-worker; fabricated story to get him fired (pg. 272)

43. Tamela - Miguel's part-time Delta Sigma Theta girlfriend; couple double-dates with Herman, Lenna (pg. 128)

44. Terrance - Helps Miss. State Univ. mile-relay squad claim NCAA title (pg. 110)

45. T.J. (aka Travis Jacobs) - Annoying, arrogant Cajun who rattles co-worker Tish (Miguel's wife) (pg. 184)

46. Troy Morris - Younger football star sibling who teases Miguel; crack addict; incarcerated (pg. 13)

47. Zac (Zachary) - Miguel's tall, dark high school track teammate, college roommate before flunking out (pg. 6)